No spoilers here. Just a tip that this one
gets better and better the deeper it goes."
—*The San Francisco Chronicle,*
Holiday Book Review Selection 2002

"An impressive performance." —*Chicago Tribune*

"Gripping . . . Evoking the feel of 1950s dramas like
"The Asphalt Jungle" and "Twelve Angry Men."
It ticks along relentlessly to a surprising conclusion."
—*Wall Street Journal*

"Brilliant! A melancholy, beautiful and—above all—
suspenseful meditation on guilt and the nature of time."
—*Time Out New York*

"Dark and enthralling . . . Cook's complicated book
is a keeper." —*Fort Worth Star Telegram*

"Cook masterfully weaves the present with the past . . .
until the killer's identity is finally revealed in a
surprising twist." —*Tampa Tribune*

"Cook knows how to build a fascinating and complex
plot and fill it full of compelling people."
—*Rocky Mountain News*

"There are plenty of twists and turns . . . with suspense
building throughout to a really surprise ending."
—*The Oklahoman*

"All of Cook's novels are master works. He is one of
the best in the suspense genre." —*The Daily American*

INSTRUMENTS OF NIGHT

"Haunting . . . The denouement took me by surprise and disturbed me for days." —*Los Angeles Times*

"An enthralling tale that cannily uses elements of the Gothic thriller."
—*The Seattle Times/Seattle Post Intelligencer*

"Hypnotic prose and fresh scenarios set [Cook's] suspenseful fiction apart . . . If you've not yet been haunted by a Thomas Cook novel, now is a fine time to start."
—*Star Tribune*, Minneapolis

"A beautifully composed tale with enough plot twists to satisfy even fans who have learned to expect surprises from this talented author . . . [Cook] deliver[s] another indelibly haunting tale that once again demonstrates that he is among the best in the business."
—*Publishers Weekly* (starred review)

"Cook teases readers throughout the narrative with tantalizing bits from Grave's own past . . . but he also saves the best—and most shocking revelations—until practically the last page." —*The Orlando Sentinel*

"This is not a novel for the faint heart . . . Cook is a master of subtlety as he weaves the past and present in and out of his own story." —*Milwaukee Journal Sentinel*

EVIDENCE OF BLOOD

"In [his] previous novels . . . Cook has shown himself to be a writer of poetic gifts, constantly pushing against the presumed limits of crime fiction . . . In this fine, new book, he has gone to the edge, and survived triumphantly." —Charles Champlin, *Los Angeles Times Book Review*

"Gripping southern drama, with its byzantine family tress, old wives' tales, and overheated memories." —*Kirkus Review*

THE CHATHAM SCHOOL AFFAIR
Edgar Award Winner for Best Novel

"A seductive book." —*The New York Times Book Review*

"Cook is a master, precise and merciless, at showing the slow-motion shattering of families and relationships . . . THE CHATHAM SCHOOL AFFAIR ranks with his best." —*Chicago Tribune*

"Intelligent . . . compassionate . . . surprising." —*The Boston Sunday Globe*

"Cook uses the genre to open a window onto the human condition . . . Literate, compelling . . . Events accelerate with increasing force, but few readers will be prepared for the surprise that awaits at the novel's end." —*Publisher's Weekly* (starred review)

"Powerful, engaging, and deeply moving . . . highly recommended." —*Booklist*

"A remarkable novel of memory and buried secrets." —*The Armchair Detective*

"Cook has crafted a novel of stunning power, with a climax that is so unexpected the reader may think he has cheated. But there is no cheating here, only excellent storytelling." —*Booklist*

"Cook's writing is distinguished by finely cadenced prose, superior narrative skills, and the author's patient love for the doomed characters who are the object of his attention . . . Highly recommended."
—*Library Journal* (starred review)

MORTAL MEMORY

"Cook builds a family portrait in which violence seems both impossible and inevitable. One of [MORTAL MEMORY'S] greatest accomplishments is the way it defies expectations . . . surprising and devastating."
—*Chicago Tribune*

"Haunting . . . Don't pick this up unless you've got time to read it through . . . because you will do so whether you plan to or not." —*Alfred Hitchcock Mystery Magazine*

ALSO BY THOMAS H. COOK

FICTION

MOON OVER MANHATTAN
(with Larry King)
TAKEN
INTO THE WEB
THE INTERROGATION
PLACES IN THE DARK
INSTRUMENTS OF NIGHT
THE CHATHAM SCHOOL AFFAIR
BREAKHEART HILL
MORTAL MEMORY
EVIDENCE OF BLOOD
THE CITY WHEN IT RAINS
NIGHT SECRETS
STREETS OF FIRE
FLESH AND BLOOD
SACRIFICIAL GROUND
THE ORCHIDS
TABERNACLE
ELENA
BLOOD INNOCENTS

NONFICTION

EARLY GRAVES
BLOOD ECHOES

ANTHOLOGIES

BEST AMERICAN CRIME WRITING
(with Otto Penzler)
BEST AMERICAN CRIME WRITING 2002
(with Otto Penzler)

PERIL

Thomas H. Cook

BANTAM BOOKS

PERIL
A Bantam Book

PUBLISHING HISTORY
Bantam hardcover edition published February 2004
Bantam mass market edition / February 2005

Published by
Bantam Dell
A Division of Random House, Inc.
New York, New York

All rights reserved
Copyright © 2004 by Thomas H. Cook
Cover photograph by Franco Accornero
Cover design by Jamie S. Warren Youll

Library of Congress Catalog Card Number: 2003062793

Bantam Books and the rooster colophon are registered
trademarks of Random House, Inc.

ISBN 0-553-58251-8

Printed in the United States of America
Published simultaneously in Canada

www.bantamdell.com

OPM   10   9   8   7   6   5   4   3   2

For Imre and Mary Greenfeld

PERIL

ONE

Bird Alone

SARA

EACH TIME she thought of it, she felt her body shiver, felt the pistol cold in her hand, the pressure of her finger as it drew down upon the trigger. And so she put it out of her mind, because if you played it over and over, the shadows would deepen around you, thicken until they suffocated you, or until you became a shadow yourself. And so she put it out of her mind because she couldn't stand the shivering anymore, the icy feel of the metal, the way her eyes had narrowed into slits at that moment, as if she were melting in this boiling pit of hatred. *Kill him,* the voice had commanded at that instant. *Kill him now!*

She whirled around and headed up the stairs to the bedroom she'd shared with Tony for the last nine years. With every step she crumbled a little, just as she had years before when she'd fled the South, headed north, already making up a new name, a new identity. She half expected parts of her body to fall away as she continued up the stairs, a tuft of hair on the third step, a hand on the fourth. But she moved determinedly despite the sensation of breaking apart, and somehow the forward movement knit her together, momentum a force in itself, driving her onward like a stone hurled through bushes, razing the path it took.

Tony's underwear lay crumpled on his side of the bed. The rest of his clothes were strewn haphazardly about the room, lifeless as pelts. He'd thrown them on the floor, probably because his father had told him that was what a man should do. Tony's father. She closed her eyes tightly and tried to squeeze him out of her mind. Even so, she could hear Leo Labriola going at Tony, laying down the law, daring him to disobey it. *A woman has to learn certain things, Tony.* One of them, she thought, was to stoop. Another was to keep quiet no matter what raged inside you. And the last, and for the Old Man, the most important, was that a woman should always be afraid.

And she *had* been afraid, she realized, and not just of Labriola or Tony or of Sheriff Caulfield on that summer afternoon he'd pulled her over, citing a broken taillight. She'd been afraid all her life—afraid to cross her father, afraid to be alone, afraid to stay and afraid to leave, afraid to say no to some things and yes to others. Now she was afraid of the future. And these large fears fueled smaller ones, so that at this very moment, in the midst of flight, she remained afraid even to leave Tony's clothes on the floor, though at last she decided to do precisely that, leave his clothes scattered across the plush blue carpet, his first clue that things had changed. When he got home tonight, he'd notice that his clothes had not been picked up, and there'd be a click in his head, audible as a pistol shot, *She's gone*.

She spun violently and strode to the closet, yanked the suitcase from the shelf, and began to pack. She took no shorts or swimsuit or sandals; she was packing not for a few days away but for the rest of her life, and she made sure there was nothing temporary about the clothes she selected, nothing that suggested she might change her mind, return to the sun-drenched house, the glittering pool. The clothes she chose were decidedly simple, the colors gray and black, appropriate camouflage for the hidden life she would live from now on. She selected them like one readying for nocturnal battle, and as she packed each item she tried to think of herself as one of the women warriors she'd read about, armored, mounted, broadsword in hand, brave in a way she'd never been but now had to be if she were going to climb out of the quicksand of her life.

The pistol, she thought suddenly, then walked to the bureau where Tony kept it, dug beneath his carefully folded underwear, felt its cold steel heft. For a moment she'd been determined to take it but now decided not to, because if she were ever cornered she would use it, and once she'd done that, taken that final, fatal step, then any dream of a better life would be forever shattered. That was where she was, she realized, poised between equally desperate alternatives, flight—unarmed flight—the only vaguely open door.

She took a moment to look over the room a final time. Everything in it looked frilly. Lacy pillows. Fringed draperies. All the colors were pastels. It was a little girl's room with muted hues and caressing fabrics, a vision of safety where there were no shadows or sharp corners. "Barbie doll," she whispered, still unable to map the route by which she'd reached this place, though she knew it had started in a field, then moved on through worlds of loss and insecurity, a grasping need for a big happy ending that appeared, at that instant, to explode before her, set her hair ablaze.

She grabbed the suitcase, raced downstairs, called a cab, and waited by the door, watching the morning light build over her neighbors' houses. Again, the irrevocable nature of what she was doing settled over her. She would never see this street again, never wave to her friend Della across the cul-de-sac or shop with her in the local supermarket. Della, like everything else on Long Island, was already disappearing from her life, growing translucent in her memory. She would call her when she got to the city, let her know that she'd made it, but all the rest—whatever job she got, where she lived—all of that she would have to keep secret for fear of being found.

The phone rang but she didn't answer it. She was terrified it might be Tony and she didn't want to hear his voice. Or it might be his father, whose voice would freeze her in place. No, she decided, the only voice she would listen to now was her own.

"All right," she whispered vehemently, "go."

And suddenly everything grew oddly weightless and insubstantial, the past years of her life, the long hope she'd nurtured for that big happy ending, all of it suddenly rising from her like the final bubbles of a dead champagne.

CARUSO

"HOW DID this fucking happen?" Labriola demanded. His eyes glowed hotly in the murky darkness of the living room.

Caruso gripped the arms of the worn Naugahyde chair and shifted nervously. "He's always been good for it before."

"And so you let him get in this deep? Fifteen fucking grand?"

"Like I say, he was good for it before, and so . . ."

"Before?" The Old Man's mouth jerked violently, spitting words like stones. "You mean before he suddenly wasn't good for it no more?"

"Yes, sir," Caruso confessed weakly.

Labriola's eyes narrowed. "Well, here's my question, Vinnie. Why the fuck do I care what he was before if he ain't good for it now?" His massive frame blocked Caruso's view of the street outside, the gabled row houses of Sheepshead Bay. "Can I spend the money this guy ain't good for?"

"No, sir," Caruso answered meekly.

Beyond the window, children played on the sidewalk and women stopped to chat, their arms filled with grocery bags or the latest baby. Caruso wondered what it would be like to live on such a street, have a house, a wife, kids, be complete and on his own. His cramped apartment surfaced in his mind, the rumpled sheets of his bed. He called it his bachelor pad, but it was no such thing. A bachelor pad was a place a guy fixed up nice and kept clean because he might meet a girl and bring her home. The room he rented in Bay Ridge was just the place where he slept and ate pizza from the box and waited for the phone to ring, summoning him here, to face the smoldering figure of Leo Labriola.

"You listening to me, Vinnie?"

"What?"

"Are you fucking listening to me?"

"Yes, sir."

Labriola ticked off all the things he couldn't buy with money he didn't have—fancy cars and whores and diamonds for Belle, his longtime mistress. And if "some broad" wanted a sawbuck for a blow job, he'd have to pass on that too, because Caruso had let this deadbeat fuck get in over his head, which wasn't going to stand, because nobody came up empty on Leo Labriola. No. Fucking. Body. Ever.

"So what I'm saying is, make him good for it," Labriola fumed. "You don't make him good for it, Vinnie, then I'll make *you* good for it."

"Yes, sir," Caruso said. His fingers rose to the knot of his tie. "Don't worry, Mr. Labriola. I'll get the money."

"You fucking better. Because I don't make threats, right? I make promises."

Labriola had told him about other promises he'd made to people who'd previously crossed him or disappointed him or simply failed him in some way. They'd ended up at the bottom of the East River or curled into the trunks of old sedans on President Street, he said. And always the stories about Russian roulette, how if you wanted to face down a guy, you offered to play it with him, took the first turn yourself, proved you had the balls to look death in the fucking eye. You did that, Labriola said, nobody ever questioned who was boss. Caruso wasn't sure the Old Man had ever actually spun the chamber and placed the barrel against the side of his head. As a matter of fact, he wasn't sure if any of the Old Man's gangland tales were true. Years before, when Labriola had first given him a job running numbers, he'd believed Labriola was a big-time mobster. Later he'd learned that in fact he was little more than a nickel-and-dime shylock. But by then it didn't matter whether the Old Man was big or small. He was the guy who'd taken him in after Caruso's father had vanished, the guy who'd given him work and patted him on the head when he did things right and yelled at him when he did things wrong and in doing that had pulled him from the boiling rapids he'd been shooting down before Labriola had yanked him from the water and given him something to do besides boost cars and raid vending machines for a few lousy bucks. Old Man Labriola had brought him under his wing, given him real work, so that he wore a suit now and looked respectable, and if you didn't know better, you might even think he was legit.

"So, you gonna straighten this fucker out?" Labriola barked. " 'Cause if you don't . . ."

"I know, believe me," Caruso said. "I'll straighten him out."

"You fucking better," Labriola warned. " 'Cause nobody screws Leo Labriola and gets away with it." He slashed the air, his hand like a cleaver. "Now get the fuck outta here."

Caruso rose and headed for the door. He'd already opened it when the Old Man's voice drew him back.

"By the way, what did you think I'd tell you, Vinnie? Huh? To just forget it? Write this fucking deadbeat a ticket? Merry Christmas. Some shit like that?"

"I just thought you should know that in the past—"

"You know what the past is, Vinnie?" Labriola snarled. "A dead body. It fucking smells."

Caruso nodded and closed the door behind him. He knew that he should be pissed at the Old Man for talking to him like he was a jerk, but each time his anger flared, he remembered how much he owed the guy, along with how much he looked forward to those moments when Labriola seemed to like him, seemed to want him around, even to think that he did a good job.

He knew that if he did enough good jobs, then one day he'd get the Big Assignment. Labriola had never told him what the Big Assignment was, but Caruso had seen enough movies to know that it was a hit that made a guy big. Someday, he thought, Mr. Labriola would put his arm over his shoulder, give him the Big Assignment, then kiss him on each cheek. At that point it would have all been worth it. The waiting by the phone, the times he'd been chewed out. At that point it would be worth it because he'd know that he was the guy the Old Man trusted to carry out the ultimate big deal, the one guy he trusted . . . like a son.

He knew that moment would come, and because of that, he couldn't get mad at the Old Man, and so he immediately shifted his anger to the deadbeat bastard who'd landed him in this fix, lulled him into false trust by always being good for it before, and in that way set him up to get hauled over the coals by Labriola. It was, Caruso concluded, all Morty's fault.

DELLA

SHE RINSED the coffee urn while Mike ate his breakfast and thumbed through the paper. Nicky gurgled happily in his high chair, his small pink fingers dunking in the milk, reaching for a Cheerio.

"Where's Denise?" Mike asked.

She turned and saw that he'd folded the paper and placed it on the table beside his plate. "Upstairs. Primping."

"Primping? Jesus. She's twelve years old."

"They start early now," Della said. "More coffee?"

Mike shook his head and got to his feet. "No. I'd have to piss halfway into the city if I had another cup." He shrugged. "Probably will anyway." He smiled that boyish smile of his, the one she'd fallen in love with nineteen years before. Then he turned and trudged up the stairs, his big, hulking shape a comfort to her, like living with Santa Claus. Once he'd made it upstairs, she listened as he moved from the bedroom to the adjoining bathroom, and back again. He'd misplaced something. His keys probably. What a lug she'd married. What a kind, sweet lug.

She walked to the bottom of the stairs. "Look in the hamper," she called. "They're probably still in your pants."

She listened as he did as he was told.

"Got 'em," he said loudly. "Thanks, babe."

She felt a modest surge of accomplishment, a sense of being useful, then returned to the kitchen and began clearing the table. She'd just finished wiping milk from Nicky's mouth when she saw Denise fly down the stairs and bolt out into the yard. Kids, Della thought, they're so crazy now.

"Okay, I'm off," Mike said as he lumbered back into the kitchen. He glanced out the window to where Denise stood waiting for her bus. "She okay?"

"Getting to be a teenager, that's all."

"Anything I should know about?"

"She talks to you as much as me." She drew Nicky out of the high chair. "Say bye to your dad."

Mike kissed Nicky on the cheek. "You be a good boy now," he said brightly. He looked at Della, and his big, clownish face warmed her. "See you tonight."

"We're having tuna melt," she told him. His favorite.

He kissed her, walked to the car, and got in. Denise offered a grudging, halfhearted wave as he drifted backward into the cul-de-sac.

Della returned Nicky to his chair, then began to load the dishwasher. The school bus arrived and Denise bounded onto it. Then the bus pulled away, and Della glimpsed her friend Sara's house across the cul-de-sac. It looked cold and cheerless and abandoned, everything *her* house was not, and she felt inexpressibly lucky to have found a guy who'd take care of her, make sure she had everything she needed, provide a life that was truly without peril.

AS HE strolled idly down the aisle of the antique shop, he thought of time, then death, then the sweetness of oblivion, how much he'd come to yearn for the end of life. So easy, he told himself, so easy just to let it go, this chain of days that stretched ahead of him. He imagined the moment, the feel of the pistol in his mouth, the shattering impact, and felt himself instantly disintegrate, burst like a vase of air, leaving nothing behind.

Literally nothing save the few luxurious items he'd purchased because the high craft employed in making them lifted his spirits and took his mind off Marisol.

But now, as he approached the anniversary of her murder, he realized that the power of a beautifully cut piece of glass or a perfectly woven scarf to change his mood had waned enormously during the preceding twelve months. He suspected that his getting older was part of it, though he was only fifty-three. The rest was loneliness, and the fading hope that there would ever be an end to it while he lived on earth. He'd loved once, and overwhelmingly lost that love in a whirl of violence, then lived on in the aftermath of that explosion, its shattering echo forever in his mind. Now, more than anything, as he admitted to himself this morning, he wanted an end to memory. Beyond life he saw a world of utter stillness and eternal dark, and yet he harbored the hope that somewhere in that darkness the soul of Marisol waited for him patiently. The nurturing of this hope, he knew, was an act of will. But if he abandoned it, Henderson would win, and Lockridge would win, and they could win only at the cost of Marisol.

Stark shook his head at the morbidity of his thoughts and glanced about the shop, hoping some small, precious thing would catch his eye.

Over the years, he'd spent almost everything he made because he saw no reason to hold on to anything. He had no wife, no children, no one whose later survival meant anything at all to him. And as for saving for that rainy day when he would be old and sick, he knew that he would never reach such a point. If he got sick beyond recovery, he would simply kill himself. When he got old, when the last small joys were gone, he would tuck the barrel of his nine-millimeter automatic against the roof of his mouth and pull the trigger. There would be no rainy days.

And so Stark spent whatever he had on clothes and restaurants and obsessive grooming. But more than anything, he spent money on delicately wrought objects, usually of glass or porcelain. They were tremendously expensive, these little statues or figurines, but in the past they'd kept him afloat. In them he'd been able to find something good in life, something done for the love of it, something to which an otherwise ordinary human being had applied the full measure of his skill.

In the past these things had soothed him like a soft, warm light.

But no longer.

"Beautiful, isn't it?"

Stark faced the dealer, noted the small rosebud in his lapel, thought it foppish.

"It's sixteenth century," the dealer added with a nod toward the fluted glass at which, Stark realized, he must have been gazing.

"Not my thing," Stark said coolly.

The dealer looked as if he'd been gently pushed away, perhaps with the nose of a silver derringer. "Well, if I may be of help . . ."

"I'll let you know," Stark said.

"Of course," the dealer said, then vanished.

Alone again, Stark strolled back down the aisle toward

the shop's front door. Scores of beautiful objects lined his path, but nothing called to him, and because of that he knew that he'd slipped out of the old reality, the one that had held him for so many years. Even though Mortimer would arrive that night with the latest payment, he would never spend another dime on what he now suddenly dismissed as collectibles.

He walked out of the shop and headed south down Madison Avenue. He knew that dressed as he was, in a fashionably cut black suit, he looked like a successful Manhattan business executive. It was a look he'd cultivated over the years and which he scrupulously maintained. It went with the false and decidedly metaphorical name he'd chosen for himself, and for the secret life he lived, and it was incontestably appropriate for the elegant bars where, if he sat long enough, a woman would finally approach him.

Marisol.

For years he'd tried to tell himself that she was just a woman, that if she'd lived and they'd remained together, they would have grown apart, their passion faded. But she had died horribly and thus became Helen still on the walls of Troy, and he had never been able to bring her down from that mythic height. He'd tried to find another woman, fall in love again, but the ghost of Marisol lingered in the air around him. She slithered between himself and any woman he caressed. Her breath stained every kiss.

And so for the last few years he'd pursued only sex, sex without affection, and except for Kiko, always with strangers. He could sense that this was just another detour from the road he truly sought and which he now imagined leading off into the shadowy and impossible distance, Marisol at the end of it, perfect and unchanged, her arms opening to receive him. He could almost hear her sensuous whisper, *Welcome home*.

MORTIMER

SITTING IN Dr. Langton's office, he felt small and un-educated, both of which he knew he was, a dull, pudgy lit-tle man with a mind that had precious little in it, at least precious little of the stuff educated people had in their minds—dates and names and bits of poetry. If he had it all to do over, he thought, he'd have gone to college, even if nothing more than Bunker Hill Community College, gotten a little polish, a little class, so that he could look a doctor in the eye and not feel the way he did now, two pegs up from a bug.

"Good afternoon," Dr. Langton said as he came into the office.

Mortimer nodded.

Dr. Langton sat down behind his desk, a wall of diplo-mas arrayed behind him. He placed the folder he'd brought with him on his desk and opened it. For a mo-ment he flipped through the pages, then he lifted his eyes and Mortimer saw just how bad it was. His stomach emp-tied in the way it had during the war when someone yelled "Incoming!"

"I have the test results," Dr. Langton said. "It's not good news, I'm afraid."

"How long?" Mortimer didn't want to be curt, but he didn't want to string it out either, because he knew that if he didn't get it quick and straight, he'd end up feeling even worse than he already did.

"That's always a guess," Dr. Langton answered. "But I'd say we're probably looking at around three months."

To his surprise, Mortimer felt a screwy sense that it couldn't be true, that a man couldn't sit in an office, feeling more or less okay, and hear a death sentence like that, three lousy months. My God, he was only fifty-six. "You're sure?" he asked.

"I wish I had a treatment for you. But in this case . . ."

"Okay," Mortimer said. The incoming round exploded somewhere deep inside him and he suddenly felt already dead. Then his mind shifted to the living, to Dottie, the wife he'd leave behind . . . with nothing.

"I'm sorry," Dr. Langton said.

"Me too," Mortimer said, though it was not for himself he felt sorry now, but for how little he'd accumulated. Nothing in the bank. Nothing in the market. Not even a little row house in Brooklyn or Queens. All of that had galloped away from him one horse at a time, galloped away on the back of some nag that finished fifth on the track at Belmont. Leaving him with nothing. No. Worse than nothing. In hock fifteen grand to a guy Caruso claimed was capable of anything. Breaking thumbs. Cutting out your tongue. And if Mortimer were, so to speak, beyond reach? What would Labriola do then? Was it really unthinkable that a guy like that, a crazy, brutal thug, might go after Dottie just to get even?

"Is there anything else?"

Mortimer looked at Dr. Langton. "What?"

"Is there anything else I can do for you?" the doctor asked.

"No," Mortimer answered. Not you. Not anybody.

Once outside the office, Mortimer glanced down Eighty-fifth Street, trying to decide what would do him the most good now, the bustle of Broadway or some secluded corner of Central Park.

He decided on the park, and after a few minutes found himself seated on a large gray stone, watching dully as the park's other visitors made their way down its many winding paths. Not far away a fat black woman bumpily pushed a wheelchair across the lawn. An old man sat in the chair, his legs wrapped in a burgundy blanket. The old man's eyes were blue, but milky, and little wisps of white hair trembled each time the wheelchair rocked. He was deathly thin, his long, bony fingers little more than skeletal. *Even that fucking guy,* Mortimer thought, *ninety if he's a day, but even that fucking guy will outlive me.*

But it was not the speed of his approaching death that rocked Mortimer now. It was how little time he had to make things right with Dottie. Poor Dottie Smith, the girl who'd been desperate enough or hopeless enough or just plain dumb enough to marry him. He had no illusion that she would miss him. He had not been an attentive husband. In fact, he'd hardly been around at all. Was that not reason enough to leave her something to make up for the thirty wintry years she'd spent with him, a guy who had never taken her out dancing, or even given her a little kiss when he left in the morning or came back at night. What could her life have been, he wondered, without that kiss? And now, after so many dull, dead years, the only kiss he had to leave her was his kiss of death.

No, he decided. No, he couldn't do that. He had to find a way to leave something for Dottie. That, he concluded, was his mission now.

SARA

WHEN THE cab arrived, she opened the door and strode swiftly down the walkway, the click of her heels so loud she felt sure it would alert the neighbors, summon them to their windows, all eyes on her now, intent, quizzical, *Where's Sara Labriola off to?*

The driver placed the suitcase in the trunk. "Getting an early start," he said.

She nodded briskly, then got into the cab, careful to gaze straight ahead as it pulled away, afraid that if she didn't, the fear would reach out like a grappling hook and haul her back across the lawn and into the house, where the voice would begin to make its hard demand—*Kill him!*—growing louder with each passing day until, inevitably, she would obey it.

At the station, the driver placed the suitcase on the curb and touched his cap. "Have a nice trip," he said.

Her fear spiked as the cab pulled away, and she was seized with the irrational suspicion that the driver worked for her father-in-law, that he was even then reaching for a cell phone, *Hello, Mr. Labriola, I just dropped your son's wife at the bus station in Montauk.* Her hands were trembling, and she struggled to still them. Her fear had reached the panic stage, so that she had to remind herself that it was the long years of listening to Labriola's stories that had created this paranoid sense that his henchmen were everywhere, whispering into cell phones, tracking her every move.

But none of that mattered now. The only thing that mattered was that she had to leave. She grabbed the suitcase and marched to the ticket counter.

"New York," she said.

The woman at the booth wore glasses so thick they magnified her eyes. The frames were bright red plastic, a gaudy splash of color in the gray bus station. "One way or round-trip?" the woman asked.

So that was what it came to, Sara thought, whether you stopped at the brink of action or pressed on against all odds, boldly took the outbound road or the circular one that forever wound you back to the scene of the crime.

"One way," she said, lifting her head, choking back her

fear, pronouncing the words loudly, determinedly, as a soldier might call out *Charge!*

The woman told her the price. She paid in cash, her credit cards left behind because she knew Leo Labriola would trace her if she used them.

"Bus leaves at ten-fourteen," the woman said.

She walked to the departing gate and waited for the bus, the fear rising steadily so that she continually glanced about nervously, wondering if Labriola had somehow guessed she was leaving, already assigned people all along the route to keep track of her. She could hear their voices in her mind, Leo Labriola's minions. *Her bus is just pulling out now. She's headed down Sunset Highway. She just reached Cold Spring Harbor. Her bus just pulled into Port Authority. She's hailing a cab at Forty-second and Ninth. Looks like she's headed downtown.*

Her eyes scanned the station for her father-in-law's shadowy agents and she saw them all around her. The teenage runaway flicking her pierced tongue; the soldier snoozing softly, his face concealed behind a newspaper; the old black man reading a tattered Bible; the business-man tapping at his laptop. Could all of them be working for the Old Man?

Of course not, she told herself, *think about something else, put him out of your mind.* She drew in a long breath. *Think about something else. Something before Tony. Before the Old Man. Something good.*

She returned to her first days in New York, the small-time cabaret singer she'd invented as herself. She'd even given her a name, Samantha Damonte, then created a person to go with it, a smoky-bar woman with plenty of experience, a burnt-out case at twenty-five. Not a bit of it had been true. In fact, as she'd finally come to recognize, Samantha Damonte was just a young woman who'd been afraid to grow up, afraid to go to college, afraid that she wasn't really special or all that talented, and so, despite the smoky-bar persona, just another girl who wanted to be taken care of. That was what Tony had dangled before her, a safe life, a chance to quiet the voice in her head, its incessantly murderous demand. She'd gone for it because she was weary of short gigs in out-of-the-way clubs, tired of agents and club owners who saw her as a mark, tired of fingers raking up her thigh, tired of the rage that swept over her like a hot wind every time some boozy customer sidled up to the piano, tossed a twenty in the glass, and nodded toward the room at the back, tired of the voice that kept rising from the smoldering center of herself, *Kill him!*

She might have gone back to Virginia, she thought now, but that door had closed long ago when her father had thrown her out, told her that her dead mother was rolling in her grave, that a singer was just a slut, that she'd either marry Billy Preston, if she could even be sure it was Billy who'd gotten her pregnant, or never show her face at his door again. She'd screamed, "Never, never, never," moved in with her cousin Sheila, lost the child three weeks later, then split for New York like a million girls before her. At a bus stop outside Philly, in a greasy diner over black coffee and a cigarette, Samantha Damonte had been born.

Okay, so Samantha Damonte was totally made up, Sara told herself, like a character in a book. But who was Sara Labriola, this woman in this particular bus station? She didn't know, and that struck her as more frightening than anything else, the fact that she could define herself now only as a woman in a rage, half wishing she had done it long ago, drawn back the hammer, pulled the trigger, given up the foolish fantasy that there had ever been a choice.

TONY

AFTER THE sixth ring he hung up, irritated that it was ten-thirty in the morning, for Christ's sake, and Sara wasn't home. He'd been calling her every half hour since seven-thirty but gotten no answer. So where had she gone so early? She had no relatives to visit. No kids to take to school or walk to the bus stop. He glanced out the office window, noted the flurry of activity, men packing fish in ice, loading crates of sea bass and bluefish that would soon be served in restaurants throughout the East Coast. In the distance, Eddie Sullivan was hosing out a truck. Seven feet away Joey Fanucci slumped against a fishing boat, smoking a cigarette, the lazy bastard, who he wouldn't have hired on a bet if he weren't a cousin and the Old Man hadn't insisted that "family is family."

He jerked open the window. "Hey, Joey. What the fuck? You got nothing to do?"

Joey tossed his cigarette into the churning water and disappeared into the warehouse.

He can hide in there, Tony thought, he can get behind a stack of shipping crates and beat his meat all fucking day. He slammed the window closed, snapped up the phone, dialed home. When no one answered, the dreadful unease flared, the corrosive feeling that something was wrong in the tidy little house he'd left only a few hours before.

He was still nursing that disturbing idea when his father burst through the door.

"Why you keep that fucking mick on the payroll, Tony? He's dumber than shit."

"He's a nice guy," Tony said.

"So what?" Labriola demanded. He strode to a chair in front of Tony's desk, plopped down in it, and spread his long, thick legs out across the floor. "So what are you telling me, that you're so rich you can keep some lazy mick on welfare forever?"

"He's not lazy, Dad," Tony said. He grabbed a pencil from a cup that bristled with them and rolled it nervously between his fingers.

Labriola eyed the pencil, then said, "What you so jumpy about?"

"Nothing."

"Nothing? I don't think so, Tony. You got something on your mind, spit it out."

"Nothing," Tony repeated.

Labriola laughed. "That wife of yours, she's probably not giving you any."

Tony slid the pencil back into the cup.

"You want to get even with her, I could have Belle fix you up."

Tony shook his head. "Stop it."

Labriola laughed again. "I told Belle I wanted her to make that thing with sole your mother used to make. You remember, with tomatoes, garlic, capers."

"I remember."

"So, you got sole?"

"Yeah."

Labriola pulled himself to his feet. "The mick can gimme it?"

"His name is Eddie."

Labriola walked to the door, then looked at Tony. "Don't let that wife of yours fuck with you, Tony."

"I won't," Tony assured him.

"Good," Labriola said curtly. "Because they try to get between us, these fucking broads."

"Between us?"

"Guys. Set one against the other. Father and son."

"Sara would never do that."

Labriola laughed and waved his hand. "Yeah, sure,

you know all about women, kid." He turned and headed out the door.

Tony watched as the Old Man slammed down the stairs and strode out across the marina, waving to Eddie with one of his get-the-hell-over-here-asshole gestures, like Eddie was his slave. He knew he should have insisted on defending Sara, but he'd been frozen by his father's mocking laughter, a laughter that had become even more hard lately, tinged with an edgy craziness, as if the Old Man were unraveling in some way, growing more violent, something in him going haywire.

Tony shrugged helplessly. What could you do with such a man? *Nothing*, he decided as always. *Nothing but stay out of his way.*

MORTIMER

BRANDENBERG HANDED him the envelope. "Tell your man he did a good job."

Mortimer tucked the envelope into the inside pocket of his jacket.

They were sitting in the lounge of the St. Regis Hotel, a place whose sumptuous decor made Mortimer feel poor and ragged. Glancing about, he wished he'd met Brandenberg in the park, where there were guys digging soda cans and scrapes of food out of the garbage. Instead, he had only the plush carpet and the thick, luxurious curtains and the well-dressed gentleman at the table to the right, some actor he vaguely recognized, though he couldn't recall the name.

Brandenberg sipped his brandy, then said, "You want a drink?"

Mortimer shook his head. "You need anything else? Some other job?"

Brandenberg considered Mortimer's questions for a few seconds, then said, "Not for myself. But I have an associate. A businessman from Saudi—"

"No." Mortimer shook his head. "Two types he don't work for. Foreigners is one of them."

"And the other?"

"Mob guys."

"I see." Brandenberg took another sip. "And why does he draw this line?"

"He got fucked. Years ago, but he don't forget."

"So you screen his clients?"

"Yeah."

"Well, then it could be kept strictly between us. I mean, as regards this associate of mine. Which is strictly a business matter, by the way. A question of internal security. Nothing . . . messy. And as far as payment is concerned, the money could come through me. So in a situation like that, how would your man know if—"

"It ain't his job to know," Mortimer interrupted.

"Fine," Brandenberg said in the crisp, cold tone of a man unaccustomed to being refused. "I suppose I admire your . . . honesty," he added grudgingly. He brought his finger to his lips, and the polished nail gave off a glint of light.

To be dolled up like that, Mortimer thought, to be all elegant and refined that way, what would that feel like? "So, I guess we're done," he said.

"It would appear so."

"Okay," Mortimer said, and on that word got to his feet and made his way out into the cheerless light.

On the street he sucked in a quick breath, felt a searing ache in his abdomen, and remembered that he was dying. He'd been close to death only once before, that day in the war when they'd come under attack from all directions. He'd felt the ground tremble, the whizzing bullets, the heat from the burning hutches, and finally the shell that had torn into his side. If it hadn't been for Stark, he'd have died right then, he thought, and suddenly the prospect of that earlier death appealed to him as few things ever had. To die abruptly, without waiting. To die owing nothing. To die young and stupid and before you'd fucked yourself over and fucked other people over, and married the first woman who'd have you, and accumulated nothing but a string of useless days. Before you'd learned just how goddamn worthless the future was. That, Mortimer decided, was a good death, and the only regret he felt as he turned and headed down the street was that he'd managed to escape it.

SARA

THE BUS cruised along Sunset Highway, through the clustered towns of Long Island. Within an hour she would be in New York. She had planned her future just that far, made no plans beyond her arrival, lined up no job, booked no hotel, nothing. At thirty-eight, she would return to the city exactly as she had first come to it twenty years before, with a single suitcase, no prospects, fleeing Long Island as she'd once fled the South, caught again in the same grim vise.

"Looks like we're going to get a little rain."

Sara glanced toward the woman who sat next to her.

"I checked the weather station before I left this morning," the woman added. "There's little spots of rain all up the East Coast." She opened a brown paper bag and took out a sandwich wrapped in aluminum foil. "I don't eat in bus stops," she explained. "Too expensive."

Sara said nothing. She wanted silence and distance, wanted only to get away from Tony and his father and from her own devouring rage.

Stop! she told herself fiercely. *Put it out of your mind, everything before right now.*

"Where you headed?" the woman beside her asked.

"North," Sara said, her voice oddly stiff and inflectionless, as if it came from stone.

The woman took the sandwich out of the foil. It was egg and bacon. She took a large bite and chewed with her mouth open. "Me too. Change for Boston when I get to the city. I got a daughter in Boston. I'm staying with her for a few days."

Sara listened as the woman prattled on and on, a low drone in Sara's mind as she detailed the route her daughter Lynn had taken through life, where she'd gone to school, the two guys she'd married, the jobs she'd had. The dragonback of Manhattan was visible before the tale wound to its end.

"I think Lynn's pretty settled now," the woman concluded.

Settled.

Sara saw a field of summer corn, felt a sweetly sickening breath in her face. She should have known at that instant that nothing would ever be settled after that because from then on, even when alone, she would hear nothing but the heavy tread of something from behind, and then the frantic scampering of prey.

ABE

HE JIGGLED the key until it opened. It hadn't turned smoothly in years. Like everything else, Abe thought, cranky and erratic, determined to thwart the smooth flow of things.

He switched on the light, closed the door, locked it. The clock over the bar read eleven-fifteen. Jake would arrive at noon, and the daily routine would begin in earnest, setting up the bar, checking the supplies, cleaning, polishing, paying bills. Jorge would show up twenty minutes later, mop the place, break down the boxes, gather up the garbage, all the drudge work of keeping the joint relatively clean. Susanne Albert, the college girl who'd worked in the place for only a couple of months, would come in an hour before opening, do the few things Jake hadn't finished, then sit in the back booth, reading some book about Hindu philosophy. And last, Lucille, the bar's only entertainment, a sixty-one-year-old former Broadway chorus singer who'd been at the bar for as long as Abe could remember, the singer he'd first accompanied all those many years ago, and who he'd kept on even after he'd bought the place.

That was it, then, Abe thought, the family.

It was a far cry from what he'd intended, but it was no doubt better than tapping out "Feelings" in some seedy lounge on the Jersey shore. He was forty-eight, old enough to know that the jazz pianist's life he'd once envisioned for himself would not have suited him very well. In fact, when he thought of it now, it was as little more than a Blue Note fantasy, like becoming a writer or an actor. Mavis had always said that he wasn't very adventurous, that all he really wanted was the anchor of a steady, predictable life. Toward the end she'd been plenty frank about it, *When you get right down to it, Abe, you're a stick-in-the-mud.*

He walked behind the bar, took the canvas cash bag he'd brought from the bank around the corner, and began to fill the register. He'd just opened the quarters into the drawer when the phone rang.

"McPherson's," he said.

"Abe. Lucille."

"You sound shitty."

"It's the mood, you know?"

"You need anything?"

"No. I'm just gonna sleep through it."

"Well, if you do . . ."

"I know, Abe."

He heard the click of the phone as Lucille hung up. Okay, he thought, his longtime chanteuse was in a mood and so wouldn't be showing up for her set. But it was a Tuesday, the slowest night of the week, so with Susanne working the tables and Jake the bar, and Jorge busing and himself at the keyboard, the bar would make it through all right.

He glanced at the old piano at the rear of the bar and remembered the first time Mavis had leaned against it, dark-eyed and looking more experienced than she should have, this woman he'd later married and who'd promised to stay with him always but had run off with a guy who'd later made it big, and whose smiling face Abe continually confronted in record stores and concert billboards. He knew what Mavis' flight had stolen from him: self-confidence, for one thing, along with the money she'd emptied from their accounts. All of that he could have gotten back one way or another, but what he'd never regained was the lightness of life, the sense of humor that had once so lifted him and made the good times roll and, more than his playing, brought buoyancy and joy to the people around him. That had gone with Mavis, and now seemed as irretrievable as the wedding ring she'd stripped from her finger and hocked at Forty-sixth and Eighth when Hell's Kitchen still smoldered on the west side of the city.

Jake came through the door and seemed to read his face. "Trouble?" he asked.

"Just Lucille," he lied.

TONY

TONY TOSSED the house keys to Eddie Sullivan. "She never locks the place, but just in case."

Sullivan pocketed the keys. "Okay, Tony."

"If the car's not in the driveway, give me a ring. But if it is, go to the door, see if she's inside. If there's some other car there, take down the license number and bring it back to me. But don't do anything else."

Sullivan nodded heavily. "Everything's okay, Tony." His smile was sympathetic. "Sara wouldn't never . . . you know."

"Yeah, well, she's seemed a little, I don't know, a little tense the last few days," Tony said. He walked Eddie out to the rusty old heap he'd been driving for as long as he could remember. "You ever gonna trade this fucking thing in?" he asked.

Sullivan shrugged. "It still runs okay. It's like an old girlfriend now." He grinned sheepishly, a thirty-five-year-old man still so shy and boyish, even the faintest allusion to women brought a blush to his face. "You know, I'm used to her."

Tony surveyed the sloping bumper and rusty under-carriage. It looked pitiful, and it made whoever drove it look pitiful. "I'm gonna give you a raise, Eddie. So you can put something down on a new car."

Sullivan's smile widened. "Thanks." He placed his beefy hand on Tony's shoulder. "It's gonna be okay. Sara, I mean."

"Yeah," Tony said, then watched as Sullivan hauled

himself into his car and drove away. He knew Eddie wasn't the brightest star in the heavens, but he was honest and reliable, and he could keep his mouth shut. A man with woman trouble could trust a guy like Eddie, a guy who lived alone, had never had a girlfriend, and might still be a virgin. Eddie took communion every Sunday at Our Lady of Fatima, and Tony guessed that he'd probably still be an altar boy if they let men his age do that sort of thing. Just the guy to check on a wife who'd been acting strange lately, Tony thought, a wife who hadn't answered the phone for hours. A piercing dread hit him, the terrible possibility that Sara had left him. He saw the red Explorer drift out of the driveway, Sara at the wheel, with that cold look in her eye.

His cousin Joey stepped out of the warehouse.

"What are you looking at?" Tony blurted vehemently.

"Nothing," Joey said, then retreated back into the warehouse.

Tony glanced out over the marina, a hundred boats precariously afloat. They seemed frail and unsteady, easily torn apart by high waves and raging winds, and for a moment he felt curiously like them, small and insubstantial before a dark, approaching storm.

STARK

HE SIPPED a martini and watched the traffic move haltingly along Fifty-ninth Street. The Oak Bar was one of his favorite haunts. He liked the dark wood and whispery conversations, the well-dressed men and women who sat together at the polished tables. He wanted the men to be arms dealers and the women to be spies, the bar itself suffused with a supercharged intrigue, something out of Cold War Vienna, the icy cat-and-mouse world of *The*

Third Man, where the only safety lay in secrecy and self-containment. In reality, the Oak Bar had nothing of this atmosphere. It was filled with out-of-towners and conventioneers. But Stark preferred to imagine it otherwise, a bar that shimmered distantly, enclosed in an elegant worldliness, cool, sophisticated, where his heart could rest unperturbed, like an olive at the bottom of a glass.

The woman who slid into the table next to his a few minutes later was in her mid-forties, but some good work had taken off a decade. She wore a dark blue skirt and white satin blouse that was partially covered by a silk scarf, black with small red roses. A gold dragon with large ruby eyes was pinned just above her right breast, wings spread, mouth open, fangs at the ready. He knew that she'd chosen it to signal that beneath the conservative clothes a voluptuous serpent twined. She ordered a brandy Alexander, swirled it with her little finger, sucked at a long, polished nail.

"I'm Evelyn," she said finally.

He nodded.

"And you are?"

"Whomever you like."

He'd responded in this way many times before, and so had learned that the woman in question either laughed and asked another question, or with a disgruntled shrug turned back to her drink and her quest, the distant hope that the next guy she approached would have no such obvious quirk.

The one called Evelyn laughed and swirled her drink. "Okay, let me think. Suppose I name you Frank."

He offered his hand. "Frank," he said. "A pleasure."

She laughed again as she took his hand. There was a slight pink stain on her straight white teeth, and this imperfection lightly touched the small, unhardened part of him. In objects, he looked for perfection, but in people, the chipped and the cracked, the all-but-invisible fray at the hem.

"And what do you do . . . Frank?"

"Whatever you say," he told her.

A carefully tweezed eyebrow drew into a lovely arch. "Really, you won't tell me what you do?"

"It's better if you make it up."

She looked at him distantly, as if unsure if he was what she really wanted, whether what she saw in him offered merely the allure of danger or the real thing.

"Okay, I'll play along," she said. "Let's say you're some kind of secret agent."

He leaned forward and looked at her gravely. His whisper was charged with conspiracy. "Our country is in danger, and I desperately need your help."

She laughed. "I'll bet you sell insurance. I'll bet your name's Harry and you're from Spokane."

"I'll be Harry if you want."

"No." She took a sip of the brandy Alexander. "No, I like your story better. Our country is in danger and you desperately need"—she hesitated, then released her final word like a small, wounded bird—"me."

SARA

SHE STOOD at the corner of Eighth Avenue and Forty-second Street, holding tightly to the suitcase. She'd known from the beginning that the moment would come when she would freeze. She'd come to New York with no idea of what to do or where to go. And so there'd have to be a moment when you couldn't figure out what you were going to do next. That was when you were most vulnerable, most gullible, most willing to take whatever hand reached out to you. Which was what she'd done with

Tony, and later hated herself for doing, and would never do again.

A voice inside her head gave the instruction, *Just keep moving!*

She lifted her hand and hailed a cab.

"Where to?" the driver asked as she settled into the backseat.

"Brooklyn Heights," she said for no reason other than that she'd sometimes strolled at night on the wide promenade, the radiant gleam of the Manhattan skyline, the great bridge shimmering above the dividing river.

On the Brooklyn Bridge, she glanced out over the harbor, the distant green of Lady Liberty, her torch hefted high. She tried to imagine herself as an immigrant, new to the country, carrying nothing but a single suitcase and some hopeful vision of the future. She labored to find something hopeful too, but her past reached for her like a bony hand thrust up from the ground, and she felt only the dreadful opposite of nostalgia, memory itself a haunted house.

"Anyplace in particular you want to be dropped off?" the driver asked as he turned off the ramp that led to Brooklyn Heights.

"Just near the river."

The cab came to a halt on Columbia Heights Street. Sara paid the driver and got out and stood, suitcase in hand, facing the river until she recalled a small hotel whose dark little cabaret room she'd once worked.

It was called the Jefferson, and the cabaret room was now just a bar off the lobby. Still, it was a place she knew and so she decided to check in for the night. The man behind the desk asked if she had a reservation. She told him that she hadn't.

"Very well," he said a little sadly, as if in recognition that a hotel where a person could just walk in off the street and get a room was a second-rate hotel, and so he must be second-rate too. "The room's on the fifth floor." He gave her the key and tapped a brass bell.

A bellhop appeared. He grabbed her suitcase. "This way."

The bellhop wore a little round cap with a strap beneath the chin, the kind she remembered on bellhops in movies from the forties, and suddenly she felt the sweet, romantic glow of those old films turn sour in her mind. Their promise of a big happy ending was no more than a cruel joke, a Hollywood fantasy in which the ones who hurt you got what they deserved.

EDDIE

AS HE pulled up to the curb in front of Tony's house, Eddie was relieved to see that Sara's red Explorer was the only vehicle in the driveway. He had not wanted to find some strange car parked there. He knew what that might mean, that there was a guy in Tony's house, in bed with Tony's wife. He didn't want to think about this because he liked Sara. She'd always been nice to him and he didn't want to imagine that she was doing the wrong thing now, something he didn't want to tell Tony, though he knew he'd have to.

He got out of the car, walked to the front door, and knocked lightly.

No answer.

He knocked again.

Still no answer.

He peered through the narrow window in the door. Beyond it, he could see the living room, but it didn't look like a room anyone really lived in. It looked like a picture in one of those magazines his mother used to buy at the corner drugstore, rich people's homes, always with gleaming floors and fresh flowers, and this feeling that no one really lived there.

He inserted the key but didn't turn it. It was someone else's house, and he felt a biting reluctance to go inside. More, it was a woman's house, a woman alone, if she were there at all. What if he came upon her when she was . . . doing something women do. He knew Tony had given him permission to go inside, even ordered him to do it. Still, he couldn't. Even if Tony's wife weren't there, he might see her things lying around, her panties, a bra, and if you saw those things, the intimate apparel of another man's wife, didn't that mean that you knew too much about her, because only Tony should see such things, touch them. He shook his head. No, he would not go inside the house.

And so he stepped off the porch and walked to the back of the house, moving along the wooden fence that enclosed the backyard. The pool was covered, the pool furniture stored in the cabana. The diving board stretched out over the vacant cement cavern.

Eddie stood on the recently mowed lawn and decided that this was an unhappy place. He didn't know how he sensed such things, and he understood that no one would pay any attention to what he thought, and yet he knew absolutely that this house was unhappy and that if Tony's wife had left it, there was a good reason for it. He would never say anything like this to Tony, of course, because no matter how it came out, Tony would hear it as an accusation. A guy always took it that way. He might rage about what a bitch his wife was, but in his heart he'd feel that in some important way he hadn't measured up.

He turned back toward the car, now resolved that he had nothing to bring back to Tony, nothing to tell him save that Sara's car was in the driveway but that she hadn't answered the door. Tony wouldn't like it that he hadn't gone inside the house, but what could be done about that? Nothing, Eddie thought, until he noticed a woman at the mailbox across the street and wondered if maybe she could help him out.

DELLA

HE WAS a big guy and she was sure Tony had sent him. As he came toward her, she noticed his hands, how huge they were, and the shoulders, enormous. So maybe it wasn't Tony who'd sent him, she thought, maybe the guy had been sent by Tony's father, one of Old Man Labriola's goons.

"Hi," the man said as he drew close.

She closed the lid of the mailbox before replying. "Hello."

"My name's Eddie," the man said. "Eddie Sullivan."

The guy smiled, and Della thought it a warm, curiously innocent smile. But then, these guys all smiled that way, didn't they? These made men who joked with you until the moment they wrapped the cord around your neck or put a bullet in your head. She'd seen guys like that in the movies, and she believed the movies were true.

"I was wondering if you know the people across the way," the man said. "Tony Labriola? Sara?"

She felt her hands tighten around the stack of bills she'd just retrieved from the mailbox. "I know Sara."

The man smiled again. He had a gap between his teeth and looked harmless, but she steeled herself against believing that he really was. A guy like that, she told herself, a guy like that could break your neck in a second, then go have a big bowl of his mother's Irish stew and forget the whole thing.

"Tony's been calling Sara all morning, but she don't answer," the man said. "He's worried about her. Maybe she had an accident, something like that. He sent me over to see if she's okay."

"I haven't seen her," Della said.

"This morning, you mean?"

"I haven't seen her in a couple of days." Della thought of her last sight of Sara. She'd looked the way women did whose husbands slapped them around, but Della couldn't imagine Tony doing that and so had supposed it was something else that was eating Sara. Maybe the fact that she'd never had any kids. Women without kids looked that way sometimes, Della knew, all hollowed out.

"Tony give me a key to the house," the man told her. "But, you know, I didn't want to . . . barge in, maybe scare somebody, you know?" He drew the keys from the pocket of a blue parka and offered them to her. "So, maybe you could take a look inside. Make sure there ain't nothing wrong."

She didn't know how to refuse, so she took the keys and walked with the man back across the street, unlocked Sara's front door, and walked into the house.

"Sara?" she called. "Sara, you here?"

She turned and noticed that the man remained outside, and suddenly he seemed astonishingly shy to her, and good, the sort of man who turned away from the embarrassment of others. "I don't think she's home," she told him.

The man stepped to the door but did not come in. "Would you mind looking upstairs? She could be up there. Sleeping or . . . something."

She felt at ease with him now. There were certain men who made women feel that way, that they lived only to protect you, that it was their mission. Mike made her feel that way. "Okay," she said.

She made her way up the stairs. "Sara?" she called again. "Sara?"

At the top of the stairs she could see into the master bedroom. Tony's clothes lay on the floor beside the bed, and the bed itself was unmade.

"She's not here," she told the man when she came back out of the house. "I looked all over."

He seemed saddened by this news but not surprised. "Okay, thanks," he said.

They walked back to the man's car. She stood beside it as he got in. She felt no fear of him now, no dread. It surprised her that she wanted to know more about him, maybe ask him how despite being so big and looking so scary, he had achieved this grace.

STARK

SHE WAS experienced, as he expected, and preferred to be on top. She kept her blouse on but unbuttoned the sleeves and rolled them up to the elbow. Her breathing came in quick, rhythmic spurts, and on the downstroke, little pleasurable bursts of vulgarity broke from her. "Oh, shit," she groaned, then took a deep breath. "Oh, fuck," she gasped. She reared back, swept her hair from her eyes, and switched to a grinding motion. "Oh, Christ." Her movements grew more rapid. "I'm going to get it," she said with a quick laugh. "I'm going to get it, baby."

Then she did, and after that rolled off him and lay on her back and gazed at the ceiling.

"Do you know what they call it in the South?" she asked. "When you get it, I mean. A nut. They call it getting your nut." She shifted onto her side, rested her head in her hand, and stared at him. "Did it bother you . . . about keeping my blouse on?"

"No."

"I've had some . . . problems, so . . ."

He touched her lips with his finger. "It didn't bother me."

She brushed back a strand of his silver hair. "You're probably married. With a couple of kids."

He neither confirmed nor denied this.

She remained silent for a time, then said, "I took the room just for the day. I do that once a month or so. To stay alive."

She was trying to explain something he'd heard before, that life was inadequate, a quick fuck at the Plaza just another survival tool. And why not? Nothing lasted. Nothing held. Life was just a long improvisation. You feinted left or right, and by that means dodged the blow.

"So, what do you think . . . Frank," she said. "Maybe we could save the country again sometime."

He shook his head.

She looked at him piercingly, and he saw a wound open up inside her. "Just not interested, is that it?" she asked.

Inevitably, the time had come to lie to her. "I'm leaving town."

Inevitably, she did not believe it. "Whatever you say, mystery man." She shrugged indifferently, but there was a bitter glint in her eye. "Too bad." She pulled herself from the bed and began to dress. He took the cue and did the same.

A few minutes later they strolled out of the Plaza and made their way toward Fifth Avenue. The circular fountain sprayed its fine mist. Chauffeurs were gathered in small knots, smoking.

"Pretty," she said. There was a mist in her eyes. "So pretty."

They walked along the avenue. The silence between them lengthened and grew heavier with each step.

At last she stopped and faced him. "May I ask you something? Do you do this . . . a lot?"

The time had come to cut the cord, and he knew that any effort to do it slowly would only make things worse. "Every chance I get," he said.

"Does it matter . . . who?"

"No."

"How very . . . romantic." Her tone suddenly grew brittle. "I should have guessed as much. All you mystery men are shits."

He gave no response but only stepped over to the curb and hailed a cab while she watched him, fuming now, from a few feet away.

When the cab pulled over he got in. "Four forty-five West Nineteenth," he said.

She bolted forward and rapped at the window, her eyes flaring vehemently. "Fuck you, mystery man."

The cab pulled away and he fixed his gaze on the rearview mirror, where he could see the driver's eyes peering at him. They were dark and sunken and they reminded him of Marisol. Her voice returned to him in a ghostly whisper, *Sabes que me matará. You know he's going to kill me.*

He closed his eyes and let the black curtain fall. When he opened them again, the cab was turning onto Nineteenth Street, and it had begun to rain.

ABE

THE OLD awning resisted him like a creature with a will of its own.

"Come on now," he blurted out impatiently.

Abe gave the crank a furious jerk, and the awning creaked out a little, covering just enough of the sidewalk to allow pedestrians to take cover beneath it but not enough for the side flap to display the full name of the bar. Rain-soaked strangers would think they were scurrying into a tavern called "McPhe," not one named for its first owner, Casey McPherson.

"Lucille's not coming in tonight," Abe said when Jorge arrived a few minutes later.

"In one of her moods," Jake added.

Jorge shrugged. "Yah, okay, thas goo." He hurried into the back.

"Thas goo," Jake repeated with a laugh. "You could tell him you'd just eaten your own fingers and he'd say 'Yah, okay, thas goo'."

Jake was nearly seventy, with sloping shoulders and a shrunken face. He seemed to slither more than walk. Behind his thin lips, it was easy to imagine a forked tongue. "As for Lucille, she should see a doctor. They got pills for it now. I seen them advertised on TV. You pop a pill and it's blue skies all the way."

Abe had advised Lucille to take medication, but it had done no good. Lucille called her dark mood The Weight, and he knew how it worked in her, falling before midnight and growing heavier every minute so that she felt that she was being slowly squeezed to death, each second dropping upon her like a stone. By dawn she'd have lost all desire to open her eyes. And why not? All she'd see was a cramped, dingy room, chairs littered with old newspapers, piles of square white boxes from Tan's Golden Dragon. Abe wondered how long it had been since she'd ordered anything but moo goo gai pan. That should have told her that it was getting worse, he thought, that The Weight would continue to fall upon her until it crushed everything—touch, taste, smell—left her with no sensation whatever except the impossible heaviness of the surrounding air.

And yet, for all that, she'd been a first-class singer when he'd met her years before. Like the best bar singers, she'd always known what the customers expected of her, how they wanted to have their spirits lifted. She'd been able to do that because she'd understood that in every man there was a knight, and in every woman a lady of the lake. The knights were fallen and the women were faded, but their vision of themselves lived on. If you kept that vision in mind, you could make each customer feel special. For years Lucille had accomplished that extraordinary feat, but at some point The Weight had crushed it, and she'd stopped singing except by rote, just mouthing the lyrics to no one in particular. He'd briefly thought of letting her go but lacked the heart to do it, and so simply had done nothing but helplessly watch The Weight grow heavier each year.

Jorge returned to the bar, mop in hand. "Okay I start now?"

"Yeah," Abe said, then grabbed a stack of envelopes from beside the cash register, walked to a booth at the rear of the bar, and began to do the bills. Casey McPherson had taught him to pay everything on time. That way, if you ever had a problem, the suppliers would cut you a little slack. Twenty years had passed since then, but Abe had yet to ask anyone to wait for the money or take less than what was owed. That's the one thing he could say, the bar had sustained him. It paid for his apartment on Grove Street and the occasional night at some cabaret joint uptown. Those were the nights he lived for, a table alone, a dark room, a singer with a trio—piano, sax, bass—an ensemble so pure in Abe's mind that there were moments, brief and a little scary, when the voice and the instruments joined in an arrangement so balanced, so inexpressibly right, it brought tears to his eyes. There were even a couple of times when he had actually hit that elusive mark himself, the unexpected D-flat he'd added at the end of his arrangement of "She Was Too Good to Me," for example. Perfect. He looked up from the bills and remembered the sound of it, the way Lucille's voice had curled around the note, so sad and lost and goddamn hopeless. That was a moment, he told himself now, smiling quietly the way he always did when he thought of something really good.

MORTIMER

THE CAR swept up beside him before he'd even noticed it, but once he saw Caruso get out, he knew he was in deep shit.

"Hello, Morty," Caruso said.

"Vinnie."

"Let's take a ride."

Mortimer climbed into the car. "I'm gonna pay you, Vinnie," he said.

"Oh, I know you are, Morty," Caruso said.

Mortimer could see that Caruso was trying hard to add a hint of the psychopath, the idea that not only would he hurt you, he'd have a great time doing it.

"It's just a question of whether you do it now or after you've maybe lost a piece of yourself," Caruso added.

"Yeah, okay."

Suddenly Caruso grabbed Mortimer's left wrist and squeezed. "Spread your fingers."

"Oh, come on, Vinnie . . ."

"Spread your fucking fingers!"

Mortimer gave in and spread his fingers, then watched as Caruso's gaze snagged on his wedding band.

"A married man," Caruso said. "Your wife love you, Morty?"

Mortimer shrugged.

Caruso released Mortimer's hand. "So here's the thing. You're down fifteen grand. So I ask myself, has Morty got that kind of cash? And I say to myself, I don't know and I don't fucking care. 'Cause if Morty don't have it, he's gonna get it. He's gonna pay me. I'm right about that. I know I am. Because you're not stupid, Morty. And you know what happens to a guy if he don't pay me. Right?"

Mortimer nodded dully.

"So what are we looking at? Week?"

"Yeah, okay."

"Good," Caruso said. He seemed glad that it was over, as if the psycho act were a heavy load he was happy to lay down. "So, we're clear then."

"We're clear," Mortimer said.

The car stopped and Caruso reached over and swung open the door on Mortimer's side. "So, you feeling okay, Morty?" he asked like a guy who'd hurt another guy's feelings and was now looking to make up.

"I'm fine," Mortimer said a little sourly, but only because the pain had suddenly swept in again, reminding him of the little time that remained, and all the time before it that he'd wasted, and how time was like a river that swept you along invisibly, taking some people to nice well-lit places and others into the deep dark wood.

STARK

THE SCOTCH was warm, and he settled back in the high leather chair and listened to Brahms's violin concerto, the final movement, where all the yearning was. So much yearning, he thought, the lone violin seemed to reach ever upward, toward some impossible height of unquenchable desire. To be captured by such longing for even the briefest moment, he knew, could change a man forever.

He closed his eyes and she was with him.

Marisol.

The odd truth assailed him once again, the fact that he'd traveled the world only to find the most beautiful woman he'd ever seen lounging in a small bar in Chueca, on the dark side of Madrid.

It had begun as business, just another day in the life of one whose job it was to find the scattered pieces of broken lives. Runaway partners, children, husbands, wives, people he tracked down and bought back to what they'd shattered when they left—homes, businesses, a lolling sense of trust. He'd always understood that it was not his job to put anything back together—blasted families, companies, estates. He simply brought back the ones who'd fled the destruction so that they could face whatever punishment or reconciliation his clients had in mind.

He remembered the small packet of information Lockridge had given him.

Lockridge, who claimed to be Marisol's lover.

Lockridge, who claimed to want her back because he loved her so.

Lockridge, who said he only wanted a chance to talk to Marisol, apologize, beg her to return.

Lockridge, who swore that if Marisol refused to go back to him, he would let her go.

There'd been a photo of the woman in question, but it hadn't done her justice. A beauty like hers was rare and deep, but it was not the beauty of a fashion model or a movie star. Nothing about her appearance seemed the product of oils and powders, the right slant of light. Her loveliness made its own light, and this light flowed over her like a stream.

"She's a seductress," Lockridge had written along the margin of the photograph, "so be careful."

Careful, Stark thought now, lifting the glass to his lips again as he recalled the moment he'd first seen her in the flesh, the way she'd looked at the little wrought-iron table in Chueca, her long, slender fingers curled around a glass of red wine to which she'd just added a burst of Casera water. Her black skirt fell well below her knees, and her plain white blouse was knotted at the front and open just enough so that the orbs of her brown breasts were slightly visible.

Her coal-black hair had thrown off small white flashes when she'd turned her head at his approach, and as he'd drawn near, he'd seen tiny drops of sweat along her upper lip. But it was her eyes he most remembered when he remembered her—dark, oval, with a hint of ancient coastal towns about them. *"Buenas tardes, señor"* was all she'd said.

TONY

HE SAT behind the wheel and stared at the house, the unlighted windows, the motionless curtains, the Explorer that rested in the otherwise vacant driveway, everything just as Eddie had described it after he'd gotten back to the marina.

She was gone. The pain of her leaving turned instantly to a wild, inchoate anger, so that he flew out of the car and strode across the lawn and bolted into the house as if carried on a boiling wave.

Once inside, he slammed through the first floor, checking each room, then stormed up to the second floor, where he did the same. In the bedroom he made no move to retrieve his clothes from the floor, his attention focused instead on the unmade bed, the way she'd left the sheets rumpled, the blanket sagging toward the floor.

A stinging heat assailed him, and in a single explosive charge he slammed his fist into the wall. The sting of the impact felt good, and so he hit the wall again and again and again, until he'd pounded a gaping hole into the plaster and bits of shattered debris lay scattered like small white bones at his feet.

When it was over, he slumped down on the plush blue carpet. In his mind he saw Sara as she'd appeared the night he'd met her, a slender young woman with shoulder-length hair who'd come on tough and worldly but had melted at his touch. He felt the sweetness of her unexpected surrender, the way she'd given herself up to him, the fever and the shuddering and the low moan, the way she'd whispered "I love you" that first time. To hear her say that again, just once, was all he wanted now.

ABE

IT WAS a slow night. By ten there were only four people left in the bar, all of them regulars, some who'd even known McPherson when he'd still owned the place and Abe when he'd played for tips, the Bordeaux glass filling slowly with crumpled bills and pocket change as night crawled toward morning, and Lucille leaned back against the piano and drew a red feather boa along her bare white shoulders and broke into the final, melancholy song before last call.

He ran his fingers over the keyboard, playing the notes of "As Time Goes By," giving it that bitter edge Mavis' betrayal had taught him.

Milo Barnes leaned back slightly, the scotch a little loose in his hand. "Where's Lucille?" he asked.

"Out sick," Abe said. He closed the cover over the keys and glanced out over the nearly empty bar. "I should probably check on her."

He picked up the phone beside the register and dialed Lucille's number. There was no answer. He'd called her a few times since early in the afternoon, attributed the fact that she hadn't answered to a nap or a brief walk or maybe that she'd gone out for groceries, her laundry. But now he was worried.

"I'm gonna check on Lucille," he said to Jake as he grabbed his hat from the wooden peg near the bar. "She's not answering the phone."

He knocked at her door a few minutes later, waited, knocked again, and when there was still no answer, unlocked the door.

The apartment was pitch black, and something in the depth of the darkness told him what he'd find when he turned on the light.

"Lucille," he said quietly as he flipped the switch.

She was lying on her back, eyes closed, one arm across her brow as if, in the last moments, she'd shielded her eyes against a blinding light. A bottle of Seconal rested on the table beside the bed, along with a half-empty glass of water. She'd left a piece of sheet music on the old battered spinet she'd once used to rehearse some song that had taken her fancy.

"Lucille," he repeated, and then stepped over to the bed and, in a distant hope he might be wrong, shook her gently. When she didn't move, he touched her face, felt a strange slackness in her skin, as if life were little more than the force that kept things taut.

The EMS ambulance arrived a few minutes later, then a couple of cops, one in plainclothes who introduced himself as Detective Melville.

"I just have a few questions," he told Abe. "You found the deceased?"

"Yes."

"And you are?"

"Abe Morgenstern."

"When did you get here?"

"Just a few minutes ago," Abe answered. "I called as soon as I found her."

"You're a friend of hers?"

"Yes. And she worked for me. McPherson's. On Twelfth Street. She called in sick this afternoon."

"How did you get into her apartment?"

"I have a key."

"So you've known her a long time?"

"A long time, yeah," Abe said, the years rushing by on a white-water stream.

There were a few more questions, all of them routine, Abe guessed, though he could not be sure, since he'd never been questioned by a policeman before.

Detective Melville closed his notebook. "Okay, thanks." He touched his hat, then went up the stairs, leaving Abe alone on the street.

He was still there when Lucille was brought down and loaded into the ambulance. Her body seemed infinitely small beneath the sheet, far too small to have contained the heavy life she'd lived, the huge obstacles she'd overcome just to get this far. It wasn't that she'd killed herself that struck Abe as particularly sad, but that she'd had to fight that urge for so long, and in that protracted struggle lost what small amount of happiness she might otherwise have grasped.

Once the ambulance pulled away, Abe walked back up the stairs and into the apartment. The super was there, looking around, as if already calculating the trouble this would cause him.

"She have any relatives?" he asked.

Abe shook his head.

"So, what you want I should do? With her stuff, I mean."

"I'll have it picked up."

The super looked relieved that clearing the apartment would fall to others' hands. "No rush. I mean, she's paid up through the end of the month."

The super left, but Abe lingered a few more minutes in her room. He was not sure why, save that some part of him simply hated letting things go. He'd hated to admit that Mavis had actually gone. Hell, he realized, he'd even felt the same about that fucking cat she'd left him with, Pookie, who'd died on him three weeks later.

He headed down the stairs and out onto the street, where he stood absently, his eyes cast upward into the misty sky, and tried to make himself believe that there might really be someplace toward which Lucille's unburdened soul was now ascending, its slender wings beating softly to the ballad she'd always used to close her set, "Bird Alone."

TONY

"SHE WAS acting strange the last few days," Tony said.

His father shrugged. "She was always a fruitcake."

Tony took the wedge of orange from the rim of the glass, squeezed it, then dropped it into his glass.

"What the fuck you drinking?" his father asked.

"Scotch sour."

"That's a pussy drink, Tony," the Old Man said. "Scotch sour. Jesus Christ. You go in a real bar and order something like that, they take you out back and stomp the shit out of you."

Tony shrugged. "Anyway, she just left, that's all. Out of the blue."

Labriola scowled. "Out of the blue means another guy, right?"

"I don't think so," Tony answered weakly.

"You don't think so?" the Old Man barked. "What are you, Tony? Stupid? That fucking bitch run out on you."

"I don't know, Dad, Sara's not the—"

"Not the what?"

"I just don't think she would have—"

"Would have what?"

"Would have . . . you know . . ."

"Fucked around on you?"

"Yeah."

"Okay, Tony, so where's her car? You said it was sitting in the driveway, right?"

"Yeah."

"So, your theory is, she leaves but she don't take the car? So what do you think, she's on foot? Walking to where? California? Jesus, Tony, think!" The Old Man slapped him lightly on the side of the head. "Think about it! This bitch ain't on foot or thumbing a ride. Or maybe you figure she's in some big fucking balloon. Floating in the air." His laugh was clanking brass. "Face it, Tony. She run off with some guy."

"I don't know what to think, Dad."

"How about money? She take any money?"

"I don't know," Tony answered weakly.

"You don't know? You ain't checked the accounts?"

"No."

"Jesus," the Old Man muttered. "Your wife takes a hike and you don't check the fucking accounts."

"I didn't think of it, Dad. I been . . . you know . . . upset."

"She played you for a chump from the beginning, Tony. Just a little hayseed singing in some fucking club, and in you walk, a meal ticket if ever there was one."

"She didn't know anything about me. I could have been—"

"Oh yeah, take me back, Tony. To that night, I mean, when you first met this fucking broad. Was you alone?"

"No. I was with Frankie and Angelo and—"

"And you paid for the drinks, right, because those two assholes never sprung for a drink their whole fucking lives."

"Yeah, I paid for the drinks."

"And you think a broad don't notice that, Tony, don't notice who's paying?"

"She was way up front, Dad, she couldn't have—"

"Yeah, yeah, up front. But she could see you, right? She ain't fucking blind. She could see you standing there with those two jerkoffs, and that it was you paying."

"Yeah, I guess she could see me."

"And how was you dressed, Tony? You have a hard hat on? Huh? You carrying a tub of fish out clubbing? You wearing some greasy, fucking work shirt, or was you dressed nice?"

"Nice."

"So she didn't have to be no fucking brain surgeon to figure it out, right? That you was a guy with cash."

"I guess not," Tony admitted.

"So there it is," the Old Man said, satisfied that he'd made his point. "That's the whole story with this bitch. Now some other asshole comes along, and she plays you for a chump." His eyes squeezed together. "I never liked her, Tony. From the South. Shit. What do you know about girls from the South? You could have married your own kind. Kitty Scalli, for example, you could have married her. But, no, you see this fucking hillbilly in some god-damn cheesy bar. End of story." He shook his head at the idiocy of it all. "You'd married Kitty Scalli, we wouldn't be having this fucking conversation."

Tony took a quick sip of his drink. "Well, the thing is—"

"The thing is, you ain't gonna let her get away with it, Tony," the Old Man said darkly. He took a noisy pull on his beer and set the glass down hard. " 'Cause if she does, you'll never live it down."

"Yeah, I know, but—"

"The problem is, you don't stand up for yourself, Tony. You ain't never stood up for yourself. A woman runs all over you, you just sit there drinking that pussy drink you got there. Your cousin Donny would never have let his wife do something like this."

"Donny's an asshole," Tony said.

"Donny's an asshole?" Labriola yelped. "Okay, let me ask you this. You think Carla would run off with some fucking scumbag? What that hayseed bitch done to you? Huh? You think Carla would do that to Donny? Fuck no. 'Cause Donny wouldn't take it, that's why. You know what would happen to Carla she done that to Donny, what your wife done to you? And there's your fucking answer. You never taught her to respect you, Tony, and this is the price you pay."

"Yeah, Dad, but—"

"No fucking buts," the Old Man snarled. "You're my son. You're Leo Labriola's son. And you know the rule I got, right? You fuck my son, you fuck me."

"Yeah, but the thing is—"

"You fuck my son, you fuck me," Labriola repeated fiercely, his eyes glowing red. "You understand?"

Tony nodded mutely.

"You got to find her and bring her back, Tony," the Old Man added sternly. "Otherwise, won't nobody ever treat you with no respect."

"Well, sure, but the thing is, I don't—"

"Don't what?"

"Don't know where she is."

The Old Man's eyes went cold. "There ain't nowhere that bitch could run to she can't be found."

"Yeah, but—"

"Nowhere, you understand?"

"Yeah, sure."

Labriola drained the rest of the beer. "I got to make a call." He got to his feet. "Then me and you are gonna shoot a little pool."

CARUSO

THE PHONE shook him from his sleep, the Old Man's voice like a fist around his throat.

"This guy, the deadbeat, he knows people, right? People who find people."

"He's connected to some guy who does that," Caruso told him.

"Okay, here it is. He gets this guy to do a job for me, I'll let go what he owes me."

"The guy usually gets thirty," Caruso said cautiously. "The bill to you is just fifteen."

"What are you saying, Vinnie?"

"That Morty's guy, he maybe won't do it for fifteen."

"Okay, so I pay the shithead thirty, and he keeps fifteen and gives the other guy fifteen."

"He shorts him?" Caruso said.

"Yeah, he fucking shorts him, Vinnie," Labriola bawled. "Or we break his fucking thumbs."

"Okay," Caruso said quickly. "Maybe he'll do that."

"Like he's got a fucking choice?" The Old Man's laugh was brutal.

"I mean . . . he will," Caruso added hastily. "What's the job?"

"Find that bitch married my son. She took off this morning. He ain't heard a word since then."

Caruso nodded briskly, as if the Old Man were in the room with him, feeling the way he'd tried to make Mortimer feel a few hours before, like a cringing worm.

"Tony ain't to know nothing about this, you understand?" Labriola added. "You just find that bitch and let me know."

"Yes, sir," Caruso said quickly.

"So make the deal with this little shit owes me fifteen grand," Labriola said. "Then get back to me."

"Yes, sir," Caruso repeated in what had become the litany of his life. He hung up, paused briefly, then picked up the phone and dialed one of the scores of numbers he had stored in the hard drive of his mind, this one under the heading "Deadbeats," the mental file to which he'd but recently added Morty's name.

STARK

HE ATE in the garden at Gascogne, surrounded on three sides by high brick walls laced with vines. Within a week the garden would be closed, and so he lingered over a final glass of brandy until nearly midnight.

After that he walked to his apartment on West Nineteenth Street. He'd bought the first-floor apartment nearly twenty years before, and bit by bit he'd turned it into a home that suited him, the walls decorated with carefully chosen oils, the floors draped with large Oriental carpets.

Once inside, he poured a glass of port, sat down in a high-back leather chair, and drew a book from the small mahogany table beside it. In his youth, reading had been his passion. He'd pored over the classics, devouring the Greeks, Shakespeare, scores of nineteenth-century novels, but now he read only for business—travel guides, catalogues filled with the latest high-tech surveillance equipment, computer manuals, private publications from the field, tips of the trade exchanged by the few people who'd made it to the top of his precarious profession.

He knew why this radical shift had occurred, and as he drank, he revisited the grim reason in a series of ghastly mental photographs—a body strewn in a Madrid alleyway, another floating in the shallow currents of the nearby river, and finally a dark-haired beauty tied to a chair, her body drooping forward, mercifully dead after what had been done to her.

Marisol.

At just past midnight, the buzzer signaled someone at the door.

He opened it to find Mortimer swiping droplets of rain from his jacket and stamping his rubber galoshes on the mat outside the door.

"Fucking wet," Mortimer said morosely. He drew an envelope from his jacket pocket and handed it to Stark. "From Brandenberg. Payment in full."

Stark took the envelope. "Would you like a drink?"

Mortimer nodded, then followed Stark inside and took a seat on the leather sofa.

Stark poured Mortimer a scotch and handed it to him. "You look a little rumpled."

"It ain't been a great day," Mortimer said. He took a long pull on the scotch, wiped his mouth with the back of his hand.

Stark watched Mortimer silently, now recalling how, after the murders, he'd had to create a new identity, find a go-between he trusted, and so had gone to Mortimer, the platoon sergeant he'd commanded through countless bloody days. Even now Stark was not exactly sure why he'd chosen Mortimer to assist him in his shadowy profession, save that there was a melancholy ponderousness to him that went well with the weighty confidences he was expected to hold. On a cold, snowy night, Stark had told Mortimer about Marisol's murder, along with the brutal penalty he had exacted from the men who'd committed it. He'd never forgotten Mortimer's reply, *Guys like that, nobody's gonna miss 'em.* He'd known at that moment that Mortimer was a man for whom moral subtlety amounted to mindless abstraction. Only the clearest lines appeared in his field of vision. On the confidence of that insight, he'd hired him immediately.

"Something bothering you?" Stark asked now.

"Me?" Mortimer laughed nervously. "Nothing."

Stark peered at him intently. "Something's bothering you, Mortimer."

Mortimer shifted uncomfortably in his seat. "Well, there is this . . . other job . . . but I don't know if you'd want to do it."

Stark eased himself into the chair opposite Mortimer. "Brandenberg again?"

"No. He had this Arab, but I know you don't want no foreigners." He took a sip from the glass. "But this other thing come in."

"What is it?"

Mortimer seemed hesitant to go on. "It's kind of personal," he said. "A friend from the old days. He called me a couple hours ago." He took another sip. "The thing is, his wife run out on him."

"That's hardly new in life," Stark said. "I'm sure you told him that in most cases the woman returns."

"Yeah, I did," Mortimer said. "But the thing is, he's set on tracking her down. He figured I might be able to help him."

"Why would he figure that?"

"He figures I know people," Mortimer answered. "I mean, not you. Just people who . . . do things."

"What do you know about the woman?"

"Nothing. And the thing is, it's embarrassing, you know? To my friend. He don't want nobody to know about it. The neighbors, relatives, people like that. So what information I get, it's got to come from him. He don't want no asking around."

"How much information can he give me?"

"I don't know. He's getting a few things together."

"I can't work on thin air," Stark said.

"I know," Mortimer said. "Believe me, I know that. And there's something else. This guy, he ain't got much money. I mean, fifteen grand at the most. I know you don't work for less than thirty but . . ."

"You said he was a friend of yours."

"Yeah," Mortimer answered. "But like I said, we're talking fifteen . . ."

"I'll take it," Stark said. "As a favor to you." He waited for Mortimer to finish his drink, then escorted him to the door.

"Good night," Mortimer said as he stepped into the corridor.

Stark nodded. "This friend of yours, you vouch for him, right?"

"Yeah, sure."

"Okay," Stark said.

"Well, good night, then," Mortimer said, returning his hat to his head.

"Good night," Stark said, and closed the door and returned to his chair as well as to his thoughts of Marisol.

SARA

"DELLA, IT'S me."

"Sara?" She lowered her voice to a whisper. "Just a sec, honey. Mike's sleeping. I'll go to the other room." A pause, then, "Tony's looking for you, Sara. He sent a guy over here and the guy saw me, and he made me go in the house and look for you. He said Tony had been calling you, and didn't get an answer, you know, and so he sent this guy. So, what happened, Sara? You have a fight, you and Tony?"

"I better go now," Sara said. "I just wanted to let you know that I'm okay."

"No, wait, Sara, where are you?"

"I have to go, Della."

"But—"

"I have to go."

"But . . . wait . . . listen . . . you're not coming back?"

"No."

"It's that bad?"

"Yes."

"He hit you, Sara? Tony hit you?"

"No, but . . . I have to go, Della."

"Yeah, okay," Della said quietly. "Sure, honey."

"So . . . take it easy, Della."

"Yeah. You too."

Sara hung up. A quick metallic click. That was what it sounded like, then, when someone dropped out of your story.

She put down the phone, turned on the television, then turned it off, and walked down the stairs and out into the night, along the Promenade, her eyes drawn to the glittering light show of Manhattan. Time passed. She was not sure how much time.

"Lady?"

She whirled, her gaze now fixed on the badge, staring at it with the same fear she'd first experienced on that summer afternoon when Sheriff Caulfield had pulled her over. *Got a broke taillight there, girl.*

"I didn't mean to scare you," the policeman said. "I just wanted to make sure you were all right."

She drew in a shallow breath. "I'm fine."

"You sure?"

"Yes."

The cop studied her for a moment, then touched the rim of his cap with a single finger. "Okay, good night, then."

"Good night."

She watched as the policeman moved on down the Promenade, waiting for him to turn around, head back toward her, the way Sheriff Caulfield had on that distant afternoon, down a dusty country road, moving slowly and without fear, superior to his prey. She felt his hand on her shoulder, drawing her from the car, confused, frightened, a teenage girl in a car with a broken taillight, eased out into the crystalline air. *Just do what I tell you and you'll be on your way.*

But this time the policeman didn't turn back toward her, and once he was out of view, she returned her gaze to the Manhattan skyline, avoiding the empty space where the Towers had once stood. They'd been like her, she thought, just standing there in the open, weaponless and vulnerable.

The memory of a sweet, liquored breath swept into

her face, and suddenly she heard the wind in the corn, saw herself glancing back to where both taillights remained intact. *But . . . Sheriff . . . my light isn't broken,* then saw him step over to the back of her car, take out his pistol, and shatter the left taillight, sending little shards of blood-red plastic onto the dusty road. *Now it is.*

The memory of that moment filled her with a burning ire, the way she'd promised herself that she would never let it happen again. Next time, *Kill him,* the voice had whispered, and she had vowed, *I will.*

TWO

Blame It on My Youth

ABE

"SO WHAT are you gonna do, Abe?" Jake lifted a glass, examined it for spots.

Abe looked up from yet another pile of bills. "Do?"

"You know, about Lucille. You gonna replace her?"

"Yeah," Abe said.

That Lucille was dead still seemed unreal to him. He'd seen her body hauled away and yet he expected her to walk through the door at the usual hour, a cigarette dangling from the corner of her mouth.

"'Blame It on My Youth,'" he said. "Lucille didn't sing that until she was forty-six, remember?"

Jake swiped the counter with a white cloth. "Made it seem like only old broads could sing that song."

"Yeah," Abe said. Then, because he could find nothing else to do, he walked to the piano, placed his fingers on the old familiar keys. "What do you want to hear?" he called.

"That peppy one she liked. I mean, when she wasn't in a mood."

Abe knew the one Jake meant, and so began a bright, up-tempo version of "Your Feet's Too Big."

When he finished, he returned to the bar. Susanne had come in by then, another book by one of what she called "the great minds" under her arm. She was a philosophy major at NYU and peppered her drink deliveries with pithy little aphorisms from her latest readings. Abe had heard scores of them during the few months Susanne had worked for him, but the only one that had stuck came from some Greek whose name he couldn't remember. Courage in a man, this Greek had said, was simply this, to endure silently whatever heaven sends.

He thought of Mavis, then of Lucille, and finally of that fucking cat, Pookie, the one he'd found dead on the kitchen floor three weeks after Mavis' abrupt departure. No, he thought, that Greek got it wrong. Courage was to endure silently whatever heaven takes away.

"So, what about Lucille?" Jake asked. "You gonna put an ad in *Variety*, something like that?"

Abe shook his head. "Nah," he said.

If he put an ad in *Variety,* he knew a thousand kids would show up, all of them scooping the notes or singing through their noses, girls with tattoos and neon hair, with pierced tongues and ears and God knows what else under their blouses or below their belts.

"How about an open mike?" he said. "We did that when Lucille left for a year. Just put a sign in the window that says Open Mike and see who drops in."

Jake shrugged. "You'll get that woman who makes all her clothes out of carpet remnants, remember her?"

Abe laughed. "Or the one who only sang songs with animals in the titles."

"But changed the titles. 'Sweet Doggie Brown,' for Christ's sake."

" 'My Funny Butterfly.' "

"Jesus, what a nutbag."

"But not as bad as the one dressed in red rubber," Abe said. "Changed the titles too, remember. 'I'll Be Peeing You.'"

They were both laughing now, and in their laughter Abe caught a glimpse of what life had been before Mavis fled. "Yeah," he said, the laughter trailing off now. "Open mike is the way to go."

MORTIMER

MORTIMER ROLLED the coffee cup in his hand and tried to keep the pain in his belly from showing in his eyes. Only three days had passed since he'd taken the deal, and here Caruso was making changes.

"This is how Mr. Labriola sees it," Caruso said. "Since he's paying the bill, he's got a right to check out the guy who's doing the job. The guy himself, I mean. Directly."

"No way," Mortimer told him.

They were sitting in a coffee shop at Port Authority, the morning commuters rushing by in noisy waves, the city in full morning frenzy. Nobody smelling the roses, Mortimer thought, though he'd never stopped to smell them either. Did anyone?

Caruso sipped a hazelnut blend from a paper cup. "That could be a deal breaker, you know, if the guy won't show."

"He won't show," Mortimer said flatly. "There ain't no give in this. He won't show . . . period."

Caruso looked offended. "So who does he think he is, fucking Batman?"

"He won't show," Mortimer repeated.

"You won't even talk to him?"

"There wouldn't be no point in talking to him, Vinnie,"

Mortimer said emphatically. "The deal don't include no meeting. He don't meet with nobody. My guy ain't never done that, and he ain't gonna start now."

Caruso leaned forward. "I just give you fifteen grand, remember?"

Mortimer remembered all too well. He could feel the envelope in his jacket pocket. The only thing, it didn't feel like bills, all silent and crinkly. It felt like thirty pieces of silver, loud and jangling, rattling through his soul.

"You gonna give a dime of that money to Batman?" Caruso asked him.

Mortimer shrugged.

"That's what I figured," Caruso said. "You're shorting him. Batman, I mean. What if he found out you was doing that, Morty?"

"He ain't gonna find out."

"What I'm saying is we got to have some trust here. Between us, I mean. I know you're shorting your guy and—" Caruso stopped, looking somewhat baffled, like a man who'd started following a thought, then lost it on the way. "Trust, that's what I'm saying. You can trust me. So your guy should show if I tell you he should show."

Mortimer took a sip of coffee, tried to act firm, businesslike, beyond intimidation. "Look, Vinnie, if Labriola wants to have a look at me, fine. But that's where it stops."

Caruso regarded Mortimer warily. "You know, I've been thinking maybe it stops with you, period. I've been thinking maybe Batman is you, Morty. That maybe you're going to grab the whole thirty grand." He took another sip of coffee. "So is there another guy or not?"

"There is," Mortimer said. "But what his cut is, that's between me and him."

Caruso shrugged. "Look, if you want to cheat your guy, so what? It's no skin off my nose who gets what in this deal, long as you come up with this fucking broad Mr.

Labriola is all lathered up about. But remember this: Labriola don't like getting fucked." He waited for that to sink in, then added, "The Old Man gets real pissed a guy tries to screw him. And on this deal, he's really steaming to get the job done. Otherwise why would he be paying thirty grand?"

"Why *is* he paying that?" Mortimer asked. "It ain't his wife skipped town."

"Close enough," Caruso said. "He don't like his kid getting screwed by this broad and her getting away with it, and all that. So he's willing to pay to get her back. But believe me, he don't like paying that much, Morty. He don't like it he's got to go that deep into his pocket to get this thing done. Put all that together, it adds up to a bad mood. He's not to be fucked with is what I'm telling you."

Mortimer glanced about anxiously. Why couldn't he have just worked in a goddamn factory like his father, or sold shoes, anything but this. And now cheating Stark? How fucking crazy could things get?

"And what steams the Old Man more than anything is being played for a chump," Caruso added.

"Yeah, I understand," Mortimer said. "But it don't change the way it is. What I'm telling you is that if Labriola wants to meet with me, I'm willing to do it. Anytime. Anyplace. But it's got to be with me 'cause nobody else is gonna show."

"I don't know if he'll go for it, Morty."

"It's the best I can do."

"Which leaves you where, exactly? If the Old Man calls off the deal."

Mortimer felt his tough-guy act crumble beneath Caruso's knowing gaze.

"It means you're back to where you was, right?" Caruso asked. "With a fifteen-thousand-dollar price on your fucking head."

"If I have to come up with the money, I'll come up with the money." Mortimer tried to sound confident but failed.

"But you don't have that money, Morty," Caruso said cannily. "If you had it, or knew where you could get it, we wouldn't be having this conversation, right? Which means if this deal don't go through, you're fucked."

"Which is why I'm ready to meet with Labriola," Mortimer said. "Jesus, Vinnie, I know I'm in a fix. But the guy I work for, he's got nothing to do with that. He don't even know about it. And there's no way I can tell him, because it wouldn't do no good, because he don't show . . . never."

Caruso considered this briefly. "Okay, suppose Mr. L. is willing to meet with you, when could you get together with him?"

"Whenever he says."

"Today?"

"Today. Tonight. Any fucking time."

"Okay, how about we make it Columbus Circle. This afternoon. Two-thirty. If I can get the Old Man to go for it, I mean."

"Fine," Mortimer said.

Caruso smiled. "And feel free to bring Batman if you can get him out of his fucking cave."

Mortimer drew in a tense breath. "There's something else. You got to supply a few details, Vinnie. Stuff about the woman. Something to go on."

"Like what?"

"Like who she is. Background. Where she might go. What she might do. My guy's got to have something to work on."

Caruso smiled. "If your guy needs that, then he should meet with Mr. Labriola."

Mortimer shook his head. "If he knew it was Labriola, he wouldn't do the job at all."

"Why not?"

" 'Cause he don't work for . . . guys like that."

"Guys like what?"

"Guys that ain't . . . legit."

Caruso looked at him quizzically.

"It's something that happened," Mortimer said. "Long time ago. It don't matter what it was, but the bottom line, he don't work for . . . you know, a certain kind of guy."

"So, who does Batman think he's working for in this deal?"

"A friend of mine, that's what I told him. He ever finds out otherwise, he'll ditch the whole thing."

"And you along with it, right, Morty?" Caruso asked with a cagey grin. He sat back, took another sip of coffee, his eyes poised like small brown marbles over the white rim of the cup. "The thing is, I don't think Mr. Labriola knows much about that fucking broad."

"Then maybe her husband's got some idea about—"

"Labriola's kid don't know nothing about this deal," Caruso interrupted. "And that's the way it stays, 'cause Mr. Labriola ain't told the kid nothing."

"The kid don't know Labriola's looking for his wife?"

"That's right."

"Why ain't he told him?"

Caruso's face stiffened. "You ask a lot of questions, Morty. First it's how come Mr. Labriola's paying so much to find this broad. Now this thing about why he ain't telling the kid nothing about it. A lot of fucking questions, Morty."

Morty lifted his hands defensively. "I'm asking, that's all. Calm down, for Christ's sake. You don't got to answer."

"All I know is, Labriola wants this broad found . . . and

quick. He's got a bug up his ass about it, that's what I'm telling you. He wants it done fast."

"So get me the information I need," Mortimer said. "Something for my guy to go on. He can't do a fucking thing till he gets something to go on."

"Okay, I'll tell the Old Man, but between you and me, ain't it Batman's job to come up with this shit?"

"Yeah it is," Morty said. "But like I just told you, Vinnie, if he comes into it at that level, it'd take him about five fucking seconds to figure out it's Labriola pulling the strings." He looked at Caruso piercingly. "If you can't keep this between us, Vinnie, then I got to pull out. That means we're back to square one with me owing the Old Man, and you having to get it out of me or he'll get it out of you, remember?"

Caruso nodded.

"So are we good on this thing or not?" Mortimer asked.

"We're good," Caruso said reluctantly. He emptied his coffee cup, then crushed it. "Just make sure your guy finds this fucking bitch."

"You get him what he needs to know," Morty said, "and he'll find her, believe me."

STARK

BUENAS TARDES, señor.

Marisol's voice was still as real to him as the first time he'd heard it.

Sitting in Washington Square Park, Stark watched the young woman who'd just reminded him of her in the way she moved so gracefully along the pathway, books cradled in her arms. She was dressed in a black skirt and blouse of dark red, and as he followed her progress through the park, Stark was once again impressed by the vividness of his memory of Marisol, how in an instant he could bring her fully into view, the dark oval eyes, the gleaming black hair, the elegant taper of her long brown legs. He knew that at first he'd reacted to her with nothing but unabated lust, and that if by some unimaginable circumstance she had accompanied him to his hotel room on that sweltering Spanish afternoon, he might simply have made love to her and in that sweaty union washed her forever from his mind. But she had looked up as he approached, softly uttered her *"buenas tardes,"* and he had sat down instead, playing the American expatriate, expecting only to confirm her identity, then notify his client that she was found. But the conversation had turned unexpectedly intimate, and he'd felt a formerly dead part of himself quicken to life, so that by the time dusk had fallen over the tangled streets of Chueca, he'd arranged to meet her the next day at the Plaza del Sol.

A breeze fingered the bare limbs of the trees across the way. He glanced at his watch, felt the crawl of time, then shifted his gaze to the right and followed another young woman as she made her way past the cement fountain at the center of the park. She did not remind him of Marisol. Instead, she directed his mind to the woman he had to find for Mortimer's friend. He didn't care why she'd left her husband or what she might be seeking in her flight. Such speculations were a waste of time. They contributed nothing to his search.

A sudden spike of memory pierced his mind. It was sharp and uncomfortable, and it vividly reminded him of that moment years before when he'd told Lockridge he hadn't been able to find Marisol, then realized that Lockridge already knew better. There'd been a look on Lockridge's face at that instant, a sense of victory, that for all Stark's caution and intelligence, he had been outwitted, and that the terrible cost of his failure would fall entirely upon Marisol.

TONY

TONY STEPPED back as the truck pulled away, loaded with the daily delivery of bluefish, cod, and grouper, and suddenly imagined Sara locked in such a van, bound at the ankles and the wrists, kidnapped. This possibility circled briefly in his mind, gathering hooks as it circled, becoming more painful until it finally burst from his mouth.

"Maybe she got snatched," he said. "Not for ransom. But for revenge."

Eddie stripped off a pair of thick rubber gloves. "Who would hate you that much, Tony? To do something like that."

"Maybe it wasn't me he was doing it to."

Eddie looked at him quizzically.

"You know how it is with my father," Tony explained. "You know the people he deals with."

"Did you ask him if maybe it could be something like that?"

"No, he'd blow up if I asked him that." Tony turned and headed back toward his office, Eddie trudging along beside him. "I think he's got somebody looking for her."

"Why do you think that, Tony?"

"Because when I told him about how Sara was missing, he started in on how I couldn't just let her go, how I had to find her and bring her back and all that shit. Then he gets up and makes a call." Tony stopped and peered out over the marina, where scores of spinnakers rocked gently in the breeze. "I think he put some guy on it. One of his guys. You know the type. Suppose this fucking guy does find her, Eddie? What then?"

"I don't know," Eddie admitted. "But look, Tony, I mean, who knows, maybe she'll come back on her own. I mean, it could be all she wants is a little break."

"A break?"

"From . . . stuff."

"Me?"

"Everything," Eddie said. "My aunt Edna needed a break. She ran off to Atlantic City, stayed two weeks, then come back. With three hundred dollars in nickels. She poured 'em out on the kitchen table. Right there, in front of my uncle. Told him to buy himself a new suit. That was the end of it. She never went nowhere after that."

"I don't think Sara went to Atlantic City," Tony said despondently.

"But maybe somewhere just to get away," Eddie said.

"Without telling anybody?"

"Without telling you," Eddie offered cautiously. " 'Cause she just wanted to, you know, be alone."

"So who would she have told?"

"Maybe nobody," Eddie answered. "Or maybe a friend. Somebody she talked to."

"Della," Tony answered. "She lives across the street. They go shopping sometimes, her and Della."

"Then maybe Sara said something, you know? You should talk to that woman, Tony. That Della woman."

Tony pondered Eddie's suggestion, looking for a way to speak to Della DeLuria without actually revealing that Sara had left him, found no way to do it, then said, "Yeah, okay."

Inside his office, safe from view, Tony stared at the picture of himself and Sara that he'd placed on his desk nine years before. It showed the happy couple on the steps of St. Mary's, Sara in a flowing white dress, Tony in a black tuxedo, his father alone and off to the right, as if in bitter surmise of his new daughter-in-law.

He never liked her, Tony thought, remembering the evening a week before when he'd come home late to find the Old Man slumped in the living room, looking sullen. Sara had come in briefly, and his father had glared at her hatefully, then gotten to his feet and left with nothing beyond a mumbled *That bitch don't know her place, Tony.*

He picked up the photograph and concentrated on Sara's face. Even on her wedding day there'd been a curious sadness in her eyes, a distance he couldn't bridge. Had it been that distance that had first attracted him, he wondered, the way she seemed to distrust love, life, everything? If so, he should have been wary of her, he told himself. But instead, that very distance had formed part of what he'd fallen for when he'd fallen for her. And he *had* fallen for her. That much was sure. He could see that even now, in the picture, the two of them on the church steps, rice flying in all directions. At that moment she had been the indisputable love of his life. The love of my life that day, he thought, then with a sudden aching clarity realized that she still was.

CARUSO

LABRIOLA'S VOICE seemed to reach through the phone line and slap his face.

"Yeah?"

"I talked to Morty Dodge about the meeting you want with this guy he works for."

"And?"

"He says his guy needs information."

"About what?"

"Sara. Things about her."

"What things?"

"For example, what she did for a living or—"

"She didn't do a fucking thing."

"Yeah, okay, but like, where she might have gone. Stuff to get the guy started, that's what he means."

To Caruso's surprise, Labriola did not protest. "I got an idea who knows that shit."

"Good," Caruso said. "I'll pass on whatever you find out."

"*You'll* pass it on? What about me? What about the meeting?"

"That's a problem, having a meeting."

"Why is it a problem, Vinnie?"

"Because the guy, he won't do it."

"I'm laying out thirty grand and this fucker won't meet with me?"

"He never shows."

Caruso could hear the Old Man breathing raggedly, like the snorting of a bull. He waited for him to speak, and when he didn't, added, "But Morty'll meet with you. I told him if it was okay you could hook up at Columbus Circle, two-thirty."

"But he's nothing but a gofer," the Old Man barked. "I don't deal with no fucking gofers."

"He's a little more than that," Caruso protested. "I mean, the guy trusts him is what I'm saying."

"So he's like a sidecar?"

"Sidekick. Yeah, something like that. But more. Loyal. A loyal friend."

"A loyal friend. You know what a loyal friend is, Vinnie? He's the other guy you toss into the fucking hole."

A small, aching laugh broke from Caruso. "That's good, Mr. Labriola. That's a good one."

"I want you to find out who this fucking guy is, Vinnie. I don't have no ghosts working for me, you understand?"

"The guy, you want me to . . . what?"

"What I fucking said just now," the Old Man screamed. "Who is he? I want to know."

"Yes, sir," Caruso said weakly.

"So, look, here's what we do. You set up that fucking meet. Say to this sidecar shithead, sure I'll have a meet. Then we meet, and we talk, and we shake hands like a couple of asshole buddies, see what I mean? Then I go my way, and the sidecar goes his. And you follow the little shithead all the way to this fucking guy he works for."

"Yes, sir," Caruso breathed.

"Understood, Vinnie?"

"I understand," Caruso said, looking about the cramped office from which he ran the Old Man's loan-sharking business.

"Okay, so, two-thirty," the Old Man snapped.

"Yes, sir," Caruso said, adding the time to a head already full of numbers, loans, payments, due dates, not one of which he had ever written down.

SARA

THE WAVERLY theater was still in the same location, and Eighth Street had the same feel to it, and their familiarity brought small parts of her former life back to her. These parts were nothing she could put her finger on exactly, only the sense that she'd packed up her youth and now she could unpack at least a little of it. Maybe that was why she'd come back to the city. Because it was the closet where she'd first secreted herself, the hole she'd burrowed into, creating an identity to go with her new name.

For a moment she peered at the coffee shop across the street, watching silently as the patrons came and went. If they only knew, she thought. She felt the ghostly grip of Sheriff Caulfield's hand on her bare shoulder, then other hands, no less ghostly but also no less palpable, the flesh of grasping fingers pressing into her flesh, sour breath in her face, the smell of drunken sweat, a man pushing her into the corn or down a narrow corridor, upright or weaving, dressed as a cop or barely dressed at all. With each memory she felt her own panic rise like a frenzied animal, trapped and panting, clawing its way out.

To keep it in, she raced to the corner, bought a paper, took it to the coffee shop and turned to the classifieds. The first order of business was to find a job, and so she looked for one among the long columns. As she searched, the paucity of her skills, how little she had to offer, grew ever more distressingly apparent. Finally, one job caught her eye. Receptionist. No experience necessary. She could answer a phone, she thought. She could take a message. She knew that thousands of others could do the same, but she hoped that somehow she'd come through the door at just the right moment, and this hope suggested to her just how depleted she was. Her only resource was now little more than a baseless grab for luck.

DELLA

SHE'D SEEN the man several times before, been introduced, shaken his hand, but even now his dark eyes seemed so lethal she could easily imagine a deadly acid spewing from them, turning human beings into mounds of glistening flesh.

"Good morning, Mr. Labriola," she said quietly.

A smile labored to form on Labriola's mouth, then gave up and curled into a frown. "Mind if I come in?"

Della stepped back and watched as he came into the foyer. He was not a large man, but there was something about him that seemed both huge and dangerous, like a boulder rolling toward you, grim and unstoppable. You either got out of its way, or it crushed you like a bug.

"You seen Tony?" His close-cropped white hair glimmered in the light. "He been over here?"

"No," Della said.

"Too embarrassed," Labriola said. "Okay, well, to make a long story short, that wife of his, she dumped him."

"Oh," Della said weakly.

"You ain't heard about it?"

She felt like a deer caught in the crosshairs of a telescopic sight. "Well, I . . ."

Labriola's bushy gray eyebrows arched menacingly. "You talked to her?"

So this is the moment, Della thought, this is the moment when the ground suddenly shifts and you find yourself teetering on the edge of a cliff. Her lips parted, but nothing came out, and in that instant of hesitation she saw Labriola's face turn grim and stony.

"You don't want to keep nothing to yourself," he said. " 'Cause I'm gonna find her, no matter what it takes."

She heard Nicky cry, and the sound of his needful voice was like a spur gouging at her side. "She called me," she said, her voice little above a whisper. "The day she . . . left."

"Where was she when she called?" Labriola asked.

Nicky was crying loudly now, an insanely demanding scream. "I have to—"

Labriola grabbed her arm and squeezed. "Where was she?"

"I don't know," Della answered. "She wouldn't tell me."

"What time did she call?"

"I don't know for sure. Late."

"And she was already where she was headed?"

"I guess she was. It was tough to hear her."

"Why?"

Della suddenly realized that she'd given out just that little morsel of information Sara had feared she might. "I don't know."

"You said it was hard to hear her."

"Yeah," Della said hesitantly.

"Traffic?"

"Maybe that was it," Della said softly.

"She in the city?"

"I don't know." Nicky's cries were like a screeching bird in her brain. "I need to change my son's—"

Labriola's grip tightened. "The kid can sit in it."

Sit in his shit. Della knew that that was what Labriola meant, and with that understanding, she knew that she had plumbed the full measure of his brutality.

He brought his face very close to hers. "She in the city?" he repeated.

"She didn't say."

"She got a man? She fucking around on Tony?"

Della shook her head. "I don't think so."

Labriola eyed her for a moment. "Okay," he said finally. He released his grip. "If she calls again, you gonna call me, right?"

Della nodded meekly and massaged her arm. "Okay."

"You're clear on that, right?"

"Yes," Della answered faintly. "Yes, I am."

"Good," Labriola said. He grabbed a pen from his shirt pocket, then took her wrist in his iron grip and scrawled a number across her white flesh, the point of the pen jabbing with a hair more than the necessary force, so that she knew the little bite of pain she felt was the old man's way of making a final point. "And Tony, he ain't to know nothing about me coming here, talking to you, nothing like that."

"Okay," Della whispered. She cautiously drew her wrist from Labriola's grasp. "I won't tell anybody." She felt crushed beneath him somehow, wriggling, Nicky screaming for her, confused that she'd not yet come to him. And yet she knew that she could not rush things with this man, could not show anything but her fear. "I won't," she repeated.

"If you do—" he began, then stopped, leaving her to conjure the consequences of crossing him.

"I won't tell anybody," Della said again. "Mike. Tony. I won't tell anybody."

Labriola stared at her silently, a smoky, hellish darkness in his eyes, so that she knew absolutely that there was nothing to stay his hand, nothing within him or without that could prevent him from committing whatever savageries he imagined.

"So, we're clear, am I right?" he asked.

"Yes," Della told him. "We're clear."

He turned to the door, then stopped and again faced her. "She tell you anything about why she run off?"

"No," Della answered quietly.

To her relief, Labriola appeared satisfied.

"Okay," he said, then opened the door and stepped out onto the small porch. His blue Lincoln Town Car rested at the curb, and Della watched as he trudged toward it, all the world curiously silent during the few seconds it took him to drive away, then abruptly jangling with a harsh and deafening noise, not just Nicky's insistent squealing, but all the clang and clatter of the world.

SHE TOOK his hands and placed them in the tray.

"So, things good with you?"

Stark nodded.

Lucia was a brown swollen berry of a woman. Her hair was black but without shine, and her voice bore the cadences of the peasant island from which she'd come. But she had a ready smile, and she did a good job on his nails, and Stark found it refreshing to be touched by someone who wanted nothing from him but a generous tip.

"You got your health, that's the main thing, no?" Lucia asked.

Stark remembered a line from Neruda, how on certain days the smell of aftershave made him sob. He knew well what the poet meant. On certain days something mournful hung in the air. Everything was draped in black crepe. He could not predict when such a day would come, nor ever fathom why it came. He knew only that on such occasions death seemed even sweeter than usual, and he felt an unmistakable longing to be rid of life's unseemly detritus, the body's crude humiliations, the idle patter of the streets, the heavy sense that nothing could be rescued from the stale water in which all things floated briefly and then sank. Each breath seemed empty, and he could find no reason to take it. It simply happened. He breathed. He didn't will it, or want it. His lungs sucked in air, and this reflexive grasp for life struck him as no less absurd than Lucia's mindless chatter, or the way her fat fingers massaged his own. It was all part of the same purely mechanistic design, without direction or purpose or will, desperate but not obviously so, the desperation built into the machine, its slimy oil. The hours were unbearable, and so you filled them with whatever you could in the same desperate way the lungs filled with air. That was the design, and Stark thought that one simple stern admonition must be tacked to the wall of every chromosome: *Just get through it.*

Lucia began to clean beneath the nails with a pointed wooden stick.

"You got pretty hands," she said. "You got hands like a woman."

Stark knew that this was not true. His hands, despite the creams and oils, were rough, his veins were raised and faintly blue. His fingers were stubby rather than tapered, and the pink nails were marked with milky-white specks. His father, the mill worker, had had rough, unattractive hands. So had his mother, the gray lady who washed the halls of the building they lived in, and in which she may well have entertained the squat little landlord on those months when she'd fallen behind in the rent.

"You want I should do the toes?" Lucia was blowing gently on his fingers now. "Some men, I do the toes."

Stark shook his head, drew a twenty from the breast pocket of his jacket, and handed it to Lucia.

"Thank you," she said happily. "I do good job, no?"

"Excellent, as always," Stark told her.

On the street he tried to admire the day, the sunlight, the warm spring air. But it continued to bother him, this thing that had begun to trouble him as he sat in Washington Square and was now dragging his mood lower and lower. At the time he'd thought it had something to do with Marisol, but now he understood that it had to do with Mortimer, the new job he'd brought him, the woman he had to find for Mortimer's friend.

Something was wrong.

And this something wrong began with the request itself, the fact that during all the long years of that association, Mortimer had never before asked a favor of him. Nor had he ever expressed the slightest hesitance in bringing him a new client. Now Mortimer had both asked for a favor and appeared unsure about the client he'd brought him. In Stark's experience, such changes never boded well. With Lockridge, he'd noticed an unexpectedly snide look when he'd told him that he'd been unable to find Marisol. This response had signaled not only that Lockridge already knew that Marisol had been found, but that finding her had been only the first stage of a darker plot. Now he had the same uneasy feeling about Mortimer.

So just who was the phantom friend Mortimer claimed to have but would not identify?

And what did this "friend" intend to do when his missing wife was found?

There was something wrong with the whole thing, Stark decided, something left out or hidden. Mortimer wasn't telling him the whole story, and in recognizing that austere fact, Stark felt a terrible sense that his old associate had crossed a fateful line. After all, Mortimer's saving grace had always been that he clearly understood his own substantial limitations, the fact that in any test of wit or will he would surely come out the loser. For that reason Stark had never doubted that Mortimer would play straight with him, if for no other reason than to do otherwise would inevitably spell disaster. But now Stark suspected that Mortimer had taken a crooked road.

But why?

SARA

SHE WAS tired by the middle of the afternoon, but she knew she had to fight it. Years before, a talent agent had counseled Sara to be "perky." A guy who owns a club is looking for a girl with spark, he'd said, even in a torch singer he's looking for a spark. Sara had assumed that she would need to show the same spark now that she'd tried to show years before. Especially since the job she sought was one that required her to greet the public, answer the phone.

And so for the past hours, in the assorted jobs she'd sought since leaving the coffee shop, she'd tried to be bright-eyed, sharp . . . have a spark. She offered a quick smile and a ready hand. But it hadn't worked, and as the minutes passed, she'd seen the interviewer slowly drift away, then rise, mutter a quick "Thanks for coming in," and escort her to the door. Nor could she blame these people for not hiring her. She was in her late thirties, a woman with no experience, her résumé a blank page. They had seen it in her eyes, seen through the sparkling mask that in some indefinable but alarming way she was at loose ends, would be trouble down the line. She knew that they couldn't guess the force that drove her, but that didn't matter. They wanted someone relaxed, someone easy, someone who believed that if you did everything right, things would work out, someone with experience but no past, a blank slate they could write their company's logo on. They did not want a woman who answered their questions quickly and added nothing, a woman in whom they could hear the aching groan of a tightly wound spring.

She thought of the man who'd interviewed her for the job of receptionist in his hair salon, the way he'd looked at her hair, like it was a nest of squirming snakes, *Thank you, we'll be in touch*. Then there was the woman at the attorney's office, dressed like a man, who talked like a man, and whose flinty gaze said *Now you're sorry, right, for wasting your life, well, too late, sister.*

The final job was located on Avenue C, a neighborhood Sara remembered well from her days in New York.

Back then it had been a dangerous place, but now, as she moved down Sixth Street, she marveled at how much things had changed. There were young professionals on the street, along with the usual tradesmen and delivery people. Tompkins Square Park, once a mire of drug addicts, was now both park and playground, a well-tended expanse of green where children scurried in all directions while their well-heeled parents looked on.

Addison Film Works was located just off the park, the building a bit more dingy than the ones around it. There was no doorman, only a spare foyer with walls painted institutional gray and an ancient elevator that creaked and trembled as it rose to the fourth floor.

The door was at the end of a corridor stacked high with cardboard boxes and black towers of videotape. The name of the company was printed in block letters on frosted glass. A single name was written in the lower left corner of the glass: *Art Gillman.*

A stubby, overweight man in a dark double-breasted suit greeted Sara as she came through the door. "I'm Art Gillman," he said. His hair was a lackluster brown, very thin on top, parted low on the left side and then swept over to cover spaces that would otherwise have been bald. "Sorry for the mess. I just got back from L.A." He shrugged helplessly. "When I'm out of the office, things go to pot."

Sara smiled weakly.

"So, what do you go by?" Gillman asked.

"Go by?" Sara asked.

"Name."

"Samantha," she blurted out before she could stop herself. "Samantha Damonte."

Something registered in Gillman's eyes. "That's good. I like that. Samantha Damonte." He stripped off his jacket, hung it on a wooden hat rack, then dropped heavily into a seat behind a cluttered metal desk. "You work in the film business before?"

"No," Sara admitted.

Gillman nodded toward the single empty chair that rested in front of his desk. "Have a seat."

Sara did so.

"It takes a little getting used to," Gillman added. "But most people catch on pretty fast." He glanced about, as if looking for an assistant. "Mildred's supposed to stay till five, but she cut out early, I guess." He eyed the small wooden cabinet to the right of his desk. "You want something to drink?"

"No, thank you," Sara replied.

"How about a cigarette." He winked. "I got a full pack."

Sara shook her head.

"Good," Gillman said. "A girl should keep fit." He leaned back and folded his hands behind his head, his belly thrust out aggressively so that Sara noticed how large and firm it was, the way it seemed to poke through the stained white shirt. "So, tell me a little about yourself, Samantha," he said.

Sara offered her best smile. "There's not much to tell."

"Start anywhere," Gillman told her brightly. "And by the way, you can call me Art. We're real informal around here."

"I used to be a singer," Sara said. "Art."

"A singer?" Gillman said exuberantly. "No kidding? What kind of singer?"

"Clubs. But that was a long time ago."

"What kind of clubs?"

"Cabaret."

"So you're used to performing for an audience," Gillman said. "That's good. 'Cause you got to deal with a lot of people in this business. People hanging around."

Sara nodded silently.

"What else, Samantha? What else can you tell me about yourself?"

Sara tried to think of something interesting, but couldn't.

Gillman continued to wait for her to respond in some way, show some sparkle, tell him something he didn't drag out of her. But all she could think to say was "I lived in New York a long time ago. When I was a singer."

"You're from the South, right?" Gillman said. "Still got a little twang there." He leaned forward, rested his hands on the desk, fingers entwined. "You don't have to like it, you know."

Sara looked at him quizzically.

"You don't have to like what you do, I mean," Gillman said. "Lots of people don't like what they do. But they got bills to pay, kids to raise. A lot of people in this business have kids, you know. Do you have any kids, Samantha?"

"No," Sara answered.

Gillman looked at her with what seemed a deep regard, as if he were trying to get beneath her skin. "How old are you, if you don't mind my asking?"

"Thirty-eight," Sara answered.

"That's pretty old for the film business," Gillman said. "It's a younger group, I mean. But the way I see it, it's the person that matters. People who see you, they wouldn't take you for thirty-eight." He looked her up and down. "Thirty tops. Well, maybe thirty-one, two." He seemed to be talking to himself again. "Yeah, that's it," he concluded. "Thirty-two tops." He waited for her to respond, and when she didn't, he said, "Have you ever been on a film set, Samantha?"

"No."

"Think it would bother you, all that hustle-bustle?"

Sara shook her head.

"Well, even if it did, it wouldn't matter, right?" Gillman said happily. "I mean, you can keep focused, I'm sure." He sprang to his feet. "Okay, so why don't I show you around."

Sara followed him out of the office, then down the corridor to a set of padlocked double doors. "This is where the action is," he told her as he fumbled for a key. "I keep everything locked up because we've had a couple things turn up missing over the years."

He unbolted the lock and swung open the door into a pitch-black room. "This is where we do the shoot." He stepped inside and turned on the lights. "It's not the Waldorf, but in this business you gotta keep an eye on the budget."

The room was a labyrinth of small cubicles, each with papered or painted walls, and set up to resemble offices, medical examination rooms, prison cells. To the right, a barn loft, complete with fake bales of hay, stood separated from a pool hall by a slender partition. There was an Arabian tent, its multicolored flaps hanging limply in the windless air, and an automobile showroom, complete with two convertibles. Toward the back a sandy beach, dotted with plastic palm trees, swept out from a large photograph of the ocean. "We can shoot just about any kind of story using these sets." He motioned her to the left, where a mattress lay on the concrete floor, stark and unadorned, covered with a single white bedsheet. "It's not up to me, you understand," he said as he approached a still camera mounted on a tripod. "Other people have a say." He stepped behind the camera and began fiddling with its dials. "Just have a seat there," he told her, nodding toward the mattress.

Gillman continued to adjust the camera. When he'd finished, he seemed surprised that Sara remained in place, glancing about, her arms stiffly at her sides. "I have to have a look," he said. "At *you*, Samantha."

She stepped back again and felt the wall behind her. She could see the door ahead and wanted to rush toward it, but couldn't. He would catch her, and she knew it. She drew her purse to her chest. "Stay away from me," she said.

Gillman stared at her. "What's the matter with you?" He stepped forward, his hands raised slightly. "Look . . . I have—"

"Get back," Sara commanded.

Gillman stopped dead. "I wasn't going to . . . do anything to you," he told her earnestly.

"Get back," she repeated sharply.

Gillman's eyes sparked with a sudden stunning realization. "Wait a second, you came for the receptionist's job." He shook his head. "Oh, Jesus. Mildred's job. You're not an . . . actress." He laughed nervously. "I'm sorry, Samantha. Believe me, I wasn't going to . . ." He glanced about the room, the grim partitions, the hanging metal lights, the cheap furniture and the plastic palms. "This place. You're scared. I'm sorry." He stepped back, his hands now at his sides, and stood completely still. "Just go, okay? Just go, and we'll end it right here."

Sara didn't move. If she moved, he would spring at her, she knew. If she turned her back, he would rush up behind her.

"I'll stay right here," Gillman assured her. "Or I'll go all the way to the other side of the room if you want."

Sara nodded stiffly.

"Okay," Gillman said, walking backward one slow step at a time. "This far enough?" he said finally.

Sara gave no answer but turned and dashed toward the door, opened it, and rushed out, taking the stairs rather than the elevator, her feet thudding loudly against the concrete steps, until she burst into the lobby, then across it and out into the air, where, she saw to her relief, no one followed from behind.

TONY

HE PULLED into the driveway, but instead of moving down the walkway to his house, he turned and faced the cul-de-sac, his attention focused on the house across the way. He didn't know Mike well, and he didn't know Della at all. But he knew that Sara and Della were friends, and that Eddie had been right in thinking that Della might have some idea of where Sara was. He'd meant to ask her about it three days before, but embarrassment had frozen him, the terrible admission that Sara was gone, and he'd taken the chance that she might simply come back, make everything right again, so that no one would have to know that she'd actually left him.

But three days had gone by and now he had no choice but to act. Still, he didn't look forward to revealing anything intimate to Della. She was Sara's friend, after all, not his, and although he didn't know the actual depth of their friendship, he suspected that Sara had told Della at least a few private things.

The thought that Sara might have had this kind of intimate conversation with Della filled him with apprehension. Suppose he asked Della straight out, *What did Sara say?* Did he really want to know? If he asked her about another guy and learned that there was one, what would he ask next? The guy's name? Why would he want that? Would he ask how long it had been going on? What good would such information do him now? Or would he simply tell Della the truth, *I don't care about any of that. I just want the chance to get her back.*

His father's face suddenly thrust itself into his mind and he knew with what contempt the old man now regarded him, his pussy-whipped son. On the shoulders of that thought, he headed across the cul-de-sac and knocked at his neighbor's door.

Della opened it. "Hey, Tony."

"I was ... I ... You haven't heard anything, right? About Sara?"

Della shook her head.

"She's missing. I mean, she just sort of ... left, I guess. ... The thing is, I was wondering if she said anything to you. You and her being friends and all, I thought she might—"

"No, Tony," Della said. "She didn't say anything to me about—"

"Yeah, okay," Tony said hastily. "I just thought maybe ... You know." He stepped away from the door. "Sorry to bother you."

"No, that's okay," Della told him. "I mean, I wish I could help you."

"Yeah, thanks," Tony said. He turned to leave, faced the empty house across the cul-de-sac, its dark windows, and stopped. "I just—" He turned back. "I don't know what to do." He started to say more, stopped briefly, then said, "Would you mind if I came in for a minute, Della?"

She looked at him in a way he'd never seen before, as if she were afraid of him.

"Just to ... talk," he added.

She nodded but he could tell that it was hesitantly.

"Of course, if you're busy ..."

"No, that's okay," Della said, her voice still oddly strained. "I'll make you a cup of coffee."

In the kitchen, Tony sat at the square wooden table, his hands folded around a brown mug, sipping it occasionally, trying to find the right words but always failing. "I think my father's looking for her," he said finally.

Della nodded stiffly and pressed her back firmly against the door of the refrigerator.

"You okay?" he asked.

"Yeah, sure," Della said.

Tony took a sip from the mug. "She didn't say anything to you, did she? I mean about leaving me?"

Della shook her head.

"You know if maybe there was some other friend she talked to?" Tony asked.

"No. I don't think she talked to anybody."

"I guess not," Tony said. An aching sigh broke from him. "She sure didn't talk to me. But then, I didn't talk to her either." He tried to smile. "You and Mike talk?"

"Yeah," she said. "Just the usual stuff. Every day. The kids."

Tony's gaze roamed Della's kitchen. He envied Mike this simple, contented wife, so different from his own. But that was what had drawn him to Sara in the first place, wasn't it? The way she was so different from the girls in the neighborhood, the ones his friends had already married or were about to. "I liked her accent," he said.

"What?"

"Her accent. Sara's. You know, southern. The thing is, I'd be good to her if she came back."

Something in Della's face altered, and she suddenly unfastened herself from the door of the refrigerator and sat down at the table. "I'm really sorry about this, Tony." She touched his hand. "Really."

He drew his hand away, feeling like a worm now, the type of guy his father hated. Not like Donny, whose wife wouldn't have dared leave him. Or Angelo, who'd never stop busting his chops if he didn't get Sara back, make her keep her mouth shut, get back to the old routine and stay there.

"Yeah, thanks," he said, and got to his feet. "I better be going."

Della walked him to the door but stepped back quickly when he turned to say good-bye, her eyes fearful again.

"I'm sorry to bother you," Tony said, though he didn't know in exactly what way he'd bothered her, and certainly could find no reason for her to fear him. Why would she? They had been neighbors for years, and he'd never done anything to cause her the slightest unease. He saw clammy dread in her eyes and knew that it was the same fear he'd seen in the cringing figures who stood before his father, men who'd crossed him in some way.

"Has anyone else talked to you about this?" he asked. "My father, I mean. Or somebody who works for him?"

Della shook her head. "No."

"I have to find Sara before my father does," he told her.

Della said nothing.

"So, if he talked to you—"

"He didn't talk to me," Della blurted, then stepped back from the door. "Really, Tony."

"Okay," Tony said.

He walked back across the cul-de-sac. By the time he entered his house he'd come to believe that Della had lied to him. It was even possible that his father already knew where Sara was. Perhaps he was already headed to some motel on the Jersey Shore, Caruso behind the wheel of the big blue Lincoln, ready to do whatever the Old Man said he had to do to bring Sara home.

MORTIMER

HE SAW Caruso first, a thin, taut wire of a guy, the type who seemed always to be walking point. In the war, they were the ones who'd usually bought it first. Bought it so quickly, Mortimer had come to the conclusion that there was something about them, all that fidgeting perhaps, that God just didn't like.

"Mr. Labriola should be here in a few minutes," Caruso said as he scurried up to him. He glanced out toward the swirling traffic. "Drives a Lincoln."

"There's no place to park around here," Mortimer said.

"Oh, he won't park," Caruso said, "the car will drive up and you'll get in." He glanced about nervously. "You better have your story straight. You don't, he could take you to some fucking car-crushing joint and nobody would ever see you again."

"You got a hell of a boss," Mortimer said.

Caruso's face turned threatening. "Speaking of which, Batman didn't change his mind, did he?"

Mortimer shook his head as a stinging pain swept across his abdomen, bending him forward slightly.

"What's the matter?" Caruso asked.

"Nothing," Mortimer groaned.

"You're pretty out of shape there, Morty," Caruso told him.

Mortimer lowered himself onto the steps at the entrance to the park. "Yeah."

"You should get on the old treadmill. Get rid of that fucking paunch you got."

"One fifty-four, that's what I weighed in the army," Mortimer told him. He could not imagine how it had happened, the physical deterioration he'd undergone since then, not only the vanished hair, the spreading belly, and drooping, worthless dick, but the lethal forces that were consuming him now, his liver going south, dragging him into the grave.

"You was in the army?" Caruso asked. "When was this?"

"Sixty-seven."

" 'Nam?"

Mortimer gave no answer. "So, is Labriola gonna show up, or not?"

"He's always on the dot," Caruso said. "Why, you got a fire to go to?"

"Time is money."

"Well, you should think of this, Morty," Caruso said. "If Mr. Labriola is a minute late, you wait for him. And if he's an hour late, you wait for him. You fucking stand here and starve to death, but you wait for him, Morty, because if you don't . . ." Caruso's eyes suddenly took on a look of animal fright. "There he is." He nodded toward a Lincoln Town Car as it drew up to the curb. "Okay, go."

Labriola was behind the wheel, and as Mortimer drew himself into the passenger seat, he felt something change in the quality of the light.

"So you're the sidecar," Labriola said.

Mortimer looked at him quizzically.

"The gofer."

Mortimer nodded as the car pulled away. "Mortimer Dodge," he said.

"I know your fucking name," Labriola snapped. "I also know you owe me fifteen grand. Fifteen fucking grand but don't want to do certain things I want you to do. For example, won't bring this guy who's working for me so I can get a look."

"I would if I could," Mortimer said.

"I like to look a guy in the eye," Labriola muttered darkly. "I like him to know what he's fucking dealing with when he's dealing with me. You know why? 'Cause once he gets a look at me, he don't have no fucking doubts about where I stand."

Mortimer remained mute. It seemed the only safe response to a man like Labriola. You didn't talk. You listened.

"So when I hear this guy won't show, I figure, okay, I'll take a look at the guy who's setting this thing up. Which is you. So, okay, now I'm having a look, and what I see is a guy in a cheap suit, with dirty shoes don't look like they been shined in ten years, and he's got a look on his face like he just poked the boss's wife. In other words, I don't like what I see. So, what you got to do is tell me what I'm seeing ain't quite right. So, go ahead, do that."

Mortimer thought fast. "You remember Gotti? The way he liked being noticed? Fancy suits. Silk ties. Big talk. Shooting off fireworks when the mayor told him not to. Well, he got noticed. But me, I don't want to be noticed like that. And that's good for me. And it's good for my guy. And it's good for you too, Mr. Labriola. Because it means that when my guy finds this woman, she won't even know she's been found. No noise. No flash. He just sees her. He don't sit down. He don't chat. He don't take no notice. He just finds her, and then he tells me, and then I tell you." He shrugged. "After that . . ."

"It's my business," Labriola said.

Mortimer nodded.

Labriola stared at him for a moment, then a loud laugh broke from him, and he grabbed Mortimer's left knee and squeezed. "Okay," he said, all boisterous good cheer now. "Okay, we'll do this thing." He grabbed the wheel tightly and gave it a jerk to the right. "So, where you want I let you off?"

"Where you picked me up is fine."

The car made an abrupt turn, cruised south on Twelfth Avenue, then swung east, Labriola silent, staring straight ahead, until the car came to a halt at Columbus Circle.

Labriola drew an envelope from his jacket pocket. "Here's that information your guy wanted."

Mortimer took the envelope.

"Stay in touch," Labriola said in a tone of grim authority.

Mortimer nodded, then opened the door and stepped out of the car. He could still feel the tremor in his fingers as it pulled away.

CARUSO

FROM BEHIND the Columbus monument, he watched as Mortimer stepped out of Labriola's car, a manila envelope in his hand. The car pulled away, and for a time Mortimer remained in place, the envelope dangling from his hand, looking curiously lost, like a guy who'd suddenly found himself in a foreign city. Then he seemed to come back to himself, glanced about, pocketed the envelope, and began walking south down Broadway until he stopped abruptly as if he'd heard something coming toward him from behind.

Caruso darted into a shop and stood, peering through the window as Mortimer cocked his head left and right like a guy listening to an argument in his brain. Fucking weirdo, Caruso thought, fucking creepy, this guy. He waited until Mortimer moved on down Broadway, then returned to the street, following at a somewhat greater distance now, his eyes peeled for the crooked shape of Mortimer's black hat.

Where the fuck is he going? Caruso asked himself, already tired now, which only suggested that he was no better off than Morty Dodge when it came to staying in shape. He'd thought of exercise, of eating better, both of which he'd considered before. He'd actually bought a stationary bike at one point, then watched helplessly as it became the world's most expensive clothes rack. He was thirty-six but looked at least five years older, a fact that wasn't lost on the women he tried to pick up. He knew that they looked at his paunch, his thinning hair, the circles beneath his eyes, and thought to themselves, This guy is fucked. And why shouldn't they think that? he wondered now. Here he was, a thirty-six-year-old guy, following this weird bastard who was probably going to lead him to yet another weirdo. The worst part was that while he and Mortimer both had to answer to Labriola, Batman didn't because the Old Man had no idea who he was. But that would change soon, Caruso thought with sudden gleeful satisfaction, as if he'd just found a way to get even with this mystery man he had never met and yet envied for his freedom, and thus wanted to bring down. He smiled. Maybe Mr. Labriola would feel the same way. Maybe he'd think that this fucking guy, this Batman-arrogant asshole, needed to be taught a lesson. Caruso indulged himself in that fantasy, imagining the Old Man's hand on his shoulder, giving him the Big Assignment. He could even feel Labriola's lips at his ear, whispering the honored instruction, the one only the most trusted men ever received, *Whack Batman.*

STARK

STARK SAT down behind the mahogany desk and reviewed the few details Mortimer had given him when they'd first discussed the job, trying to divine which of them were true.

The facts themselves were spare.

A woman had left her husband.

She'd done so only three days before.

She'd left from Montauk, Long Island, and gone to an as-yet-unknown place.

She had not taken her own car.

Mortimer had offered nothing beyond these scant details save that his "friend" did not wish to reveal himself but promised to supply considerably more information about his wife, at least as far as where she might have gone and by what means she'd gone there.

In itself, his client's reluctance to identify himself was not unusual. In such situations people on the other end of the arrangement were often jealous of their privacy. He'd worked for politicians, high-profile businessmen, actors, and musicians. No one was safe from the eternal tendency to fuck up. That was one of the things Stark had learned over the years, that rich, famous, and even quite intelligent people could suddenly find themselves neck deep in trouble. Their personal relationships abruptly spun out of control because they'd screwed the wrong person or trusted some grifter who'd promised five bucks for every nickel they invested. Human life went forward on a sputtering wave of such mindless improvisation. On some otherwise normal day a line drive went foul. A man met a woman, took her to bed, awoke to find a psycho in his arms. Or he let a stranger buy him a drink, talked a little about money, turned over half a million to a thief. There were a thousand ways for a life to go disastrously awry. And when it did you looked for a way out that didn't blow what was left of you to smithereens. You found someone who could make the necessary correction, have some face time with the face you wanted to wipe out of your life. Oftentimes, the job reduced to simply that, a single eye-to-eye confrontation, one Stark always ended with a standard chilling statement, *This is over . . . as of right now. Whatever you thought you were going to get, you're not going to get it. From this moment on, you only start to lose. How much you lose is up to you.*

He'd delivered these words scores of times, to distraught mistresses and wily con men and well-heeled drug dealers, and the look in his eye and the tone in his voice had rarely failed to do the trick. No matter how venal or stupid or psychopathically greedy people were, they never failed to know when the man they were dealing with couldn't wait to die. A man who regarded life as nothing more than a long, boring wait at the airport held the ultimate means of intimidation. No one wanted as his enemy a man whose only friend was death.

Of course, there'd been those few exceptions even to this rule. People who didn't trust what they glimpsed in Stark's eyes, didn't really believe he was what he appeared to be, dismissed his lethal stare as a bluff.

But Stark never bluffed. That was, he thought, the ultimate secret of success. If you said you'd walk away, you walked away. You said to yourself, I don't fucking care, and you turned and you didn't look back. And if you said you would do a thing, you did it no matter what the cost. You said to yourself, I don't fucking care, and you did it, and it was done, and you never calculated the risk you'd taken, nor ever the size, be it large or small, either of the penalty or of the reward. Not to care what you won or lost, this was the cold, hard ground of dignity, and standing on that ground was the only thing that made life bearable.

Stark knew that he could convey all of this in a single deadly glance. But he also knew that inevitably some people would fail to read that glance correctly. And so, on those very rare occasions when he'd had some doubt that the point was made, he'd simply ratcheted up the stakes, drawn the nine-millimeter from his jacket, and kindly asked the offending person to open his mouth. The object of Stark's attention always did so, his eyes widening as Stark pressed the blunt steel barrel into their gaping mouths, careful to scrape the sensitive roof with the metal sight, and thus cause that little nip of pain that so eloquently underlined the desperate nature of the case.

The problem at the moment, however, was that Stark was no longer sure of what his assignment was. Mortimer had asked for a favor, but reluctantly. He'd never done that before, and it was this odd twist in the road that now chewed at Stark relentlessly, urging him to get to the bottom of Mortimer's strange behavior.

But how? He decided he would pretend that he believed Mortimer's story. He would tell himself that whatever peculiarities he sensed in the deal might well be harmless, and on that assumption he would work in the normal way, using whatever information Mortimer brought him as the springboard for further investigation.

He took a regional map from the file and spread it across his desk. Since the runaway wife hadn't taken her own car, the husband would first need to determine if his wife had taken a cab either to her destination or to some other form of transportation. There were several small airports in the vicinity of Montauk. It would not be hard to determine if the woman had used any of them. There were also several bus depots in the area, as well as a single commuter train. The bus or train could have taken her into New York, from which she could have gotten passage to anywhere on earth.

The trick, then, was to narrow the field, shrink the wide world of possibility into a small, tight knot of likelihood. But that couldn't be done until the husband supplied the added information he'd promised Mortimer. Until it came, Stark could only wait.

But waiting was hard, and even as a child Stark had noticed how little patience he had for the undone deed. He liked to be on the hunt, and if he were haunted by anything, dreaded anything, it was the idle time between jobs. During those intervals, he felt his life grow numb. It did not surprise him that soldiers of fortune were prone to suicide. For how could a man who thirsted for danger possibly endure the absence of it, the long days when he felt himself imprisoned in an empty and unlighted room. He knew the usual means by which such men made the clock move. Drugs. Alcohol. Whores. But the drugs wore off, and the alcohol drained away, and the whore finally had to dress and find another john. And after that, the soldier lay in the dull aftermath and dreamed of jungle fire-fights, the thrill of being cornered, wounded, left for dead, the ecstasy that ever accompanies the narrowest escape. Denied this primal excitement, how banal and uneventful the rest of it must seem. And so why not press the barrel to your head if the hourly alternative offered nothing more than the unbearable pall of the commonplace?

Stark drew the nine-millimeter from the drawer of his desk, caressed it with affection, thought of Marisol, and marveled with what dreadful accuracy Neruda had hit the mark, understood that in the sickly sweet smell of aftershave the total horror was revealed.

ABE

ABE RECOGNIZED the man who came toward him from the front of the bar as a semi-regular, a guy who came in sporadically, took a place in the darkest corner he could find, and ordered scotch without designating any particular brand. He wore a faded black suit, with shiny pants that fit him badly, and an old hat that looked as if it had been run over by a truck, then pounded back into shape. Over the years, they'd had a few conversations, but Abe had learned little beyond the guy's first name and the vague notion that he was some kind of investigator, though exactly what type the man had never said, save that he "found people."

"How you doing, Morty?" he asked now.

"Abe," Mortimer said. He slid onto the stool opposite. Abe smiled. "What'll you have?"

"Scotch," Mortimer said.

Abe usually poured the house brand, a cheap blended scotch that wasn't all that bad. But Mortimer looked so hangdog, he decided on a better one, grabbed a smooth single malt and poured a shot.

Mortimer knocked it back quickly, with no sign that he tasted any difference.

"Another?" Abe asked.

"Yeah," Mortimer said.

Abe poured a second round.

Mortimer knocked that back, then placed the shot glass on the bar and wiped his mouth with the back of his hand.

Abe tried to lighten the atmosphere. "You don't sing by any chance, do you, Morty?"

"Shit," Mortimer said glumly.

Abe poured another round. "Sip this one," he said. "You might enjoy the taste."

Mortimer did as he was told.

"What do you think?"

"Good," Mortimer said.

"You look a little . . . I don't know . . ."

"Fucked," Mortimer said.

"Yeah, that's the word," Abe said. "What's the trouble?"

Mortimer's eyes suddenly lifted from the glass, and Abe could see just how deep the trouble was.

"I got these fucking tests back." Mortimer looked surprised that the information had flown from his mouth so suddenly. "A death sentence. Three months on the outside." He rolled the glass slowly between his hands. "Liver's shot."

Abe had no idea what to say, and so he said, "Shit."

"Yeah." Mortimer shrugged. "No hope. Couple months, on the outside."

For a moment the two men sat silently. Then Abe said, "I'm really sorry to hear it, Morty." He poured a fourth round. "On the house. From now on," he said.

"From now on," Mortimer repeated, his voice oddly filled with emotion. "You're a real friend, Abe. Always there for me."

Abe stared at him, astonished that Mortimer could regard him in such a way. Before now he could remember no conversation that hadn't included the weather.

Mortimer put out his hand. "My best friend."

Abe shook Mortimer's hand lightly.

Mortimer smiled at him warmly, then finished off the drink. "I didn't tell Dottie yet."

"Dottie?"

"My wife." Mortimer ran his finger around the rim of the empty glass. "I ain't told nobody but you, Abe."

"You should tell your wife," Abe said, now suddenly aware that this was Mortimer's best friend talking.

"The trouble is, I got nothing to leave her." Mortimer shook his head despondently. "Horses, you know?"

Abe realized that for Mortimer this amounted to a heartfelt confidence. "So, what are you going to do?" he asked. "I mean . . . about . . . what was your wife's name?"

"Dottie."

"Yeah, Dottie."

Mortimer considered Abe's question briefly, his eyes gazing into the empty glass as if it were a crystal ball. Then he sat back and lightly slapped the bar with both hands. "I better get going." He grabbed Abe's hand and squeezed. "Thanks, Abe," he said as he eased himself off the stool.

Abe came around the end of the bar and followed him out onto the street. It seemed the minimum he could do. Briefly, they stood together, watching the breeze riffle through the trees that lined the street.

"Let me know if there's anything you need," Abe said finally.

Mortimer snatched a pack of cigarettes from his jacket, thumped one out and lit it. "You got a safe, Abe?"

"Yeah."

Mortimer lifted the match and stared at the small, guttering flame. "Maybe you could do something for me."

"Sure."

Mortimer drew an envelope from his pocket and handed it to Abe. "Fifteen thousand. It's for Dottie. If something happens to me, make sure she gets it."

"That's a lot of cash," Abe said warily.

"I do a cash business," Mortimer replied. "And the thing is, if I keep it, it'll ride off on some fucking nag at the track." He dropped the cigarette and crushed it with the toe of his shoe. "You don't see me around, look me up in the book. Mortimer Dodge. Eighty-sixth Street. That's where Dottie is."

"Okay," Abe said. He put the envelope in his pocket. "But, hey, maybe you'll beat this thing."

Mortimer shook his head. "If it was a light switch, I'd flip it off right now."

"If what were a light switch?"

"Life," Mortimer said, turned, and trudged wearily down the street, head bowed, shoulders hunched, as if headed for that place where the firing squad stood waiting for him, talking idly and smoking cigarettes.

CARUSO

FROM BEHIND the limited concealment of a tree, Caruso watched Mortimer trudge up the street. He'd seen him pass an envelope, but the guy he'd passed it to didn't remotely resemble the sort of guy he'd have taken for Batman. But that didn't matter, Caruso said to himself. If this fuck was Batman, and the Big Assignment came his way, then it didn't matter if the guy looked the part or didn't look the part. Either way, the guy was history.

Now, as he fell in behind Mortimer, following him at a distance, he wondered just how many guys Mortimer would see during the night, how long the list he'd have to whittle down, eliminating one guy at a time, until he knew which one Batman really was.

Mortimer reached Fifth Avenue, then headed uptown again. It was a clear, cool night, but as far as Caruso was concerned, the air's crisp clarity did nothing to recommend a long nocturnal stroll up the blue spine of Manhattan. What if Mortimer were a drunk? Caruso asked himself. What if the poor hopeless bastard was one of those guys who spent his nights going from bar to bar but always managed to appear sober the next morning. Caruso considered this possibility, then instantly believed that Mortimer was precisely this kind of guy. From that unappetizing conclusion, he imagined himself tailing his black-hatted quarry from one gin mill to the next as the hours dropped dead one by one, and dawn at last broke over the bleary face of the city.

But as Mortimer continued north, he seemed hardly to notice the taverns he passed. Instead, he appeared entirely lost to the world around him, hardly noticing the speeding traffic or his fellow pedestrians. When an old woman's small white dog leaped at him, snarling and straining at the leash, he seemed barely aware of it. He didn't flinch away or alter the pace of his forward momentum but only sailed onward, holding to his course like a battered old steamer churning its way home.

At Nineteenth Street, Mortimer turned westward, his gait now so weary and unsteady he seemed perpetually jostled by a rude, invisible crowd. The signs from the bars did not beckon to him. He passed them like strangers, wobbling on through the nearly deserted street until he reached a building whose address Caruso could clearly read: 445 West 19 Street.

It was a five-story brownstone that looked carefully maintained. Two black wrought-iron railings led up seven cement steps to a polished wooden door. Four windows faced the street, and there were terra-cotta flower boxes in each of them. Some kind of greenery rose from the boxes, but there were no flowers. There was a large brass knocker on the door, but Caruso noted that Mortimer pressed a small buzzer instead, then waited until the door opened.

STARK

MORTIMER STOOD at the door, the same oddly morose look on his face that Stark had noticed at their last meeting. "I hope it's enough," he said as he drew the envelope from his jacket pocket.

Stark looked at Mortimer pointedly, took in the drawn, desolate face, the sense of something frayed beyond mending. If something were wrong with the deal, he thought, and Mortimer knew it was wrong, then what desperation would have compelled him to go through with it? He thought of the years they'd worked together and decided, just this once, to offer an out.

"Do I need to know anything else, Mortimer?" he asked. "Anything else before I go to work on this?"

"You mean about the—"

"About anything," Stark interrupted.

"No."

"Are you sure?"

Mortimer looked unnerved by the question but said only, "Yeah."

All right, Stark thought, what's done is done. He took the envelope from his hand. "I'll get back to you."

With that, Stark expected Mortimer to retreat down the corridor, but he remained in place, staring at the envelope.

"What's the matter?" Stark asked.

"I thought I'd wait."

"For what?"

"For you to see if you got enough to do the job."

"What's the hurry?"

"No hurry," Mortimer said quickly, nervously, like a guy covering his tracks. "It's just that my friend, he's anxious to get moving on this thing, so if you can't do it, he needs to know."

"I can't read it now," Stark told him. "I have an appointment."

"Okay," Mortimer said weakly. He stepped away from the door. "So, you'll let me know when . . ."

"I'll be back here at midnight," Stark said. "You can call me then."

"How about if I just come by," Mortimer asked.

"You're not going home now?"

"Dottie's on the warpath. I'm giving her a little time to cool."

Stark looked at Mortimer doubtfully. "Why is she on the warpath, Mortimer?"

Mortimer looked like a guy caught with his hand in

the till. "This other broad," he sputtered. "She thinks I got this other broad."

Of all the answers Mortimer could have given, Stark thought, this was the most ludicrous, and because of that, he knew that it had been yanked from a mind unaccustomed to deceit.

"I see," Stark said coolly.

"She's real hot about it," Mortimer added with a sideward glance.

"No doubt," Stark said, though he knew that this, too, was ridiculous, since everything Mortimer had ever said about his wife suggested that she was a woman who asked little and demanded nothing, a dull, moonless planet that revolved around Mortimer in an orbit that never varied in its shape or speed.

And so the question was why had Mortimer bothered to concoct such a shallow, pointless, and transparently absurd lie. The only possible answer was that he'd done so in order to conceal some deeper and more dreadful falsehood.

Stark hated both the question and the answer. He looked at the envelope Mortimer had just given him and felt sure that something was seriously wrong in this whole matter of the missing wife.

"The woman," he said. "Did you know her?"

Mortimer looked as if he'd just been hit with an electric shock. "The one who's missing?" he asked. "No, I . . ."

"But she's your friend's wife, right?"

"Yeah."

"And yet you never met her?"

"I met her," Mortimer said. "But I didn't really know her."

"So you're not involved in it," Stark said. "In her being missing."

"Me?" Mortimer's face froze in shock. "How could I be involved?"

"I don't know, Mortimer," Stark told him. "Maybe you and the woman are . . . close."

"Close?" Mortimer yelped. "You mean like . . . close . . . like that?"

"Maybe she's the woman your wife is worried about."

"No!" Mortimer blurted out. "Nothing like that. I never really knew the woman. She don't mean nothing to me."

Stark let Mortimer squirm for a moment, then said, "All right. Come back around midnight."

Mortimer looked like a schoolboy suddenly released from the clutches of a disapproving teacher. "Okay," he said hastily, then turned away and trudged back down the stairs.

Watching him, Stark recalled how emphatically Mortimer had denied any connection to the missing woman it was his job to find. If this were true, he thought with a renewed and steadily sharper sensation of disturbance, then Mortimer was in Lockridge's position, hired to find a man who could find Marisol for another man, in this case, Mortimer's "friend." But who was this friend, Stark wondered, and was he like Henderson had been, a scorned man, bitter and enraged, the missing wife—if she were his wife—now the sole object of his boiling wrath.

CARUSO

AS HE followed Mortimer westward, Caruso thought of the man at the top of the stairs, and the more he thought of him, the more one thing seemed clear. This guy looked a lot more like Batman than the barkeep he'd seen talking to Mortimer minutes before. For one thing, he'd had a book in his right hand. A very old book, like the ones Caruso had seen in movies about rich people who had huge country estates and whole rooms filled floor-to-ceiling with books you never saw in bookstore windows because they'd probably been made for the people who read them and nobody else. He knew that such people were phonies, that they would shake his hand, then quickly wash. He would always be low and dirty and disreputable to such people.

Okay, so forget about the barkeep, Caruso thought, it was this guy he'd love to waste, this smart and arrogant guy, with the fancy book in his fucking hand. He could put a bullet between his eyes and walk away smiling. He imagined doing just that, getting the word from Mr. Labriola, *Whack Batman,* then coming up behind this fuck and whacking him good. He thought of the shiny thirty-eight revolver he'd bought eight years before and which he kept, fully loaded, in the glove compartment of his car. When the moment came, he knew he'd be ready.

The only problem was that even if Labriola gave him the Big Assignment, he couldn't be sure if this guy was really Batman. Because if he were Batman, then wouldn't he want to look like he wasn't instead of like he was?

Mortimer had made it to the Seventh Avenue subway by the time Caruso had run the various permutations through his mind. By that time he no longer felt certain which of the men Mortimer had visited was actually the man Labriola had hired to find his daughter-in-law, and this left Caruso utterly perplexed as he watched Mortimer descend the stairs to the station, then finally disappear.

Nothing was easy, that was the bottom line, Caruso concluded. Everything required more than you thought it would. More investigation, he decided, he needed more investigation before he could tell Labriola who Batman was and be sure that he was right. But how could he check out two different guys at the same time? That was a real mind twister, and as he made his way down the stairs, still vaguely on Mortimer's trail, he tried to figure out a way to do it. The obvious answer was that he could hire some punk to keep an eye on one of the guys while he kept an eye on the other, but the punk would want money, and Caruso didn't have any money, and he knew Labriola wouldn't spring for an extra dime.

A problem, Caruso thought, as he watched Mortimer step onto the uptown number one, a real fucking problem.

SARA

SHE'D BEEN lucky, and she knew it. She was lucky because she hadn't brought the gun. If she had, the commanding voice would have been too loud and insistent for her to ignore. In her mind she saw the little bald man stagger backward as the plume of blood spread across his chest, a look of horrified amazement on his face. One more step, and what she now envisioned would have been real.

And so she had to be careful. That was the lesson she had to learn. She had to check everything out. She had to be street smart. She couldn't allow herself to be cornered again.

Still, there was no choice but to go on. And so she took the paper from her bag and once again turned to the classified section. She scoured its pages, noting the varied skills she did not possess. She knew nothing of computers, nothing of bookkeeping, nothing of management, nothing of organization. She couldn't set a broken leg or clean a tooth. She couldn't fix anything or assemble anything or break anything down once it was assembled. She knew nothing about the theater, nothing about carpentry, nothing about recruitment. She had no experience in retail, had never sold a skirt, a greeting card, a record. The only thing she'd ever sold was herself, her voice, and that was probably long gone.

She folded the paper and considered just how little she'd learned in her life that anyone else could use. She knew scores of old songs, could play a little piano. But so what? The world was full of people who could do these things. The point was to be able to do something that someone else wanted done and would pay you to do. Or maybe just something you had that someone else wanted. Maybe no more than your body.

She froze, appalled by the idea that she could think so little of herself. And yet, what did she actually have to offer? What could she do that a thousand other people couldn't do better?

She knew that these were devastating questions, and that if she pursued them, she would fall and fall and at the end of her fall she would reach the bottom of her will and there lay prostrate and defeated, a woman fit only to be scooped up and tossed into the backseat of a car and driven back to Long Island.

And so she decided that there were some realities that no one could afford to stare in the face, because if you did, you saw only the heartless truth of your situation, and if you did that, you'd give up on everything. The winners were the ones who ignored the facts, because the facts were like whirling swords, forever slashing at your hope, and against which you had only the armor of your refusal and avoidance and denial, whatever you needed to say *Not me*.

She rose and made her way back across town, pausing briefly in Washington Square Park to watch the street musicians who gathered there. Some were singing folk songs and strumming guitars. There were a couple of rappers, and near the fountain, a lone crooner of the old standards. He was in his sixties, Sara supposed, his voice a bit gravelly, and yet somehow perfect for the world-weary lyrics of "But Not for Me."

Listening to him, she realized how little she'd known about life when she'd sung the old romantic songbook. She was sure she could sing these songs more truthfully now, because of all that went wrong and faded and vanished, all that betrayed and disappointed you, the things that never added up and the things that never made sense, and because she knew that for her to sing them in any other way would be to sing a lie.

CARUSO

SO, COULD Piano Man be Batman? Caruso wondered as he sipped his beer. The guy sure didn't fit the image he'd had in his head. But facts were facts, and he'd watched from just across the street and seen Mortimer talking somberly to this same guy who sat, playing the piano, utterly ordinary, nondescript, and who for all the world didn't look like he could find a black guy in Harlem, much less some crazy broad who ditched her husband and sure as hell didn't want to be found.

He grabbed his beer and strolled to the back of the bar.

Piano Man had just come to the end of a song, so it seemed to Caruso that it was a perfect time to chat him up.

"You worked here a long time?" he asked.

"Seems like forever," the man answered.

Caruso took a quick sip of beer, then glanced about the nearly empty bar. "Slow night."

"It's early," the man said. "We get a better crowd at night."

"So, you got entertainment." Caruso nodded toward

the piano. "I seen the sign outside. Abe Morgenstern at the piano."

Piano Man shrugged. "I just like to keep from getting too rusty. We used to have a singer."

"This all you do, piano?" Caruso lit a cigarette.

"No, I own the place," Piano Man answered.

"Own the place, no shit," Caruso said. He smiled. "My father had a small business," he lied. "A bakery. Lived right over it. All night he could smell the work he'd done that day. Never got away from it. It eats you alive, a small business."

"It takes up a lot of time, that's for sure," Piano Man agreed.

"So, you're like my dad, you live upstairs?"

"No," Piano Man answered. "I got a place over on Grove Street."

Caruso smiled cheerfully. He couldn't tell if Piano Man was lying, but he hoped he was. He loved being lied to because it confirmed a truth he needed for his work, the fact that people were scum, so whatever you did to them, they fucking deserved it.

But that wasn't the point at the moment, Caruso realized. The point was to nail the guy down, get something for Labriola to chew on. "So, I was wondering," he began. "If I was looking to get a place in this part of town, would Grove Street be good?"

"Yeah, sure," Piano Man said.

"What kind of rent would I be looking at?"

"A bundle."

"Like how much?"

"Depends on how big. You got a family?"

The fact that he didn't have a family stung Caruso briefly, like admitting to another guy that he couldn't get it up. "No," he answered quietly.

"So a studio, that would be enough?"

"A studio, yeah."

"I would guess a couple grand at least."

"A month?" Caruso gasped, momentarily taken in by his own ruse, the absurd notion that he was looking for a place in the city. He wasn't, of course, and he told himself that immediately. Still, the fact that he couldn't afford to live in Manhattan even if he wanted to made him feel like a guy who would always come up short, have a car, an apartment, a girl that was a couple notches down from the ones he really wanted. But this was a point uncomfortable to pursue, and so he returned to the issue at hand. "So the bar, it makes you a good living, I guess."

Piano Man shook his head. "No, I barely scrape by."

Caruso smiled delightedly. If this were really Batman, then he was lying through his teeth. Because Batman probably had plenty of dough. The trouble was that Piano Man didn't look like he had a nickel. He wore a faded shirt and flannel pants and talked about how he was just scraping by, and if Piano Man was Batman, then all of that was bullshit. The problem was that the pose was solid. Piano Man actually looked like a down-at-the-heel guy. He talked like one too. Simple. Direct. He gave nothing away. Put it all together, Caruso reasoned, and it was the secret of his success. If it were all a disguise, no amount of small talk could cut through it. The guy was good. A real pro. Caruso realized that he could stand around and yap all night and not get through the mask.

"Well," he said, "I better get going." He downed the last of the beer and stared Piano-Man-Maybe-Batman right in the eye. "Take care of yourself," he said.

"You too."

Caruso headed for the door, but before going through it, looked back. Piano Man was making his way toward the front of the bar, his expression curiously vacant, his thoughts obviously somewhere else. *On the woman maybe,* Caruso thought, *the one he's tracking down.*

SARA

SHE'D NOT noticed the place before, but now she saw that it was McPherson's. Years earlier she'd heard a singer there, a pretty good one, she recalled. The sign in the window said "Singer wanted. Open mike."

She knew what that meant, every would-be Broadway ingénue in New York would take a turn. They would be young and bright and full of great expectations.

Even so, she walked across the street and peered through the window, expecting to see the latest arrival from Georgia or Minnesota singing her heart out, trying to make an impression on some potbellied agent or well-heeled producer, or perhaps just singing for herself, honing her skills, along with trying to keep hope alive. But the mike stood alone before the old piano, the man at the keys looking down for the most part, absently studying his fingers as if trying to remember what they were for.

She knew that if she were like Della, believed that the Great Something Out There inevitably provided for the lost sheep, the fallen sparrow, she would stride into the little bar, introduce herself, step up to the mike, belt a great number, get a full-time job on the strength of that one performance, and turn her life into grist for some inspirational film.

But Sara believed none of that. Instead, she believed in the raw play of chance, in opportunities as easily missed as seized, the wheel's random turning. In long walks at the mall, she had argued her position with Della, knowing all the while that no matter how sound her arguments, how proven by the facts, Della would hold to the golden chord of her claim that nothing in the universe was truly accidental, that she had met Mike not by chance at a movie theater but because through past millennia their souls had converged. The meeting at the movie theater, where Della had dropped her change and Mike had picked it up, was merely part of the Plan, the way you achieved the Big Happy Ending.

Through the bar's hazy window, Sara stared at the vacant mike and the battered old piano and guessed that the bar was barely making ends meet. This was not necessarily bad news, however. For it could be argued that what the bar really needed was a singer to revive it, a voice that drew people in, made them hang around a little longer than they might have otherwise, linger for the final set, maybe even still be there when the barman sounded last call.

Last call.

She heard the wind in the corn, felt her body pushed into the enveloping green, Sheriff Caulfield behind her, telling her she had to play along, keep her mouth shut, which she might as well do anyway, since he ran things in Cumberland County, and who would listen to a white-trash tenant farmer's daughter?

And so she'd played along and kept her mouth shut, and the thing was done, and she'd pulled herself from the ground and staggered back toward her car, the voice screaming in her ear, *Kill him! Kill him now,* a voice she'd managed to silence only by promising absolutely and forever that it would never happen again.

She closed her eyes and tried to squeeze all that had happened after that from her mind. When she opened them again, the sign shone dully before her.

Singer wanted. Open mike.

Last chance, she thought, though she wasn't sure it

was even that. Still, it was a job, if she could get it, and at least there'd be no more searching the paper and going on interviews and sitting silently while they looked at her from across their polished desks.

Okay, she decided, why not, and on the wave of that decision walked to the door.

THREE

Mean to Me

TONY

TONY SNAPPED the cell phone closed and looked at Eddie. "He won't tell me a thing," he said.

They had been driving aimlessly for an hour, through a string of Long Island towns, Tony talking to his father, trying to get some idea of who he'd put on Sara. "He just says he'll find her, and when he does it's up to me."

"Up to you?" Eddie asked.

"What I want to do about it."

"So, what you want to do, Tony?"

"I don't know," Tony admitted. "Talk to her, I guess."

They rode in silence for a time, before Eddie said, "So, what will you talk to her about, Tony?"

"I don't know." Tony pulled down the visor to shield his eyes from the bright midmorning sun. "There's something eating at him," he said. "My father." He considered his father's gruff, angry tone, the spiking rage he seemed to feel at the mention of Sara's name. "Maybe I should just tell him to pull this guy off, you know."

"She could come back any minute," Eddie said consolingly. "Like that aunt of mine."

Tony stared out at the dull suburban landscape. "She never liked it here," he said. He tightened his grip on the wheel and shook his head. "I don't know what I want anymore, Eddie. I mean, what's the good of her coming back if she can't be happy?" He thought a moment, then shrugged. "But I don't think she was ever happy. Except maybe right at the beginning, before—"

"Before what?"

"Before the Old Man started coming over all the time. Always beefing about this or that."

Eddie nodded silently.

"I don't want him to find her," Tony continued. "Him, or some guy he's got looking. It would scare her, you know? Some goon coming up to her, telling her she's gotta come with him, maybe grabbing her arm, pushing her into a car." A scene from his boyhood sliced through his brain, his mother on her knees in the kitchen, holding a bloody cloth to her mouth. A terrible dread seized him, and he suddenly steered the car off the main road and brought it to a halt on a secluded beach. "I got to find her before this goon does," he said emphatically. He studied the empty expanse of the sea briefly, then turned to Eddie. "I figure it's Vinnie Caruso that's looking for her. Who else would my father use for something like this?"

Eddie nodded heavily. "Yeah, it's probably Vinnie."

Tony studied Eddie's doughy features a moment, then said, "You go back a while, right? You and Caruso? I noticed it. When he shows up at the marina, he always says hello to you."

"We go back, yeah. High school."

"You were friends?"

"We hung out together," Eddie said. "Weekends, you know? Over at Buddy's Grill, with other guys that didn't have no dates."

Tony tried to imagine Eddie and Caruso in Buddy's Grill on a listless Saturday night, both of them losers, no girls in sight, staring at each other over chili dogs and Cokes, two guys without prospects, two of life's innocent bystanders, dodging stray bullets, getting hit or not, but always and forever within the line of fire.

"Vinnie wasn't a bad guy back then," Eddie added. "But he got picked on. Stuart Brock used to beat him up."

Tony guessed what Eddie had left out. "Until you made him stop, right?"

Eddie nodded silently.

"So Caruso owes you," Tony said.

Eddie looked at Tony without comprehension.

"He owes you a favor," Tony explained.

"I guess."

"Do you think he'd be willing to tell you if he found Sara? Before he told my father, I mean."

"I don't know, Tony. Vinnie's real tight with your father."

"But it wouldn't hurt to ask him, right? At least I'd find out if he's the guy my father has looking for her."

"No, it wouldn't hurt to ask," Eddie said.

Tony touched Eddie's shoulder. "I won't forget this, Eddie." He hit the ignition. "Believe me, I won't forget."

On the way to the marina Tony once again surveyed the world around him. There were good schools and playgrounds, soccer fields and tennis courts. The little malls hummed with shoppers. It wasn't for Sara, but it was not so terrible a place, he thought. The argument he'd made that they should live here rather than the city seemed valid enough even now. So the problem wasn't that he'd gotten it wrong about Long Island, he decided. The problem was that he'd gotten it wrong about Sara, never gauged how isolated she would feel, how bored. But there was more than that, he realized. Some part of her had always been withheld from him, buried deep, something inside of her he couldn't reach. He wondered if all women had this little room they wouldn't unlock for you. Maybe even Della DeLuria had a room like that, one Mike couldn't enter but sometimes thought about, wanted to know what Della kept in there.

At a traffic light, a shiny Ford Explorer pulled up beside him. The woman behind the wheel was about Sara's age, with close-cropped brown hair. She held loosely to the wheel, a thick bracelet on her wrist, a small diamond winking from her finger. There were two kids in the back, but the woman seemed hardly to notice their frantic scuffling or the maddening noise they made. Her eyes were fixed on the road ahead, and she seemed determined to make it to the next light, then the next, until the day had passed, and she was at home again, in her bed, nestled beside her sleeping husband, her eyes open in the motionless dark.

He had to admit that even now he had no idea what thoughts came to Sara when she lay in the ebony silence of their bedroom. Her flight was all the evidence he needed that she must have been desperately unhappy. Years before, his cousin Donny had told him women were always unhappy, and that the only way a man could be happy was not to care. That was what he'd tried to do, he decided now, he'd tried not to care that Sara was bored, lonely, or that he'd broken the promise he'd made that once his business was off the ground they'd move to the city. For a time she'd made the case for returning to New York, but his father had supplied the reasons he'd given her for not doing it (Manhattan was far from his business. Long Island was better for the kids that would be coming along), though to the old man there'd never been any point in giving Sara a reason for anything since it was the man who was supposed to decide where his family lived. He could hear his father's relentless call to arms, *Be a man, for Christ's sake!* And so he'd done that. He'd been a man. And now he was a man alone.

"I'll do it," he blurted out suddenly.

Eddie looked at him quizzically.

"I'll do it," Tony repeated. "Move to the city, if that's what she wants. That's what I'll tell her if I get to her first." He stared at Eddie desperately. "But I got to get to her first. Help me, Eddie. Talk to Caruso."

Eddie seemed to see the depth of his desperation. "Okay, Tony," he said. "Okay."

Tony turned his gaze westward and considered the limitless expanse that presented itself to him, his country from sea to shining sea, the vast landscape into which Sara had disappeared, his mind now focused exclusively on one question: *Where could she be?*

SARA

SHE SAT at the window, the skyline of the city so close she could almost touch it. It was the phone that seemed far away and deadly silent. Perhaps she'd get a call, perhaps she wouldn't. The guy had said he liked her singing and taken her number, but an odd look had come into his eye when she'd told him that she was living in a hotel. Maybe at that moment he'd figured her for trouble, a woman at loose ends, a drunk, maybe, or worse—anyway, undependable.

She tried to put the bar and the open mike out of her mind, along with whatever hope she'd briefly harbored that she might actually get the job. She couldn't even be sure that she'd sung all that well. It didn't matter anyway, because the guy who owned the place had no doubt noticed how jittery she was, the way her eyes darted around like a frightened little bird. Who would want a singer like that, nervous, strung out, probably on the run?

On the run.

She recalled her first days in New York, how she'd waited by the window as she did now. The only difference was that now someone could show up suddenly, Labriola in his big blue Lincoln, pounding on her door, kicking it open, dragging her down the stairs and through the lobby while the little bellhop looked on, aghast, but ready to take the fifty Labriola slipped him, along with the icy command, *Keep your fucking mouth shut.*

She had no doubt that the bellhop would do precisely that. After all, it was what she'd done years before. In her mind, she saw Caulfield standing above her, zipping up his pants, telling her to keep her mouth shut. She'd known instantly that she would do it, let him just walk away, back to his car, and after that go home to the little shack she lived in with her father, hoping somehow she could put it all behind her.

She'd almost done it too, she thought now, almost gotten clear of it. She'd come to New York, landed enough work to keep a roof over her head, married Tony, moved to Long Island, where, despite the little nagging problems and disappointments that plagued any life, she'd almost made a go of it.

In her mind she heard the heavy thud again, a beast closing in upon her from behind.

Almost, she thought, *but not quite.*

ABE

HE KNEW only that her name was Samantha, that she lived in a Brooklyn hotel, and that from the moment she'd begun to sing he'd felt the old, forgotten stirring, felt again what a song can be, along with something more, something extra, a small, barely detectable charge.

He looked over to where Jake stood at the bar, slicing a lime. "That singer who came in last night, how old you think she is?" he asked.

"Thirties," Jake said.

"Yeah, that's what I was thinking." In his mind he saw her standing by the piano, heard her voice again. "She sings older though."

"You wish she was older," Susanne piped in with a laugh. "You wish she was older but still looked like a chick."

"Chick?" Abe asked. "I thought that was sexist, that word."

"No, just sexy," Susanne returned. "At least for old guys."

"Upbeat would be good," Jake said absently. "Lucille was always singing those downers."

"Lucille was a torch singer," Abe reminded him.

Jake dropped the slices into a white dish. "Used to sing 'Fly Me to the Moon,' remember? Like it was bullshit. Like nobody could do that for nobody else." He shook his head. "Fucking depressing, the way she sung it." The knife suddenly stopped. "So, you're going to hire this broad?"

"I don't know."

"Oh, sure you are," Susanne said with a laugh. "I could see she was getting to you."

Getting to you? Abe asked himself. Was that the small charge he'd felt as the woman sang?

A sudden agitation seized him, the sense of something broken loose and rolling about inside him.

Getting to you.

He walked out of the bar and stood on the street and tried to forget that a woman named Samantha had come into the place the night before, sung a song, and somehow shaken something loose.

Getting to you.

If that were true, he had to stop it, and so, at that instant, he decided not to call her, just let her find a gig somewhere else and leave his life alone. That would be the safest thing, he thought, just to leave things where they were, Jake slicing limes and Susanne straightening tables and Jorge in the back, stacking cases of beer, and himself standing alone on the street or sitting at the piano, his fingers resting without movement on the ever-yellowing keys.

CARUSO

"SO, ANYWAY, like I said. I see you give Morty the envelope and you pull away, and so I follow him and he starts walking downtown."

Labriola kept his eyes on the road as he steered the Lincoln off the Henry Hudson Parkway and headed east along the Cross Bronx Expressway.

What, Caruso wondered, could he possibly be thinking? One thing he knew, that whatever it was, it wasn't good. In the few days since Tony's wife had disappeared, a strange darkness had settled over Labriola. It was like a stain that seemed to sink ever deeper into his mind. It was thick and black, and it kept him grimly focused on finding her to the exclusion of other, more important matters, like who'd paid him recently, or what should be done about Toby Carnucci, who should maybe be slapped around a little, the fucking deadbeat.

"So, anyway, when Morty gets to Twelfth Street, he swings east," Caruso went on. "He makes it almost to Fifth, then he stops at this fucking bar."

Caruso had gone over all of this once before, but Labriola seemed to want to hear it all again, as if he were hunting for something, or pondering secret calculations.

"Like I said, the place is called McPherson's," Caruso added. "So, anyway, I go to the window and look in. Morty don't see me, but I see him clear as day. He's talking to this fucking guy at the bar, who turns out to be the piano player, but like I find out later, also owns the place."

"Owns the place," Labriola muttered.

"Owns the place, right," Caruso said. "So, okay, like I said, I figure this is maybe Morty's hangout, you know, that maybe he's a regular, so I wait and he has a couple of drinks and I don't see he ever pays a nickel, and him and the other guy are talking away, and then they stop, and Morty gets up and heads for the door. So I run across the street 'cause I don't want this fuck should see me watching him, and he comes out and the same guy is with him. And right there on the street, Morty gives this guy the envelope, which I figure is the same envelope you give him when he had that meet with you."

"You seen him pass the envelope to this other fucking guy?" Labriola blurted out with a sudden leaping virulence. "With your own eyes, you seen it?"

"With my own eyes."

Labriola glanced out the window and surveyed the neighborhood the expressway had destroyed. "You ever live in Tremont?"

"No," Caruso answered.

"That fucking Jew tore it down," Labriola said bitterly.

"Jew?"

"That fucking Moses." Labriola continued to stare wistfully out the window. "It was like Arthur Avenue still is. A real neighborhood. But that fucking Jew tore it down to build this piece of shit."

"What piece of shit?"

"This ugly fucking road is what."

"Oh."

Labriola's face contorted. "Somebody should have put a bullet in that fucking kike."

Caruso said nothing. Since he had nothing to add to this latest outburst, his only choice was to wait it out, just sit tight and let Labriola chew on whatever he was chewing on until he swallowed it.

"That's when I moved to Brooklyn," Labriola said. "That's when I knew the Bronx was finished." He shook his head disconsolately. "Tremont," he said mournfully. "Tremont was beautiful in them days, but that fucking Jew tore it all down." He suddenly turned from the window and leveled his gaze on Caruso. "A bullet in his head, that's what he needed."

Caruso stared at Labriola, utterly baffled by the Old Man's sudden interest in his old neighborhood, but heartened that he was thinking in such terms, moving perhaps toward the Big Assignment, maybe to whack Toby Carnucci, the stupid bastard, or better yet Batman, the arrogant fuck, if the guy with the book really was Batman, which he still didn't know for sure but was beginning not to care, since whacking the guy with the book would feel great whether he was Batman or not.

"Sometimes a bullet is all that can do the job," Labriola said. "Am I right, Vinnie?"

Caruso smiled broadly. "You're dead right, Mr. Labriola."

He saw that his answer pleased the Old Man, and so he added, "You ask me, a bullet in the head is too fucking good for some people."

"Too fucking good, Vinnie," Labriola repeated.

Caruso cautiously returned to the matter at hand. "So, anyway, I figured I knew who Batman was, you know?"

"Batman?"

"The guy Morty works for. That's what I call him."

"Why you call him that, Vinnie?"

" 'Cause he's all mysterious and shit."

"Oh."

Caruso waited for Labriola to add his own comment, but the Old Man said nothing.

"Anyway," Caruso began again, "anyway, at first I figure Batman must be the guy at the bar, on account he give the envelope to him, you know? But then, Morty don't go straight home after meeting this guy. He goes to Chelsea. Meets another guy. And not only that, he gives something to this guy too. An envelope."

Labriola looked at Caruso intently. "You see my problem here, don't you, Vinnie?"

Caruso blinked.

"You only know one place where that guy works."

"What guy?"

"That fucking piano player you're talking about."

Caruso stared at Labriola without expression.

"Work. That ain't a good place. It's the same like I only know where a guy lives. If I want to pop some fuckhead, and I only know where he lives, then I got to pop him with maybe Mrs. Fuckhead sitting there, maybe with a couple little pint-sized fuckheads running around."

Caruso nodded. "So you—"

"What?" Labriola snapped.

"So, you've decided to pop this guy?" Caruso asked.

Labriola glared at Caruso. "Did I say that, Vinnie?"

"Well, no . . . but."

"But nothing," Labriola barked. "Put your hands out, Vinnie."

"Huh?"

"Put your hands out, Vinnie. Far as you can."

Caruso did as he was told.

"Wiggle your fingers."

Caruso did.

"That's how far you look ahead, Vinnie. Just as far as your fucking fingers. But me, I got to look ahead. Like to what I do if this fuck fucks me."

Caruso started to draw back his hands. "How would he—"

"Keep your hands out there."

Caruso straightened his arms.

"Wiggle your fingers, Vinnie."

Caruso wiggled his fingers.

"You're gonna keep your hands out there like that until you start seeing farther than your fucking fingers. Now, that question you asked me. What was it?"

"I can't see how he'd fuck you," Caruso answered cautiously, since he was not at all sure that this was the question Labriola had in mind.

"You can't see it 'cause you ain't looking no farther than your fingers."

Caruso looked at his fingers.

"Here's how. He don't do the job. What I do then, Vinnie?"

Caruso hazarded a wild guess. "Well, you . . . could make him give you your money back."

"Money?" Labriola bawled. "A guy don't do a job for me, I don't want his fucking money. I want *him*, Vinnie."

Caruso nodded briskly. "Sure. Right." He cautiously lowered his hands. "I see what you mean."

"So what can you tell me about this guy besides where he works?"

"Which guy?"

"The one you told me about. The one in the bar. What else you know about him?"

Caruso remained silent.

"What else you know, Vinnie?" Labriola repeated. "About the guy at the bar or that other guy who maybe is . . . what'd you call it . . . Spider-Man?"

"Batman."

"Yeah, him. What else you know?"

"Well . . . nothing."

"That's right. Nothing. Which is bad, 'cause I need to know about both these assholes," Labriola said darkly. "You understand, Vinnie? Where they go. Who they see. All that shit."

"Yes, sir," Caruso said lamely. "I'll find out about them."

"Make sure you do, because whichever one of these fucks is supposed to find that bitch, if he don't do it, you got to pop him, Vinnie."

Caruso felt a surge of excitement. "Pop him, right," he repeated. "I would have to pop him. And I would too. Whatever you say, Mr. Labriola."

Labriola seemed not to hear him. Instead, he again focused his gaze on the ravaged neighborhood of his youth, staring at the buildings that lay alongside the expressway as if they weren't really standing, save as the ruins of some long-forgotten war.

For a time, Caruso watched as Labriola continued to stare out the window. Then he drew his gaze away and stared straight ahead, down a road whose twists and turns had wonderfully delivered him into the Old Man's trust.

STARK

THE MATERIAL Mortimer had brought lay strewn across the desk. It could hardly have been more useless. Nothing but a picture of a woman in her mid-thirties and a random assortment of more or less incoherent observations, all of them scrawled on legal-size yellow pages in a disjointed handwriting whose legibility strained Stark's eyes and strengthened his suspicions that there was something in this deal that didn't quite add up.

As to facts, Stark learned only that the missing Sara was originally from the South, had come to NYC as a young woman, worked as a nightclub singer, met and married the anonymous husband, and "done nothing" since then. She had no children according to this information, no living relatives, and no resources since she'd taken nothing from her husband's bank accounts.

As to where Sara might have gone, the notes offered no assistance. She had left her car in the driveway, but there was no indication as to whether another party had picked her up, or, if such were the case, who that individual (friend, lover, taxi driver?) might be. She'd also left most of her clothes and all of her jewelry, including both wedding and engagement rings, which indicated that she either had limited means or that she expected her needs to be met by someone other than herself.

The more Stark reviewed the notes, the more useless they seemed. But it was not just the uselessness that bothered him. There was a disturbing look to the notes. The handwriting was an angry scrawl, the angles sharp, the words disjointed. Even on the page they seemed to sputter madly.

He reached for the phone.

"It's me," he said when Mortimer answered. "The notes you got from your friend are useless."

"He's a little . . . he ain't . . . open with everything."

"He's very angry."

"Yeah."

"I've seen this before, Mortimer."

"I know you have."

Mortimer's answer seemed clipped, as if he were hurrying away, on the run himself in some way, seeking someplace to hide no less desperately than the missing woman.

"I think we need to talk," Stark said. He waited for Mortimer to offer something that could quell his growing misgivings. Then he said, "My house. Three-thirty."

"Okay," Mortimer said weakly.

Stark hung up the phone, returned the notes to the plain manila envelope, and placed the envelope in the top drawer of his desk. He could feel something evil stir around him. It coiled in the fractured handwriting of the notes.

He closed the drawer, walked to the window, parted the thick curtains, and looked out at the street. Years before he'd done the same from his hotel window in Madrid and seen Lockridge standing by a lamppost, smoking, with one hand sunk deep into the right pocket of his black leather jacket, his freckled fingers no doubt caressing the blade he would later use on Marisol.

MORTIMER

MORTIMER STARED disconsolately at the television. The Yankees were losing, but he didn't care. He had no money on the game, but that wouldn't have mattered anyway. He had bigger fish to fry than a Yankee win, even if he stood to gain a few bucks in the deal. He had bigger fish to fry. A dreadful sense that Stark had caught on to something, the dark edges of the deal.

"You gonna be home for dinner tonight, Morty?"

He glanced across the room to where Dottie stood, draped in a sleeveless floral housedress, leaning on one flabby arm, her pendulous breasts, as Mortimer saw them, all but touching the floor.

"I don't know for sure," he said.

Mortimer returned his attention to the game and tried to put everything else out of his mind, all the thoughts that were rolling around inside his head, banging against his skull like stones. He didn't want to think about Stark, or what Stark might be thinking, or how what Stark was thinking could affect him. He wanted to think about a horse that won, a bet that netted him a bundle. But his horses had always lost, and he'd netted nothing, and this dreary conclusion turned his thoughts to death.

He was going to die very soon, and he knew that this was a big deal, and yet he seemed unable to focus on it. He was going to die soon and he didn't have a nickel of life insurance or a nickel in savings, and in fact was in hock to the Prince of Darkness for fifteen grand, and even this seemed little more than a small bump in the road. The problem was that he kept thinking about his life rather than his death. How small and drab a thing it had been. How little he'd gotten out of it. Within a few months it would be over, and yet what exactly was this life that would soon end? What had it amounted to? Nothing, Mortimer concluded, absolutely nothing. But that conclusion did not bring his speculation to an end. Instead, the problem only got larger. If he was nothing, then why was he nothing? That was the one question he wanted answered. How had he come to this bleak place, and was there any way he could escape it, however briefly, before the final curtain fell?

"You can't give me no idea?" Dottie demanded.

"No."

Dottie jerked her hand from the doorjamb, clearly irritated. "How about you give me some idea, Morty," she said. "So I know to make dinner or not make dinner, you know?"

"Don't make dinner," Mortimer told her. He knew she was glaring at him, but he didn't care. Bigger fish to fry, he thought, than a pissed-off wife.

He rose, walked to the door, and yanked his jacket from the wall rack beside it. By then Dottie had swept up behind him in a flutter of garish colors, menacing as a huge, angry parrot.

"Where you going?" she demanded.

"Out." A sudden pain streaked across his stomach. "Shit."

"What's the matter with you?" Dottie said, though with neither sympathy nor concern, his pain just another source of irritation.

He was amazed at how unnerved it made him, this single stinging cramp. "Fucking gas," Mortimer answered. He placed his hand on his stomach and squeezed. "I gotta go." He started to open the door, but Dottie closed it.

"You'd tell me, wouldn't you, Morty?" she asked.

"Tell you what?"

"If something was wrong."

"What are you talking about?"

"Wrong, I mean, with us?"

Wrong with us? Mortimer couldn't imagine such a question. Nothing had ever been right with them. Their marriage had been a long slide down a muddy chute, love and passion only things they saw in movies, people rushing toward each other through woods or on the beach. For as long as he could remember, Dottie had been dull and overweight, like himself, and when he thought of them together, he thought of comic figures, people in commercials. Human jokes.

"You'd tell me, wouldn't you?" Dottie insisted. "If something was wrong?"

She looked at him silently, waiting for his answer, and he saw that he'd lied to her so often, she expected only lies, and even thought of them as kindnesses.

"There's nothing wrong, Dottie," he growled as he stepped out into the corridor.

"Okay," Dottie said with a shrug, then softly closed the door.

And so, seconds later, he was standing on Eighty-sixth Street, the usual crowds rolling up and down the busy thoroughfare, but utterly alone in their midst. He had always been alone, he knew. Movies talked about guys who stood alone, and it was supposed to be a good thing, but when you got hit by cancer, or got some other really awful news, when death or something almost as bad stared you in the face, you yearned for someone to share the dark tidings, maybe feel a little bad for you. They didn't need to lend you money or overdo the pity. You just needed to know that it was bad news for them too.

He thought of the one person in the world who'd probably feel that way. It wasn't Dottie. And it wasn't Stark It was Abe who'd looked sad when he'd told him about the cancer, looked sad and poured him a round on the house and then said he could drink for free until he died.

What a guy, Mortimer thought to himself with a surge of true devotion to Abe Morgenstern, *my best friend.*

DELLA

THE PHONE rang. Della picked it up.

"I just wanted to let you know I'm still okay," Sara told her.

Della thought of Leo Labriola, felt again the hard grip of his fingers on her wrist, the bite of the pen, and knew that her friend was not in the least okay. She could warn her, but what would be the consequences of that? What if the Old Man found out about it? There was Nicky to think about. And her daughter. And Mike. You save one person, you put another in danger. Because there seemed no way to act rightly, she said only, "That's good, Sara." She added nothing else, because the important thing was to get off the line as quickly as possible, learn as little as possible about where Sara was or what she was doing. That way, if Labriola really used muscle, she'd at least have a weapon against him, the fact that he could squeeze and squeeze and she still wouldn't know any more about Sara than she already knew, and so there'd be nothing he could get out of her.

"Have you seen Tony?" Sara asked.

Labriola's warning sounded in Della's mind, *If she calls, don't tell her nothing.*

"Listen, Sara, Nicky's sick. He had a fever this morning, and I got this appointment, so . . ."

"Sure," Sara said. "Sure, Della."

"I'm sorry to rush off like this but, you know . . ."

"I understand," Sara said. "Take it easy, Della."

The click of the phone swept over Della in a deep, relieving wave. But then the wave receded, and the relief turned to accusation. Her friend was being hunted by a vicious old bastard who'd stop at nothing, and she, Della, could do nothing to warn her. She had mentioned

Labriola's visit to no one, not even Mike, and she'd lied to Tony, though at least he'd figured that out and so knew without a doubt what his father was up to. None of that removed the stain of her cowardice, however, the fact that she'd not only betrayed her friend but that she was at this very moment being drawn deeper into that betrayal.

"Who called?" Mike asked as he came into the kitchen.

Della stepped over to the sink, began rinsing the dishes. "Just one of those calls. Somebody selling something."

"What this time?"

Della thought fast. "Insurance."

"Insurance?" Mike said doubtfully. "I didn't think insurance companies did any telemarketing."

"I guess some of them do," Della said weakly.

"I thought you might have a secret admirer." Mike drew her into his arms.

She laughed. "You'd know it if I did."

His eyes drifted away, and she knew that he was staring at the wifeless home across the cul-de-sac. "Well, it took Tony by surprise, didn't it?"

She abruptly drew herself from his arms. "Sara didn't have a . . . she wasn't doing anything like that." She turned back to the sink. "I mean, some other guy."

"How do you know that, Della?"

She picked up a plate, began moving a yellow sponge over its floral surface. "I just know, that's all."

Mike's large hands gripped her shoulders, turning her to face him. "What's going on?" he asked.

"Nothing," Della answered, but saw instantly that he didn't buy it.

"Della, what do you know about this? Did Sara talk to you?"

"No."

"Did Tony?"

"Tony? 'Course not. I don't know anything, Mike. Really."

He considered this briefly, then said, "Okay," but in that voice that meant "for now."

She smiled and quickly changed the subject. "I'm going to drop Nicky off at my mother's this afternoon. Then a little shopping."

"Okay," Mike said. He kissed her lightly, then went back upstairs, grabbed his jacket, and came tromping down again, the jacket slung over his right shoulder.

"I've got an early tee-off time," he said as he headed out the door.

"Have a nice day," Della called to him, though no longer sure she herself would ever have another. After a moment she heard the car as it backed down the driveway. From the kitchen window she could see Mike as he drifted into the cul-de-sac then drove away, and this entirely familiar scene suddenly struck her as infinitely precious, something that had seemed so sure and firm before but now gave off a sense of being terribly at risk.

EDDIE

HE DIDN'T like it, but he had to do it. When you were a guy's friend, you helped that guy out. And so, with no further consideration, he picked up the phone and dialed the number.

"Caruso."

"Vinnie, it's Eddie. It's been a while, huh?"

"Since what?"

"Since we seen each other."

"I was down at the marina a couple weeks ago."

Caruso was right, and Eddie thought it was pretty stupid how he'd said it had been a while when it really hadn't. He thought fast and said, "Yeah, but we didn't really have time to talk, you know. So, listen, I was thinking maybe we could have a drink sometime. I mean, like tonight."

"Tonight?"

"Yeah."

There was a pause, during which Eddie tried to imagine what Caruso was thinking.

"Eddie, let me ask you something," Caruso said finally. "You okay?"

"Yeah, sure."

"I mean, that little shit fire you, something like that?"

"Little shit?"

"That little shit you work for. Fucking Tony. Did he fire you is what I'm asking."

"No."

" 'Cause if he did, I could do something about it, Eddie," Caruso said. " 'Cause Mr. Labriola, he trusts me, you know, like a son."

"Tony didn't fire me," Eddie told him. "How come you think that?"

" 'Cause I figure you want to see me 'cause you need a little cash, maybe."

"Oh, no, it's not that."

"But, Eddie, if you need cash, you don't come to me like you would some fucking shylock, you know? You come to me like a friend."

"I don't need money, Vinnie."

"You don't need money?"

"No."

"So, what do you need, Eddie?"

Eddie sensed that the phone was not the best place to

tell Caruso what he was after. A guy would say okay to a certain kind of favor over the phone, but there were favors that called for a guy to really put something on the line, and when you asked for one of those, you needed to look the guy in the eye.

"I was thinking we might have a drink, Vinnie. I could tell you then."

"And it don't have to do with money?"

"Money, no. It ain't about money."

The fact that it wasn't about money seemed to put Caruso on alert.

Eddie tried to ease his mind. "It ain't nothing bad, Vinnie. Nothing to worry about. Just a favor."

"Okay," Caruso said. "Where you want to meet?"

"How about Billy's Grill?"

Caruso laughed. "Jesus, Billy's Grill. I ain't been there in fifteen, twenty years."

"But we used to hang out there, remember?"

"I remember. Especially that night when I was all . . . fucked up."

Eddie recalled that night well. Caruso had gotten all steamed and decided to whack Rudy Kellogg for stealing Cindy Mankowitz even though Rudy had done no such thing and Cindy had gone out with Vinnie only once, and that on a dare from Kathy Myerson.

"I would have done it, you know," Caruso said. "I would have done it if you hadn't got that knife away from me."

Eddie doubted that Vinnie would have done anything at all, but this didn't seem the right time to say so. "So, Billy's Grill?"

"Sure, okay."

They settled on a time, then Eddie listened while Caruso boastfully jawed about the easy money he had and the big expensive things he bought with it. After that,

Vinnie yapped away about the nightspots he preferred, and even claimed to have a few babes who just couldn't get enough of him. Eddie doubted that any of this was true, and the fact that Vinnie felt compelled to spin such stories suggested that the awkward, orphaned kid he remembered from his boyhood had been a better guy than the man Eddie was scheduled to meet at Billy's Grill later in the day. It was because he'd gone to work for Old Man Labriola, he supposed. You couldn't work for a guy like that and not have some of it rub off on you. It was like working in a coal mine, Eddie decided, only the black dust was on your soul. *Too bad,* he concluded when he finally hung up. *Too bad Vinnie went that way.*

SARA

THE PHONE rang. She picked it up.

"Samantha?" a voice said. "Damonte?"

The guy, Sara thought, surprised, the guy at the bar. "Yes."

"This is Abe, the guy owns the place that had the open mike deal last night? Morgenstern? We talked for a couple minutes?"

"Yes."

"Well, the thing is, I liked the way you sang, you know? I liked it a lot."

"Thank you."

"So, I was wondering. Would you be interested in coming by again?"

"Coming by?"

"I'd like to talk to you about, maybe, developing an act, you know? For the bar, I mean. Would you . . . well . . . would you be interested in that?"

"Yes, I would," she told him.

"Okay, so, when could you drop by?"

She thought of the brief conversation she'd had with the man the night before. He'd seemed easygoing, a guy who probably never got mad or snapped at anybody. A boss like that was what she needed, she supposed, because she was jumpy, on edge, always looking over her shoulder, felt in every heartbeat a little ache of fear. "Would this afternoon be okay?" she asked.

"Yeah, fine," the man said. "How about two-thirty?"

"Okay."

"See you then."

She put down the phone and felt a little burst of hope. Not much, she admitted, but maybe just enough to get her through the day.

ABE

OKAY, SO, that's done, Abe thought as he hung up the phone. He had not intended to do it, but there it was, acting on impulse, one of the many things that had driven Mavis nuts, usually because when he did it, it was a screwup. As this might be a screwup too, Abe thought, this woman he didn't even know but liked for no good reason except that she sang well and there was something about her that . . . well . . . got to him.

He sat back and glanced around his office, and it seemed to him that everything he saw confirmed that, impulse or not, he'd done the right thing. Going through the motions, that was what his life had become, a daily going through the motions. There were the bills on his desk, the orders in the box, the file cabinet stuffed with forms and catalogs and tax receipts, and God only knew whatever else he'd crammed in there. There were the boxes of whiskey, overflow from the storeroom, stacks of promotional material dropped off by the salesman, a bottle of wine Mrs. Higgins had brought back, claiming it was corked, which it was, and so he'd refunded her money, and now was supposed to contact the distributor for a refund of his own, but never would because . . . well . . . why bother since he'd sold it to her illegally, as a favor, McPherson's being a bar, not a liquor store, and besides it was only twelve bucks, and his time wasn't worth it.

But what *was* his time worth, he asked himself now. What were the days and hours that remained to him actually worth if he lived on as he now lived? Not much, he decided, which was why he'd changed his mind about that singer, gone with that little charge Susanne thought was so funny, but which, he knew, even "old guys" felt, perhaps old guys felt even more sharply than young guys because the horizon was closing in and the next chance you had might well be your last.

So, okay, he thought again, now rising with a curious energy, *so, okay, done.*

MORTIMER

HE FOLLOWED Stark over to the large antique desk, where the contents of the envelope had been spread out for display.

"You didn't look at any of this, did you, Mortimer?" Stark asked.

Mortimer knew that he was being instructed to look at the few spare items Stark had assembled on the desk.

"The notes, if you can call them that, are very general," Stark said. "And the photograph, I don't even know how recent it is."

Mortimer had never seen the missing woman before, and he was struck by how kind she looked for a woman who was supposed to be such a raving bitch. In fact, she had the delicate beauty of women he worshipped from afar, and it was hard for him to believe that anyone had been so stupid as to drive her from his life.

"How old is the picture, Mortimer?" Stark asked. "Did the husband tell you?"

"It's recent," Mortimer answered, though he had no idea if this was true. But what did it matter now if he lied to Stark again and again? With the first lie, the dam had broken, and he knew that the poisoned water was now destined to leak out until not a drop was left. "She's in her thirties. That's all I know."

"She's never had a job." Stark nodded toward the single sheet of notes. "Except years before. A singer. She's from down south originally. She took none of the husband's money. She left her car in the driveway. Do you have anything to add to this?"

"No."

"Well, that's a problem, Mortimer, because there's nothing to go on in any of this," Stark said. He picked up the photograph and the notes and returned them to the envelope. "This friend of yours has to give me more."

"He won't," Mortimer said.

Stark sat down behind the desk and stared Mortimer dead in the eye. "This is a favor I was willing to do for this man," he said. "But really, I was doing the favor for you."

"I know."

"You told him this?"

"Yeah. And that you was doing it on the cheap."

"He understands that I don't owe him anything, correct?"

"Right."

"And that I don't need his money?"

"He knows that, sure."

"So where does that leave me, Mortimer?"

"Leave you?"

"Yes, leave me. Because I can't do what he wants me to do if he doesn't give me more information."

"I don't think he'll give nothing more," Mortimer said.

"If that's the case, then there's nothing more I can do." Stark scooped the notes and picture into the envelope and held it out to Mortimer. "You can return all this to your friend with my best regards."

Mortimer didn't take the envelope from Stark's hand. "You can't do that," he said, and immediately realized that he'd made a terrible mistake, that Stark would hear the sudden hint of dread in his voice.

"What do you mean, I can't?" Stark asked.

"You have to go through with it."

"Why?"

Mortimer labored to make his answer genuine. "Because you agreed to do it, and he's counting on you."

"Your friend is counting on me?"

"Yes."

"But he won't give me any additional information?"

Mortimer hesitated. He knew he was in a box, that Stark would drop the case if more information were not provided. But he also knew that there'd be no more information. Unless he made it up.

"Well?" Stark demanded.

"I'll talk to him," Mortimer said. "I'll get it out of him. Whatever you need."

Stark watched him intently. "Does this friend of yours have any idea where his wife might be?"

The cityscape beyond the window provided the only answer Mortimer could think of. "Here," he said. "He thinks she came to New York."

"Why does he think that?"

Mortimer shrugged. "He figures that she just wants to disappear, and so she'd come to the city. Disappear into the crowd." He could tell one part of Stark's mind was willing to accept the modest logic of this, while the other part labored to peel back his skin, peer into his brain, find the elusive something that Mortimer was holding back.

"All right," Stark said finally. "I'll give this friend of yours one more chance to provide something useful. One chance, Mortimer."

"Okay," Mortimer said.

For a moment the two men peered silently at each other, a gaze Mortimer found uncomfortable.

"This friend of yours," Stark said, "what does he intend to do when he finds this woman?"

Mortimer had no idea, but said, "He just wants her to come back to him."

"Are you sure that's all he wants?"

Mortimer knew that Stark was thinking of Marisol. "He wouldn't hurt her. He wants her back, that's all."

Stark's gaze bore into him, and he knew that if his eyes rested on him in that way just a moment longer, he'd spill his guts.

"I gotta go," he said, then turned quickly and headed for the door.

He'd just reached it, when Stark called to him.

"Mortimer, we can trust each other, can't we?"

Mortimer turned toward Stark, saw something unexpectedly troubled in his eyes, as if he were working hard not to believe something he couldn't stop himself from believing.

"Yeah, sure," he answered lightly. What else, he wondered, could he say?

EDDIE

THE BEER was growing warm in his hands, but there was nothing to do but wait. Vinnie Caruso had never been a stickler for getting to a place on time, and Eddie had long ago accepted the fact that he came when he came. In the meantime, Eddie tried to think of the right approach, what he'd say once Vinnie had downed a couple of beers, loosened up, dropped the wise-guy routine, and returned to the kid Eddie had known years before, a nice guy, like so many others, but with lousy parents, the mother a lush, the father missing altogether. What could you do but feel sorry for a kid like that, a little guy, picked on. Eddie had saved him from a bully once, and after that Vinnie had hung close for a few years. Then they'd gone their separate ways until one night they'd met again at the Saint Lawrence Hotel, where Vinnie ran a shylocking operation from the office of an otherwise legit car service. Vinnie had ushered him into the little cubicle he used for business, and the two of them had talked for a few minutes, Vinnie propped back in his chair, his feet on the desk, puffing a cigar that was almost as long as his arm, acting the made-man routine, though all Eddie had to do was look around to know just how little-made he was, just how low on the pecking order. But it was the moment he'd started to leave, Eddie recalled now. He'd gotten up, smiling as always, started for the door, when Vinnie, still seated, had called him back, *So, Eddie.*

Eddie had turned around to find the little guy staring at him intently, the cigar lowered, the old Vinnie peering at him, almost sweetly, so that Eddie knew that Vinnie was remembering how Eddie had saved him from that bully so many years before. *So, Eddie, how you doing, huh?*

That was the moment, Eddie thought now, his large hands wrapped around the mug, that was the moment when he could have asked anything of Vinnie Caruso. If he'd been in debt, the money would have been there. If some guy had been giving him trouble—on the job, say, or anywhere else—that guy would have been spoken to by Vinnie or some thug Vinnie sent, and the trouble would have instantly gone away. But Eddie had only shrugged and said that he was doing fine. Then they'd shaken hands, and Vinnie had tapped the side of his head, and said his parting words, *You was good to me, Eddie. And when somebody's good to Vinnie Caruso, he don't forget.*

The problem was this. Eddie didn't like asking favors. He didn't like doing it ever, and normally wouldn't have done it at all. You didn't do a guy a good turn because you expected to get something back. The priests had taught him that. If you do good to get good, they'd told him, it wasn't really good at all. But now, as he thought about it, he hadn't helped Vinnie Caruso all those many years before because he'd expected to get something back. So it was okay, he figured, asking Vinnie for a favor now, as long as it was just this one.

Caruso came through the door with the peculiar swagger he'd adopted over the last few years, and which Eddie thought he'd probably gotten from mob movies, especially the one where this wiry little guy talks big and screws this gorgeous blonde, and backs up everything he says with sudden bursts of annihilating violence.

"Hey, Eddie," Vinnie said brightly as he strode up to the booth. "How they hanging?"

"I'm good," Eddie said. "Want a beer?"

"Nah," Vinnie said. He stripped off his jacket and hung it on the metal hanger beside the booth. "I'm a scotch guy." He snapped his fingers and the barmaid appeared. "You got Glenfiddich, sweetheart?"

"Yeah."

"Two cubes. Three fingers."

The barmaid looked as if she'd just bitten into a lemon. "Okay," she said, then turned on her heel and disappeared.

"So, how you doing?" Vinnie asked.

"Good," Eddie said. He took a sip of warm beer.

"At the marina, right? That was the last time?"

Eddie started to answer, but the barmaid returned with the scotch, placed it on a small paper square in front of Caruso, then stepped away.

Vinnie lifted the glass. "To old times."

"Old times," Eddie echoed.

The glasses clinked together and each man drank.

"You been waiting long?" Vinnie asked.

Eddie shook his head.

Vinnie leaned forward. "So, what's on your mind, Eddie?"

There seemed no way to edge around it, close in slowly, so Eddie said, "You know about Tony, right? That his wife left him?"

"Yeah, I heard about it."

"Tony says his father is trying to find her."

Vinnie's fingers tightened around the scotch. "So?"

"So I was wondering if he asked you to do it."

Vinnie took a quick hit from the scotch, then set the glass down hard. "I don't talk about business, Eddie."

"That means yes, right?"

"That means I don't talk about business is what that means."

"The thing is, Tony's spooked," Eddie said.

"Spooked? Why?"

" 'Cause he don't know what his father has in mind."

"For that wife of his?"

"Yeah. He don't want nobody strong-arming her."

"Who said anybody was gonna strong-arm her?"

"He's afraid, that's all," Eddie said. "You know how Labriola is."

"Mr. Labriola just wants to find his wife for him," Caruso said. "Then he'll tell Tony where she is and Tony, he goes and talks to her."

"He told you that? The Old Man?"

"Yeah," Caruso said.

"So you're looking for her?"

"In a manner of speaking," Caruso admitted. "But like I said, Mr. Labriola, he just wants they should talk, Tony and his wife, work things out, you know what I mean? Make nice. He don't like it when things don't go smooth."

Eddie looked at Vinnie doubtfully.

"What?" Vinnie asked crisply.

"And if the wife didn't want to make nice, you wouldn't do nothing to her, would you, Vinnie?"

"What would I do?"

"You wouldn't do nothing is what I'm asking."

"Why you asking me that, Eddie?"

"I'm asking because suppose you find Tony's wife and she don't want to have nothing to do with Tony. What then?"

"What then?"

"What do you do?"

"To the broad, you mean?"

"Tony's wife, yeah. Supposing you find her and she don't want to . . ."

Caruso laughed. "Suppose I ain't actually the guy looking is what you should be supposing."

"You ain't looking for her?"

"No," Vinnie said. "Not me personal."

"Who is?"

Vinnie laughed. "I ain't sure myself. All I know is this. Mr. Labriola had me pay a guy to find Tony's wife. So I did."

"You paid a guy?"

"Paid him plenty."

"What guy you pay, Vinnie?"

"A guy ain't connected to Mr. Labriola or me or Tony or nobody else you ever heard of." Caruso laughed. "Mr. Labriola mulled over some guys. Burt Marx, remember him? I told the Old Man, I said, 'Burt Marx? That fucking guy couldn't find a chink in Chinatown.' "

"So who's looking? Who's the guy?"

Vinnie suddenly glanced about nervously. "You think I can tell you that, Eddie?"

"Vinnie, you remember that night when we come up on each other there at the hotel?"

"Yeah, sure."

"And we talked awhile, right, you and me? And then I got up to leave and you said, 'So, Eddie, how you doing?' Remember that?"

"Yeah."

"Okay, so, this is how I'm doing. I need to know who this guy is, Vinnie. The one looking for Tony's wife."

"What's it to you?"

"It ain't for me," Eddie answered. "It's for Tony."

"What does he care who's looking, long as she turns up?"

"He wants to know what's going on, that's all. It's his wife, you know, so he wants to know."

Caruso downed the last of his scotch. "Okay, suppose I give you this guy. What then?"

"I'll keep an eye on him, that's all."

"Just you?"

"Yeah."

Caruso laughed. "You can't watch a guy twenty-four hours a day."

"As much as I can, then. When he turns in, I'll turn in."

Caruso considered this for a moment, then said, "You know what Mr. Labriola would do to me, don't you, Eddie?"

Eddie nodded.

"You get any idea the guy's maybe getting suspicious, maybe catching on to you, you got to back off, you understand? And I mean fast, Eddie. You don't look back. You just back off and he don't see you no more."

"Okay."

Caruso plucked a cigar from his jacket. " 'Cause let me tell you something, this guy, he'll drop the deal he gets wind of something. And you know what would happen if this guy dropped the deal he has with Mr. Labriola?" He lowered his voice to a desperate whisper. "I'd have to whack him, that's what."

"You?"

Caruso lit the cigar and waved out the match expansively. "Who else would Mr. Labriola trust with a job like that?"

Eddie gave no answer.

"So we're clear on this?" Caruso asked.

"Yeah."

Caruso rose and motioned Eddie to follow him outside. They walked to Caruso's car and got in. "Okay, Eddie, here's the deal." In the car's shadowy interior, Caruso's eyes gleamed eerily. "There are two guys could be looking for Tony's wife. I ain't sure which one. There's a guy runs a bar on Twelfth Street in Manhattan. Morgenstern. It could be him, but I don't think so. The other guy lives in Chelsea, 445 West 19 Street. Right off Ninth Avenue. You pick."

"The bar guy, you don't think it's him looking for Sara?"

"My guess, no."

"Okay." Eddie offered his hand. "I'll keep an eye on the other one."

"Up to you," Caruso said with a light shrug.

"Yeah, okay, the other one. Chelsea."

"Good enough," Caruso said. "I only seen the guy once. Fifties, I'd say. White hair. Tall. Thin." He grasped Eddie's hand. "One thing, though," he added. "Whatever you find out about this fuck, you gotta let me know."

"Yeah, sure," Eddie said. He drew his hand back, but Caruso held on to it.

"I mean it, Eddie," Caruso warned. "This is business, and you tell me you're going to keep me posted, you gotta do it." He released Eddie's hand. "You don't, then favors, friendship, that's all in the shitcan now."

SARA

SHE SAT across from him in a booth at the back and listened as he detailed the terms. The basic salary was decent, and she'd get a piece of the music charge, and even better, a piece of the bar, which she knew was more than fair. They never liked to give a piece of the bar, and she couldn't remember ever having been offered it until now. But here this guy was, giving her a piece of the bar, and yet, as she listened, the cold, hard truth kept pressing against her mind, the fact that she simply couldn't do it, couldn't take the offer, the whole thing was impossible.

"So, what do you think?" he asked.

She had to tell him and she knew it. She had to tell him right now that she'd made a big mistake, that she couldn't possibly take the job, this great deal he was handing her. She had to tell him that she'd been taken in by her own pathetic fantasy of being a singer again, even stupidly blurted out her old stage name, and that now she was sorry, really sorry, that she'd wasted his time.

"Samantha?"

Okay, she thought, I'll do that. I'll tell him that Samantha Damonte is a phony name, that I'm married and on the run, and that the only job I could possibly take would be one I could hide behind, a job in the back or in the basement.

"Does it sound fair?" Abe asked.

"Fair?" she asked weakly.

"Is there something else you want?"

She shook her head at how crazy she'd been to let herself get caught up in this fantasy that she could return to a singing career, erase Tony and his father, take any kind of job other than one she could crawl into and pull over her head like a thick blanket. A singer? Ridiculous. Even in a little bar like Abe's, the singer's name and photograph would be taped on the window or the door, her face for the whole world to see.

"I mean, we could . . . negotiate a few things," Abe said.

She imagined Vinnie Caruso or some other of Labriola's thugs seeing her picture, reporting what he'd seen to the Old Man. She could see Labriola's smile, feel the wrath sweep over him, his desperate need to find her. She knew that he would stop at nothing to accomplish this, and on that thought she realized that she had now put this guy in danger just because she'd come into his place, sang a song, and been offered a job she couldn't possibly take. The stark nature of her circumstances swept over her in a shivering wave, the terrible truth that she was not only in danger herself, but like some Long Island version of Typhoid Mary, infected everyone she touched.

"Are you okay?" he asked.

She could feel his gaze like a hand, pressing her back to the wall. "Yeah, sure."

"So, what do you think? Sound good, the deal?"

It sounded better than anything she could have imagined, but she knew no way to accept it. "It's a very good deal," she said quietly.

"So?"

She shook her head. "I can't."

He looked at her quizzically. "Can't what?"

"Take the job."

He leaned forward, his eyes very intent. "Why not?"

She began gathering her things. "I can't." She felt her own sudden frenzy, the desperate clawing of her fingers as she reached for her purse.

"What are you going to do?" he asked.

"Hide," she answered before she could stop herself.

"From who, what?"

She was on her feet, turning, the door of the bar before her now like an escape hatch.

"For how long?" he asked.

She looked at him, the word chilling her spirits with its fatality. "Forever," she said.

DELLA

HER MOTHER poured the coffee, then sat down. "So, how's Mike?"

"Fine," Della said. She wiped a scattering of crumbs from Nicky's mouth.

Mrs. DaRocca smiled. "They all like graham crackers. You liked them. Your brother."

Della nodded crisply. "You heard from Chuck?"

"Not in a couple weeks," Mrs. DaRocca said. "He's got a new girlfriend. When he has a new girlfriend, he forgets to call."

Della thought of her kid brother, remembered his tendency to mischief, the way she'd always tried to pull him out of whatever trouble he got himself into. She wished he were home now rather than on some army base out west, and so unable to help her, or even give advice. Unnecessarily, she brushed again at Nicky's mouth, then glanced at her mother, recognized the look in her eyes.

"You and Mike having trouble," the old woman said.

It was not a question, but a declaration, and for a moment Della thought it might be easier if it were true. Married trouble stared you in the face. There were ways to deal with it. A priest. A counselor. With married trouble, there was a line of defense, a method for dealing, maybe even a solution somewhere down the road.

"Another woman?" her mother asked.

"No, Ma," Della said. "Nothing like that."

"Money?"

"No, Ma," Della repeated. She started to draw Nicky into her lap.

"Leave him where he is," Mrs. DaRocca snapped.

Della obeyed instantly, like a little girl.

"Look me in the eye and tell me nothing's wrong," the old woman demanded.

Della knew she couldn't do that.

"It's not you, is it? You're not cheating on Mike?"

"No!" Della cried indignantly. "Ma!"

The old woman leaned forward. "So what is it, Della?"

There was no escaping her, and Della knew it. Her

only hope was to come up with a story her mother would believe. "It's my neighbor," she began, making it up as she went along. "His wife left him. He came over. He thought I might know where she went."

"Do you?"

"No."

"So, how come you're upset about this?"

She shrugged, thought fast. "I don't know. You just get to thinking, you know, about . . . things."

"What things you thinking about, Della? This ain't got nothing to do with you, so what things you thinking about?"

She was like a crab, Della thought, her mother. Once she grabbed on to something, she never let go. "You know, how a person can live with a person and maybe not know . . . anything. That's the way it is with this guy."

"What guy?"

"My neighbor. He didn't have any idea she was going to leave him."

"Like he's the first," Mrs. DaRocca said with a laugh.

"Anyway, it makes you think."

The old woman waved her hand. "It makes you think because you're a worrier, Della. Always worrying about something."

"Yeah, okay," Della said, hoping to drop the subject.

But this only made her mother more intent. "Mike, he comes home every night, right?"

"Yes."

"And you, you make dinner. You see everything's clean. The other stuff, you know, private. That's okay too, right?"

"Yeah, Ma, it's fine."

The old woman looked at her sternly. "So stop worrying about that neighbor of yours. It ain't your problem."

"Right," Della said. She saw Sara in the city, trying to start over, unaware of the mad dog that was hot on her trail, a vicious old dog that was tracking her relent-lessly but one she could not tell Sara about for fear that it would turn on her as well. "Right," she repeated. "Not my problem."

And yet if that were true, she wondered, then what was this pain she felt and which seemed to grow larger by the minute. She felt nothing but that deepening distress for a moment, then glanced up and saw that her mother's eyes were bearing down with the old relentlessness she re-membered from her girlhood, questions fired like rockets toward her ever-crumbling defenses, *That boy treating you good? You letting that guy touch you? You pregnant?*

"Mike raise his hand to you?" the old woman asked sharply.

"No!" Della shot back. "You know Mike. He wouldn't—"

"Della," her mother said, cutting her off. "I look at you, and I see scared. Something's scaring you." She planted her fleshy arms on the table and leaned forward. "Now, what's scaring you?"

There was no point in lying to her, Della realized. For nearly forty years, the old lady had seen through her like a sheet of cellophane. "I don't know what to do, Ma."

Her mother's scowl was dark and fearsome. Even sit-ting, even completely still, she looked as if she were strap-ping on a gun.

"You tell me right now, Della," she commanded. "And don't leave nothing out."

Della hesitated briefly, then said, "It's Leo Labriola."

Her mother looked at her as if she'd just blurted out the ingredients of a secret recipe. "How you know him?"

"My neighbor. Labriola's his father."

"What's that got to do with you?"

"His wife ran off, like I said, and Mr. Labriola is looking for her. He came to my house. He wanted to know if

I knew anything about Sara, that's my neighbor, Tony's wife, the one that ran off, who Labriola is looking for. And he . . . threatened me, Labriola did."

Her mother's face seemed to gray and flush at the same time, like firelight on a stone. "He done what?" she asked.

"He threatened me," Della repeated. "Grabbed my arm. Right there." She rubbed her arm softly. "He scared me, Ma." Her face was wreathed in shame. "And I didn't tell Sara about it. That he was looking for her, I mean. But more than that. The way he's looking, you know?"

"What way?"

"Like . . . mean. I didn't tell Sara about that."

"How could you tell her? You talked to her?"

"Yeah."

"You know where she is?"

Della nodded. "But not exactly."

"What do you mean, not exactly?"

"She always talked about the city. I figure that's where she went."

Mrs. DaRocca offered a surprisingly bright smile. "I'll straighten this out, Della," she said.

"What?" Della asked unbelievingly.

"I'll straighten it out," Mrs. DaRocca repeated. She patted her daughter's arm. "Stop worrying about it."

And Della, to her vast surprise, did exactly that.

CARUSO

HE FELT smart, and he loved it when he felt smart. He'd always wanted to feel smart more than he'd wanted to feel anything else. More than he'd ever wanted to be good-looking or tough. You could be tall, dark, handsome, but none of that lasted very long. And in the end, nobody really admired a guy just for his looks. You admired a guy who was tough, could take a trimming, give back what he got, but only if he weren't a dope at the same time. A moron with guts was mostly just a moron. But a guy with brains, that was a guy everybody admired. He'd heard somewhere that when a dolphin met a shark eye-to-eye in the ocean, it was the shark that blinked. That was what brains did for a guy, he thought, made the idiots give way.

A soaring wave of self-esteem swept over him, and on the crest of that wave he picked up the phone, dialed the number, smiling pleasantly until Labriola answered.

"I got it done," Caruso told him.

"Why you talk to me like a dope, Vinnie?" Labriola barked. "Huh? Why you do that?"

Caruso felt the hot-air balloon deflate. "Well, I . . ."

"I answer the fucking phone, right? And you don't say who it is I'm talking to. You don't say what it is you're talking about. So answer me this, Vinnie. How do I know I'm not talking to some fucking cop, huh?"

"I thought you'd—"

"What?" Labriola snapped.

"Recognize my voice," Caruso said lamely.

"Your voice?" Labriola cackled. "Like you're Marilyn Monroe, or something? Why would I recognize your voice, Vinnie?"

"Well, I mean, we talk a lot and so—"

"Forget it, Vinnie," Labriola interrupted irritably. "What's on your mind?"

Now Caruso hardly knew what to say, all his cleverness gathering like a pool of urine at his feet. Not smart, he told himself, not smart at all.

"Vinnie!" Labriola yelped.

Caruso shuddered. "Uh . . . I just wanted you to know that I'm doing it."

"Vinnie, you think I got all fucking day to pull shit out of you? What the fuck you talking about?"

"Them guys," Vinnie answered, working to control the lacerating contempt Labriola made him feel for himself. "I got . . ."

"What guys?"

"The ones could be looking," Caruso answered. "For Tony's wife."

"What about them?"

"I'm keeping an eye on them. Like you asked me."

"So?"

"I just . . . well . . . I . . ."

"I told you to keep an eye on them, didn't I?"

"Yes, sir."

"So, why wouldn't you be doing it?"

"I just—"

"You just nothing, Vinnie," Labriola said. "You just woke me up for fucking nothing."

Caruso's head drooped forward. "Sorry," he muttered.

Labriola's voice sawed into him. "The next time you call me, you better have something I want to hear."

"Yeah, I'll . . ."

A click at the other end, and the phone went dead.

Caruso held the cold black receiver in his hand. It felt as dark and thick and lifeless as the inside of his skull, a dense, unlighted thing that only fooled him when it seemed to spark.

ABE

THE SUPER swung open the door and waved Abe into the room. "You caught me just in time," he said. "I was gonna call the Salvation Army to come get the rest of this stuff."

Days before, Abe had gone through Lucille's meager possessions, selecting a few mementos, leaving the rest for the super to dispose of in any way he wanted. Now he was relieved to see that the piano remained, along with a scarred kitchen table and a second table Lucille had used as a desk. "You said she was paid up till the end of the month, right?"

"Yeah."

"I have this woman who—"

"Gotcha," the super said with a leering grin.

Abe looked at him sternly. "Needs a place," he said emphatically. He peered about the room a final time. "No creeps in the building, right?"

The super shrugged. "There's creeps in every building, but the ones we got here, they wouldn't hurt nobody."

"Okay," Abe said.

On the way back to the bar, he replayed the last few minutes of his encounter with Samantha Damonte, saw again the desperation that had suddenly overtaken her. He knew that no matter what he might have done at that moment, she would have raced away, told him nothing more, simply disappeared, leaving nothing behind.

But she had left something behind, a tiny bit of information, and he was going to use it.

"Hello."

Her voice still bore the same strain he'd heard when she'd fled the bar.

"It's Abe," he said. "Morgenstern." He waited for her to respond, but she offered nothing. "You okay?"

"Yes." Her tone was very nearly metallic.

"You remember telling me that you lived in a hotel?"

"Yes."

"Well, that singer, the one I told you about, the one who died? She had a place in the Village, not far from the bar," Abe said. "She had a month left on her rent. So, the thing is, I thought you might want to stay there instead of where you are." He could not interpret her continued silence, so he took a bold swing. "It would be free until the end of the month. I don't know . . . I mean . . . what your . . . situation is . . . but staying at a hotel, that's expensive, right?"

"Why are you doing this?" she asked quietly.

From her voice, he couldn't tell if she were suspicious or mystified, felt him a threat or just an enigma.

He wasn't sure himself, he realized. Maybe it was that little charge he'd felt at his first look at her. Or maybe it was the strain in her eyes, the trembling in her hands, the way her voice turned icy when she'd said "Forever," then left the bar.

"I don't know," he admitted. "It's just that . . . there's this room, and I figure, who better to have it for a few weeks than—" He stopped and tried to ease her with a quick chuckle. "Than another torch singer."

Another silence.

"So, you want to take a look at it? I could meet you there, show you around a little. Tomorrow morning, maybe, before I go to the bar."

"Okay," she said. "Thanks."

Abe gave her the address, then took a chance and said, "May I ask you a question?"

A pause, then, "All right."

"Are you . . . is something—" He stopped, thought better of his question, and decided on another direction. "Whatever it is, you can beat it, Samantha."

He heard a soft breath through the line, though "Thank you" was all she said.

EDDIE

HE CHECKED the address, then the nameplates, confirmed that one was blank.

What now?

Nothing, Eddie decided, but wait.

And so he sat down on a cement stoop across the street, watching as the late-afternoon pedestrians made their way down Nineteenth Street. He had never actually lived in the city, nor ever wanted to. Manhattan was not his kind of place, and the people could hardly have been more different from himself. First off, they were educated. Everyone who lived in Manhattan, he supposed, had gone to college. His cousin Patsy had done that. She'd gotten a scholarship to Columbia, then landed a big job with a law firm whose offices were on Park Avenue. At Christmas parties back home, she tried to be nice to everybody, but despite the effort, she looked as if she were in a dentist's waiting room rather than at home with her family. You could tell she wanted to get back to Manhattan, to her smart, well-dressed friends. Because of that, the cousins usually started talking about her once she'd left. They called her stuck-up and snooty and said she should just stay in the city if she thought she was so great, so much better than the people who'd never left the old neighborhood. But Eddie had never added his voice to their condemnations. If anything, he'd felt sorry for Patsy, sorry that she'd let go of something that seemed precious, the hold of family, which was, he thought, the fortress you lived in, and which kept you safe. That was it, he thought now, that was what made him jumpy in Manhattan and eager to leave it as fast as he could. It wasn't just that he didn't feel at home in the city. It was that he didn't feel safe when he was out of his own neighborhood, away from his own kind, didn't feel that he could just be Eddie Sullivan . . . and survive.

His gaze drifted up the building, then along the line of windows on the fifth floor, hoping to get a glimpse of the man who'd been hired to find Tony's wife. He imagined him as a tall, thin ice pick of a man. They had a tendency to look like that in movies, but Eddie knew the guy could just as easily be short and pudgy. The thing he had to keep in mind was this guy might be dangerous, might be capable of anything. That's what a bad man was, Eddie thought, a guy who would do anything if the money was right or he was scared not to do it, a guy who lived without a line. Eddie couldn't fathom how such men went through their days with no sense of limits. He'd never been sure of what he wanted to be, only that he didn't want to be *that*.

It was nearly an hour later when the man finally appeared, and despite the hazy light of early evening, Eddie had no doubt that he was the one Caruso had described the night before. He was around five ten, dressed in a black suit, and carrying a tightly wrapped umbrella. His hair was gray, and there was plenty of it, but it was the graceful way he moved down the street that pegged him for sure. This was a man who knew how to handle things, who could think his way out of a real pickle, then make all the right moves. He had that assurance, that look of being in control, or at least able to get control of any situation.

Eddie followed at a discreet distance, watching carefully as the man continued east until he reached Fifth Avenue, where he turned south and made his way to Washington Square Park.

There was something about the way he moved, never looking right or left, that gave Eddie the idea that this was a walk the man often made, perhaps routinely at this same hour every day. He decided that he would station himself opposite the building at the same time tomorrow, check if the man came out again, walked to wherever he was going. If so, then he'd have established at least a portion of the man's routine, could predict, though not with absolute certainty, where he could be found at a particular moment. He knew that this wasn't much, but at least it was something he could report to Tony, let him know that he was on the job.

TONY

HE WAS on his fourth drink and nothing was getting better. If anything, he could feel his mood darkening, growing dense, with something hateful rising out of the smoky depths, the red-eyed terror of his father.

"Hey, Tony."

He looked up from the glass and saw that she'd swung into the booth and was now sitting firmly opposite him.

"You been nursing that one for a while," she said.

Her name was Carmen, and she worked for some guy who kept a boat in the marina, or maybe she was his girl. Anyway, she was dressed in bright colors, as always, with huge hoop rings that sparkled in the smoky light.

"You wanna buy me a drink?" she asked.

Tony straightened himself abruptly and pressed his back against the wooden booth. "Carmen, right?"

The woman laughed. "As in Miranda. That woman with the fruit basket on her head." She laughed again. "And some opera singer too."

Tony blinked absently. "So, what'll you have?"

"How about a Bloody Mary?" Carmen said.

"Done." Tony snapped his fingers and Lucky, the waiter, came trotting over. "Bloody Mary for the lady."

"Coming up, Tony," Lucky said, then trotted away again.

Carmen brought a long, bright-red fingernail to the corner of her right eye. "So, you out alone tonight?"

"Yeah."

"She lets you off the leash like that, your wife?"

Tony nodded.

The bright-red fingernail made a slow crawl down the side of Carmen's face until it came to rest at her lower lip. "Not me. If I had a handsome guy like you, I'd hold tight."

Tony considered the options, his eyes lingering on the face before him, the dark brown eyes and black hair and slightly olive skin. Carmen wasn't bad looking, and she would probably get a real kick out of being with him, even if for only a night. She would tell her girlfriends about it, and in the story he would be stronger and more handsome and better in bed than he really was, because Carmen Pinaldi needed to believe that the guy she was with was strong and handsome and great in the sack, because if he were less than that, then so was she. So he should just do it, he told himself, just take her back to his house or to some motel and just do it. Sara had left him, after all. So why shouldn't he just buy Carmen another drink, chat her up for a few minutes, then whisk her away to a shadowy bedroom and huff and puff and get it done and feel the sweet revenge of having done it?

Revenge, Tony thought. That was the problem. He would do it only for revenge, a way of getting back at Sara. And because of that it would be without pleasure, and laced with pain, and during every moment of it he would be thinking of Sara.

He took a long draw on the cigarette, then crushed it in the square glass ashtray. "I better be going," he said.

Carmen looked surprised and offended and seemed to see her face in a mirror and not like what she saw. "Oh, okay," she said coolly.

He didn't want to hurt her but knew he had. "Sorry," he said quietly.

She shrugged dryly. "You gotta go, you gotta go."

He rose and paid the tab and walked out of the bar and into the dark, dark night. He could hear the muffled sound of the jukebox in the bar, the equally muffled sound of the people inside, little bursts of laughter that seemed aimed at him, at his situation, at how much he'd screwed things up. He turned and walked toward his car, away from the music and the talk and the laughter until he was safely beyond all these things and stood alone in the silence, beneath a canopy of rain-gray sky. Briefly, he peered upward and in his mind painted his wife's face in the low-slung clouds, the weight of her loss growing ever more immense, crushing him beneath it, grinding him to dust—the tiniest speck, the blindly whirling atom— becoming smaller and smaller with each passing second until at last he felt smaller than the smallest thing that ever was.

He got into the car but couldn't turn the key or press his foot down on the accelerator. And so he sat, frozen behind the wheel, remembering their first days together, the later wedding with its ecstatic night, the morning after, both of them famished, laughing over toast and orange juice, the long walk along the Bermuda shore, the azure water lapping at their feet, and then the parade of days that followed, all that happiness, her sparkling eyes, the smile, the way she raked her finger along his chest, the sound of her quiet sigh, all of it coming back to him in wave after shuddering wave so that later, when he'd finally turned the key, pressed the pedal, pulled away, he couldn't recall the actual moment that he'd begun to cry.

STARK

HE WALKED to the unlighted window and parted the curtains. Across the street, he saw him again, a large, awkward man in an old blue jacket, the one he'd noticed as he'd made his evening stroll to the park earlier, then again as he'd returned home, and now, past midnight, this same man sitting on the stone stoop across the street, patting himself against the early-morning chill. He'd disappeared for a while, but had now returned to rest like a crouching gargoyle on the steps, then rise abruptly and pace back and forth along the deserted street.

The man rose suddenly, turned left, walked a few paces, then wheeled around and retraced his steps, a journey repeated several times before he returned to his earlier place on the stoop and resumed his watch.

A rank amateur, Stark thought. He'd never known anyone to blow his cover more thoroughly. Still, there was no doubt that the man had been sent to keep an eye on him. The only questions were why he'd been sent and who had sent him.

Stark had little doubt that the answer to the second question was Mortimer's friend, the overly discreet husband in search of his vanished wife. In the years since Marisol's death, he had always expected a husband or lover to attempt the same dark plan, hire him to find a woman he intended to kill. The only surprise was the sudden rage he felt at the prospect of it being done again. It was raw and biting, as if all the passing years had done nothing to quell the fury he'd felt so long ago. He recalled the morning he'd arrived at Marisol's apartment, the door slightly ajar, the way he'd called her name, waited through the following silence, then eased open the door and stepped inside. The carnage that greeted him still burned in his mind, Marisol's naked body slumped in a chair, ankles and wrists bound, her hair swept over the top of her head. He'd lifted her head to see a face beaten beyond recognition.

Stark's dream of vengeance had flared up from that bruised and battered face, the brown eyes swollen shut, the fractured jaw and split lips. And now this rage swept over him again as his eyes bore down upon the figure on the stoop. He imagined the missing wife in the guise of Marisol, tender and forgiving, kind beyond any man's deserving, full of the leaping energy of life, wanting only to begin again, the man in the blue jacket like Lockridge, hired to follow him until he found her, then deliver her to Henderson, the man who wanted her dead, Mortimer's shadowy friend.

Of course, he couldn't know if the two cases were exact parallels. He couldn't know if the man in the blue jacket was the husband Mortimer had spoken of or whether he'd been hired by the husband. But in the end, it didn't matter. One way or another, a woman was going to be hurt, and the man who paced sleeplessly on the street below was the instrument of her harm.

Stark's eyes focused like death rays on the man below, watching as he suddenly stopped and slumped against the leafless tree, then nudged himself away, paced, returned to slump against the rain-slicked trunk again. It was not hard to imagine the source of his restlessness, the rabid impatience that kept him in constant physical agitation. Lockridge, the man who'd followed him to Marisol, had been afflicted with the same frantic movements, and because of that Stark knew precisely what he was thinking, that he was close, very close to the hapless woman whose destruction he sought. They all plotted the same horrors, these men. And only other men, cold, brutal, vengeful men like themselves save for their targets, could stay their hands.

ABE

HE SAT at the bar, his feet planted on the rail, his fingers knotted around the half-empty pilsner. The room was silent, the piano covered, all the lights out save the few small ones that burned all night even when he wasn't in the place. He wondered how many nights he'd spent this way, sitting alone after the place had closed, staring at his own face in the mirror across the bar. That was the thing about being alone, it numbed you after a while, so that you really didn't notice just how alone you were. Then suddenly, someone showed up, and she had a certain look and spoke a certain way, and you realized how much you'd lost.

What he had not imagined was the sheer, heart-stopping excitement he felt in the simple thought of her. The moment she came into his mind, all the old songs made sense again. He felt their tingle and their fever, and the strange exquisite jeopardy they conveyed. He wanted to put his foot down, get a grip, but he knew he couldn't, not with this one. He wanted to believe that she was just a woman, like others, just a woman passing through his life. But each time he tried to do that, he remembered some little thing about her, and all his will went flying out the window, and he knew that she was not at all like any other woman he'd ever met.

But what made her different?

The answer came so quickly, he knew that it was true. What made her different?

A courage so raw, he could almost see it bleed.

He didn't know what was eating at her, whether it was real or something inside her head. He knew only that she was trying desperately to stay ahead of it, and that you had to have guts to run that long and hard, always alert for the sound of footsteps behind you, always glancing over your shoulder. He didn't know how long she'd have to live this way. He knew only that it was part of the package, something you signed on for if you signed on for her.

And that's what he'd done, he knew, he'd signed on. But for what exactly? He shook his head at his helplessness. If it were a movie, he'd know what to do. If it were a guy bothering her, he'd be like Gary Cooper or somebody like that. *Man of the West,* that was the movie he thought of. He'd be like Gary Cooper in *Man of the West.* The problem was that in the movies it always ended with that final showdown. No cops came around later to investigate. No guys in lab coats examining fibers. No grand jury mulling it over. No fourteen-page indictment, no lengthy trial, no heart-stopping conviction . . . no consequences at all. In the movies, a bad guy was dead, and, quite rightly, nobody gave a fuck.

The door opened and he saw Mortimer's face hanging like a funeral wreath in the air.

"Hey, Abe," he said.

"Mort," Abe answered dully, his mind still on Samantha, how at sea he was.

Mortimer took off his hat and flopped it down on one of the stools while he slid up on the one beside it.

Abe poured him a drink.

"Thanks," Mortimer said. He knocked back the scotch, wiped his mouth with the sleeve of his jacket. "So, what's new?"

"Not much," Abe said. He'd meant to say nothing more, but suddenly he thought of Samantha again, and despite the fact that Mortimer was hardly the guy he'd normally have talked to about anything important, he said, "I met this woman."

Mortimer seemed delighted not by what Abe had said, the fact that he'd met a woman, but simply that Abe had mentioned it to him. "No kidding," he said. He idly circled the rim of his glass with a single finger. "Good for you." His finger abruptly stopped its circuit and he looked at Abe like a guy who wanted to give good advice. " 'Cause we ain't got long, you know?"

Abe wiped the bar with a white cloth. "No, we don't."

Mortimer glanced away, his eyes now fixed on the front window, the gray, cascading rain. "So don't let this one get away," he said.

"I may have to," Abe said.

"Why's that?"

Abe realized that he didn't know Mortimer Dodge nearly well enough to be talking to him this way. He laughed. "Ah, nothing. She doesn't talk about it, but, I don't know, it's got me thinking maybe I should start packing a gun."

"A gun?" Mortimer asked. "What for?"

Abe waved his hand, now sorry that he'd brought it up, since the whole thing had finally sunk into nothing more substantial than a cowboy movie fantasy. "In case some guy's bothering her, which maybe there is and maybe there isn't."

"More like a chance of it," Mortimer said thoughtfully. "Like it could be a guy."

"Yeah."

Mortimer nodded. "So, you got a gun, Abe?"

Abe laughed. "Of course not," he said. He poured Mortimer another drink. "So, what's new with you, Morty?"

"Same," he said without emphasis.

"Nothing new on your . . . condition?"

"I'm a dead man," Mortimer said. "So what?"

"So what?" Abe asked.

Mortimer looked at him without expression. "It ain't like I got much to lose."

"It's harder, I guess," Abe said, thinking of Samantha again. "It's harder when you do."

EDDIE

HE BLEW into his cupped hands, then rubbed them together rapidly. It was nearly two thirty-four in the morning, and he'd decided that if the man in the black suit did not come out again before three A.M., he'd leave. On the other hand, if he reemerged from the building, Eddie would fall in behind him, follow him wherever he went, wait until he came out again, resume the tail.

It was boring labor, especially in the spitting rain that had now begun to fall. It was cold and dark and boring, but that was the price of real friendship, Eddie decided. Helping Tony was something he had to do because he could not imagine doing otherwise. He remembered the day the Towers fell, how his cousin Tommy had survived the collapse, called his wife, Celia, and told her he was okay. She'd begged him to come home, crying all the time they were on the phone together. But Tommy had said no, that there were other firemen buried in the rubble, that he had to stay. Celia had kept crying, and Tommy had finally just hung up on her. It was a little like that, Eddie concluded, this thing he had to do for Tony. Not as terrible as the thing Tommy had gone through, but one of those moments when there really wasn't a right thing to do, so you just did the thing that seemed less wrong.

A blast of wind struck him, shaking raindrops from the tree above him in a splattering shower. He brushed the shoulders of his old blue jacket, then pulled off his cap and slapped it against the side of his leg. When he returned it to his head, the man in the black suit was already coming down the stairs.

He eased himself behind the tree but saw that it was too late. The man had already caught him in his eye. But so what, Eddie thought. He was just some guy on the street, no one likely to be noticed. And yet the man seemed to notice him, and as Eddie watched, he glanced left and right down the street as if checking to see if anyone else was around, then stepped off the curb and made his way across the street, walking slowly, deliberately, until he made it to the other side, where he stopped, his body in profile under the streetlamp.

He was only a few feet away now, and Eddie could make out the gaunt face, the shimmering white hair. He looked like a guy in the movies, an aging film star, the Cary Grant type, but with a silent, sinister edge. For a moment he stood very still, his hands thrust deep into the pockets of the black overcoat, his collar turned up against the wind and the rain. He seemed to be looking at the brick wall that faced him, staring at it intently, as if reading instructions that only he could see. Then he turned, his face now in full view, so that Eddie could see the curious sadness that wreathed it and gave it the lost, hopeless look of a man who didn't like the things he had to do.

"It's over," the man said.

The words had come so suddenly and with such finality, Eddie wondered if they'd actually been meant for him at all.

"What?" he asked.

The man took two broad steps with a quickness and agility that made it seem as if he'd been blown across the pavement by a sudden gust of wind. "It's over."

Eddie stared into the unblinking eyes. "What is?" he asked.

"All your plans," the man said.

"I don't know what you—"

He felt the man's hand at the collar of his jacket, then the sharp bit of a blade at his throat.

"Don't say a word," the man said.

Eddie wanted to speak but could think of nothing to say, and so simply obeyed helplessly.

"Now," the man said. "Come with me."

FOUR

For All We Know

STARK

TO HIS surprise, he'd stayed the night, something he'd never done before, and which told him that new arrangements were being made, preparations for the moment, that something deep inside him had pronounced the last rites.

"You want to have breakfast?" she asked tentatively.

He shook his head. "I have an appointment."

It was the only answer he'd ever given, but on this morning, with her eyes upon him so oddly, as if studying some previously unnoticed feature of his face, he felt a curious impulse to say more. "I don't mean to be so aloof," he said.

She laughed. "Aloof doesn't begin to describe you, Stark."

Her name was Kiko, and she was the only lover who'd lasted. And yet, even with Kiko, he'd maintained his usual distance. She called him when she had a free afternoon, which happened about once a month. They met at her apartment on the Upper East Side, a place that was always immaculately clean and smelled faintly of lavender.

The bedroom was small but beautifully appointed, with Kiko's own small paintings on the pale blue walls, flower gardens that had a vaguely sensuous feel to them, though in a chilly, refrigerated sort of way. Amid these motionless blooms they "did" each other, as Kiko liked to call it, then went their separate ways.

"My father's pretty sick," she said.

Stark had never met Kiko's father, nor anyone else in her family, nor any of her friends. And so it surprised him when he said, "I hope he'll be okay," with an unmistakable sympathy.

"He won't be," she said.

"It's like that?"

"Yes."

He had no words for her, and so walked over to the bed, leaned forward, and kissed her softly.

She looked at him quizzically. "You're in a strange mood."

He stepped away and continued to dress.

She watched him somberly for a moment, then cocked her head to the right, almost playfully. "By the way, there's something I've never asked you. Are Asians better? I hear guys think we are."

He stood by the window, knotting his tie. Outside, a brief autumn rain had come to an end. "I don't rank women by ethnic group," he told her.

She propped herself up in the bed. Her hair lay thick as a blanket over her small and perfect breasts. She had flawless skin and gleaming oval eyes. Everything about her was perfect, particularly her forthright acceptance of herself, the utter lack of self-importance.

"Okay, so how do you rank them, Stark?" she asked.

"By how much I care," he told her.

"You're serious."

"Yes."

"So where am I on that list?"

"Second from the top."

Something in her face changed. "We've been together for a long time."

He gave his tie a final pull. "Yes, we have."

"What's our secret?"

"That we're easy, I guess," Stark answered. "That it's no big deal."

She drew her knees up and planted her chin on them. "That is so the wrong answer, Stark."

He plucked his jacket from the chair across from the bed. "Maybe it's time for you to move on, Kiko."

She heard it, and he knew she'd heard it, the air of finality in his voice, its declaration, clear and ominous, that he'd turned a corner in his life, was taking no one with him.

"You're not coming back, are you?" she asked.

He said nothing but only drew on his jacket and buttoned it.

"Can you at least tell me why?"

He walked to the door, then turned and faced her squarely. "Because you need to find someone else and go over the falls with him."

"Over the falls."

"You need to fall in love, Kiko," Stark said. "Everybody needs to do that . . . just once."

Her eyes glistened suddenly, and her long black hair trembled. "Good-bye, Stark," she said.

At the door he wanted to look back but knew he shouldn't. "Good luck" was all he said.

TONY

THE LITTLE rooming house was neat but very shabby, with furniture that looked scavenged from the street.

Eddie's room was equally spare. A small refrigerator rattled in one corner. A single-eyed hot plate sat on a tiny wooden table, fit only for heating water or canned food.

"He ain't suppose to have a hot plate," the old woman who ran the place said sourly. "Fire code don't allow it."

Tony stood at the center of the room, hoping to get some idea of where Eddie had gone. He'd never been in Eddie's room, he realized, nor anywhere else with him save at the marina or one of the little diners in the nearby village. And yet, during all that time, he'd thought of Eddie as his best friend, the person he'd turned to to help find Sara, and who had now vanished without a word.

"He didn't come into work this morning," Tony said. "Didn't call. So I was wondering, you know, if maybe something happened."

The old woman plopped down in the room's single, overstuffed chair. Her hair was white and stringy, her eyes a filmy brown.

"He don't talk much, Eddie," she said. "Keeps to himself."

Tony wondered if this amounted to loneliness, or if Eddie was simply one of those solitary souls who prefers the quiet, the lack of fuss, a life without strings.

"When was the last time you saw him?" he asked.

"Yesterday," the old woman answered.

"What time?"

"In the morning. About nine, something like that."

Tony glanced toward the open closet, where a few shirts hung limply from wire hangers, along with a couple of wool jackets and three pairs of flannel trousers. "It's not like him not to show up for work, not to call in. It's just not like him."

"So, where is he, you think?" the old woman asked.

"I don't know," Tony answered. He walked to the window and peered out at the street. The neighborhood was like Eddie's closet, drab and untended, its faded brick buildings lined up like old shoes. "Did you notice him going off with anybody?"

The old woman shook her head. "But I don't keep an eye on the men who live here. And Eddie, I didn't even know he was missing."

And so no one would be hunting for Eddie Sullivan, Tony thought, no wife or kids or friends save for Tony himself.

"You think he's in trouble some way?" the old woman asked.

Tony peered at the empty parking space where Eddie's old Ford should have been parked. "I'm sure he'll turn up."

But he was not sure Eddie would turn up, and if he didn't, he had no one but himself to blame. For a moment he reviewed the circumstances that had led to this pass. He'd asked Eddie to talk to Caruso, and after that Eddie had disappeared. And so it stood to reason that if anyone knew where Eddie was, it was probably Caruso. Even so, Tony didn't know what to do about it. Caruso worked for his father, and the Old Man would be furious at the thought that Tony had tried to come between him and his trusted gofer.

He was still pondering the situation when he got back to the marina. He'd hoped to see Eddie's beat-up old car in the lot, but it wasn't there, and because of that Tony now felt a slowly deepening dread settle upon him.

He walked into his office, glanced out the window, hoping against hope that Eddie would miraculously appear, sauntering down one of the wooden piers in that ungainly way of his. But Eddie didn't materialize, and so he turned from the window and sat down at his desk. For a time he once again considered his options. They seemed to grow fewer with each consideration, and finally he concluded that there was nothing to do but take the bull by the horns. He picked up the phone and dialed the number.

"Yeah?"

"Vinnie, it's Tony Labriola."

Silence.

"I'm calling about Eddie Sullivan."

Silence.

"I thought you might know where he is."

"Why would I know that?"

"Vinnie, this is serious."

Silence.

"Are you listening, Vinnie?"

"Yeah, I'm listening."

"I know he talked to you about Sara."

Silence.

"About how my father's looking for her."

Silence.

"You hear me, Vinnie?"

"Yeah."

"So, what did you tell him?"

"I didn't tell him nothing."

"Vinnie, are you listening to me? Eddie's missing."

Silence.

"Vinnie, I can't let this go. I know Eddie talked to you about Sara. Now, listen, did you tell my father that Eddie talked to you?"

"No."

"Tell me the truth, Vinnie."

"I didn't tell him nothing. Your father, I mean."

"What did you tell Eddie?"

"Nothing."

"Vinnie."

"Nothing."

"Where is he, Vinnie?"

"I don't know."

"Where is he, Vinnie?" Tony repeated evenly.

"I'm telling you, I don't know," Caruso answered.

"I know you talked to him."

"Okay, so what? I ain't saying I didn't talk to him. But that don't mean I know where he is. Last I seen him we was at Billy's Grill. Like you say, he wanted to know was I looking for your wife. I told him no, and that was the end of it."

Tony listened for something further at the other end of the line, a word or caught breath, some hint that signaled truth or lie, but nothing stirred, and so, after a moment, he said, "Vinnie, we got to meet."

"That ain't a good idea, Tony."

"You got to meet me. I won't say a word about it to my father, but I got to talk to you. We'll go out on my boat. Nobody'll see us. You got to do this, Vinnie. I got to find Eddie."

"But I don't know nothing about Eddie."

"Vinnie, this thing is getting out of control."

Silence.

"Come to the marina," Tony said.

Caruso did not respond.

"Vinnie, if you don't meet me, I got no choice but talk to the cops."

"The cops? What they got to do with it?"

"Plenty if something happened to Eddie."

"Nothing happened to Eddie."

"How do you know?"

"I just know, that's all. Eddie don't never get in trouble."

"So where is he, Vinnie?"

Silence.

"So, you gonna come to the marina or not?"

"Yeah, okay," Vinnie said.

"Can you be here in an hour?"

"All right."

Tony heard a quiet sigh from the other side, waited for more, and when none came, gently returned the phone to its place.

CARUSO

CARUSO HEARD the soft click as Tony Labriola returned the phone to its cradle. He had lied and lied, but the strange part was that he wasn't sure why he'd lied, save that in the world he knew, the truth was never a good idea.

Fuck, he thought as he hung up the phone. Then he posed the question starkly, *Where the hell is Eddie Sullivan?* When no answer immediately presented itself, he rose and walked out of the cramped office he maintained in the basement of the Caldwell Hotel, past the usual losers, who hung like old coats in the corridor, and into the brisk autumn air.

The spitting rain that had drenched the city the night before had finally relented, but the cloudless blue sky gave Caruso no relief. Instead, he sensed that far away a little bulletlike particle had suddenly assumed a trajectory that would inevitably send it crashing directly between his eyes. Eddie Sullivan was missing, and he could be missing only because something had happened to him, something really bad.

But what?

Caruso stared into the empty blue and considered possibilities that were as far beyond him as the infinite spaces that dwarfed him from above.

Labriola.

That was the obvious answer. Somehow, the Old Man had gotten wind that Eddie was working for Tony, and so, to flex his muscle, show that pussy-whipped son of his that he meant business, he'd done something—snatched, beaten up, murdered, any or all of the above?—poor, stupid Eddie Sullivan.

This was certainly possible, Caruso reasoned, because Labriola was really lathered up about something, and when he was that way, he was capable of anything. But if you added reason to the brew, even the small amount that battled to maintain itself within whatever storm was currently blowing in Labriola's mind, then doing something bad to Eddie made no real sense.

Caruso leaned against the side of the building and ticked off the reasons why it was pointless to hurt Eddie Sullivan.

First off, you didn't need to. A stiff warning would be enough. At most, a slap, a punch in the stomach. Eddie would have inevitably reported such crude disciplinary action to Tony, and in response Tony would have immediately pulled Eddie out of the game.

Second, why should Mr. Labriola give a shit what Eddie did? Eddie was just a guy who worked for Tony. Why should Labriola worry if Eddie trailed Batman until he found Tony's wife? As long as she was found, it didn't matter who found her, right? Okay, so forget Labriola. Chances were he had nothing to do with whatever had happened to Eddie Sullivan.

Which left Batman.

The more Caruso considered the matter, the more it seemed to him that if Eddie had come to harm, it was Batman who'd done it to him. He was a secretive guy, after all. Morty Dodge had made that clear. A guy so secretive he'd refused to meet Labriola. *He won't show.* Those were Morty's words. Now, Eddie Sullivan was no pro at tailing a guy, so suppose he burned his cover, which he probably did. What would a secretive, probably nutty guy like Batman do in a situation like that? The answer, given Morty's sinister mutterings, was that he might do anything. Which meant that Eddie Sullivan might very well be dead.

The more Caruso pondered this explanation, the more it hardened in his mind. At first, it was a distinct possibility. Seconds later it was a definite probability. Before a minute passed, Eddie Sullivan was without doubt sleeping with the fishes.

This was a serious conclusion, and now Caruso's mind shifted to its equally grave implications. Within a few days he had gone from a guy hiring another guy to find a broad to a guy who'd hired a guy who'd killed a second guy who was trailing the guy who was trailing the broad. Caruso's mind dipped and whirled as he tried to nail down what, from a legal standpoint, he had done.

One thing was sure. His ass was in a crack, and the guy who'd put it there was Batman. The question was how to get back out of it. The answer seemed obvious, and the beauty was that he longed to do it anyway. The answer was to whack Batman, the murdering, psychotic bastard.

For a moment he imagined doing just that. He saw the silver-haired figure strolling down a midnight street, that fancy book in his hand, feeling all smart and safe and above everybody else, completely unaware of the figure who'd fallen in behind him, a little guy with a pencil-thin mustache who now moved closer and closer, pulling his neat little thirty-eight from his trouser pocket, waiting for just the right position to do a gorgeous job.

Then, BAM!

Caruso smiled with satisfaction as the rest of the film unspooled in delicious slow motion. Batman falling forward, knees buckling, that fancy book of his sliding across the gritty sidewalk and tumbling into the gutter wash, Batman now facedown, eyes open, staring, astonished that he'd actually been whacked, the snooty bastard, that his brains and his secrecy and having Morty Dodge as his personal gofer hadn't protected him from that little cylinder of lead Caruso had sent hurtling into the back of his fucking head.

There was only one word for it, Caruso thought as the movie came to its glittering end. *Beautiful*.

MORTIMER

HE WATCHED Dottie as she made his usual breakfast of bacon and eggs. She seemed to roll rather than to walk, a huge round ball of a woman draped in the same tattered housedress she'd worn for years. Or was it the same? Mortimer didn't know. He didn't know Dottie either, he realized suddenly, and now there would never be any time to discover who she was at the moment or had been all these years. The pain in his guts made it clear that they would not grow old together. He would not be with her during her final illness, and so there'd be no one beside her bed when she drew her last breath. How sad that seemed to him now that she would die alone, that after having given her so little, he would not be able to give her at least the comfort of his presence when the light dimmed and the room grew cold.

They'd met someplace twenty-eight years before. A party of some kind, he recalled, probably having to do with a game or some other sporting event. He'd explained how the odds worked and she'd smiled and smiled and tried to look fascinated though he doubted that she'd given a rat's ass about a single thing he'd said. How thick he must have been not to have known that she was only trying to make him feel comfortable, or like a big shot, or whatever way a homely girl thought she ought to make a guy feel so he'd take an interest. Still, it was sweet of her to have tried to make him feel good about himself, Mortimer thought. But then, she'd always been good to him, he supposed, never one to bitch all that much, never one to complain when he wasn't around. Just a decent person, Dottie was, a woman with a big, kind heart. The salt of the earth, he told himself, his wife was the salt of the earth.

"Dottie," he said quietly.

She didn't turn from the counter. "Yeah."

"Dottie."

He heard the plaintive sound in his voice and knew that she'd heard it too, because she turned toward him slowly, a quizzical look in her eyes.

He smiled quietly and patted his lap. "Come here."

She didn't move but simply stared at him wonderingly, a slice of white bread in her hand, a pink plastic knife in the other. "I'm making lunch," she said.

"Come here," he repeated.

She came forward reluctantly, bringing the bread and knife with her, and sat down on his lap.

"Dottie," he repeated. He could feel her great weight on his legs, the vast round bulk of her, soft and doughy, like holding a huge sack of flour.

"Dottie . . ." he began again, but the words stopped in his throat and he could only stare at her mutely, a strange sense of failure descending upon him as he admitted to himself that there was nothing he could do for her, nothing that would comfort or protect. It was too late. And so he simply patted her back softly and said, "Get up."

She looked at him oddly.

"Get up," he repeated, now remembering the one person on earth he might still help in some way.

"Morty, what's the matter with you!" Dottie asked.

Mortimer gave no answer, but merely strode into the bedroom, pulled out the top drawer of the bureau, and dug around in a tangle of socks until he found the pistol. "I gotta go," he told Dottie as he came back out of the room.

"You ain't having lunch?"

"No," he said. He yanked on his coat and the old rumpled hat and fled out into the dreary corridor, then down the unpainted stairs, floor after floor, the stabbing pain in his abdomen increasing with each step until he burst out into the crisp autumn air, all but running now, dodging traffic as he crossed Eighty-sixth Street, then stopped dead and drew in a long, shaky breath, his gaze rising up the lightless windows of his building until it reached the terrace of his apartment, where he saw Dottie standing in her old faded housedress, peering down, searching for him in the crowd.

He fled into a nearby shop, and from that vantage point watched his wife give up the search and shrink back into the apartment, where he imagined her at the kitchen counter again, smearing mayonnaise on a piece of white bread.

Even now he wasn't sure what he'd wanted to say to her as she sat on his lap. *Dottie, you know I love you, right?* No, that wasn't it, because he didn't really, and never had. *Dottie, I got some bad news.* That couldn't have been it, because he wasn't at all sure she would find the news of his impending death all that difficult to take.

Then suddenly he knew what he'd wanted to say: *Dottie, is there anything I can do* . . . That was what he'd intended to ask her. *Is there anything I can do to make it up to you?* A dumb question, he thought now, which was why the answer had come to him so quickly, *No, asshole, there's not a damn thing you can do for her.*

The pistol sagged down in his jacket pocket, and as he felt its weight he thought again of Abe. Abe had done him the only favor that mattered to him now. He said he would hold on to the fifteen grand and give it to Dottie when the time came. He was a friend, Abe, and even though fifteen grand was nothing, a lousy year's rent, still when he'd asked Abe to hold on to it, Abe had agreed without the slightest hesitation. He curled his fingers around the handle of the pistol. Okay, then, he thought, one good turn deserves another.

MRS. DAROCCA

SHE HAD never learned to drive, and so she walked now, moving her heavy body through the old neighborhood as if it were a stone pushed by the lithesome young girl she'd once been.

She walked past Our Lady of Fatima Parochial School and remembered Sister Amelia's shocked response, the accusatory gaze of Father Santori the day he'd escorted her through the iron gate and on to the hard concrete walkway, grasped her shoulder, turned her brusquely, and sent her home with a cold final word, *I'll be speaking to your mother.*

She walked past the row house her longshoreman father had finally managed to buy and recalled the mist in her mother's eyes when the old priest left her house later that same afternoon and she came up the stairs to her prodigal daughter's room and told her flatly that she'd shamed the family, *This will break your father's heart, Celia.*

She walked past the little park where she'd met Frankie DaRocca and told him everything in a burst of anguished confession, recalling the soft touch of his hand on hers, *I'll marry you, CeeCee,* past the stone church where he'd made good on that promise, past Frankie's house, where she'd lived with Frankie and his widowed mother for the first five years, past the hospital where her son had been born, taking the name DaRocca, just as she had taken it seven months before.

In the space of a few blocks she passed all the remaining architecture of her youth, walking like the condemned young girl she'd been so many years before, the old landmarks of her neighborhood still wreathed in hostility and disappointment so that she picked up her pace as she moved through the last of them, rushing like someone running a gauntlet, her white orthopedic shoes padding ever more rapidly against the concrete sidewalk until she stopped before the house she sought, so much bigger than the rest, noticed the big blue Lincoln in its gated driveway, and so knew that he was home.

She had never been in Leonardo's house, and as far as she knew neither of his parents had ever known about her. They'd behaved like the aristocrats Leonardo's father had always claimed they came from, American only in that they rode in fancy cars rather than in fancy carriages. They'd had high hopes for their only son, and early on Leonardo had appeared perfectly suited to fulfill them, a tall, handsome boy with jet-black hair who'd been the pride of Our Lady of Fatima's track team, a boy on the way to some big school, maybe even Notre Dame. How could she ever have expected him to throw all that away over some dumb Sicilian peasant girl pregnant with a little boy whose small dead body she could still see cradled in Frankie DaRocca's slender teenage arms.

She made her way up the stairs, surprised that one of Leonardo's thugs hadn't suddenly appeared to block her way. She knew he'd gone in that direction, gotten in trouble with the law, gone to jail, then come out again to become some kind of small-time gangster, a downward and disreputable course that must have humiliated and enraged Leonardo's parents. She'd heard that they'd disowned him after he was nabbed in a stolen car ring, but she'd heard only scant news since then. Clearly he'd inherited the family home, or perhaps bought it after his parents' death. It was the sort of thing she could see him doing just to get even with them, buying back the house of his boyhood with the dirty money his parents would never have taken. He was like that, Leonardo, a guy in whom hurt quickly turned to anger. She'd seen that early on, and so had never told him about the little boy he'd fathered on a rainy night in a Queens parking lot, and who now lay still and dead in the DaRocca family plot.

The door opened and he stood in the shadowy light of the foyer, an old man in a floral shirt and baggy pants, the handsome face ravaged by time or worry, or just the corrosive things she knew he'd done. His hair was white and thick, but beneath its silver crown the young man she'd once known had entirely run to ground. Deep lines ran in jagged gullies down the sides of his face and spread out from his eyes, creased his forehead and gave his face the look of desert soil badly raked.

"You want something?" he barked.

"It's CeeCee," she told him. "CeeCee Maganara."

She'd fixed herself up slightly, applied a little rouge and lipstick, worn the dress she'd bought for Della's wedding and which, though tight, still showed her figure to good advantage. Now she realized that these considerations meant nothing, her little allurements added in vain. There was no glimmer of romantic appreciation left in Leonardo Labriola, and so she knew that what little power she thought she might have had over him had long ago dropped away.

He blinked dully, his eyes on her eyes, wandering

nowhere, so that Celia knew that she was as unrecogniz-
able to him as the little boy he'd sired, no less a foreign,
unknown, crumbling thing. And yet he had loved her
once, hadn't he? He had said he did, and she had believed
it. He had whispered it in her ear softly, gently, and
through all the years that had passed since then, she had
harbored the belief that it had been true. But now a
wholly different truth emerged, the terrible nature of her
gullibility, the lie she'd swallowed and then nurtured
through the years, telling herself that once she'd been
loved by a smart boy, a handsome boy, a boy with class,
with a future, a boy on his way to college, that once, just
once, she'd possessed the looks and manner of one who
could summon the love of such a person. She had come in
the hope of reluming that memory in the man who stood
before her. Now she realized that no such possibility existed, or had ever existed, that she was merely one of
many others he'd known briefly, then discarded.

"When we were . . ." she began, then stopped since
there was no point in appealing to the past, the night in
the car, the talk of love. All of that was dead. And so she
said, "My daughter lives across the street from your son.
That's what I got to talk to you about, Leonardo."

The way she'd used his first name appeared to drop a
stone in the deep well of his consciousness, release a few
small ripples into his mind. "What'd you call me?"

"Leonardo," Celia answered. "I called you that in high
school."

Labriola's eyes squeezed together but without recognition.

"The thing is, I want you to leave my daughter alone,"
Celia said.

"You what?"

"You came to her house," Celia said, but without the
boldness she'd hoped to show him. Instead, she felt a

rising fear she met the only way she knew how, which was to harden and grow more bold. "You threatened her. You came to her house and threatened her."

Labriola leveled a lethal stare in Celia's direction and stepped out onto the porch. "What I do is none of your fucking business."

She could see the full depth of what he had become, the serpent that lay coiled within him. She felt like a small brown sparrow, he the hawk circling overhead. Her only choice was to act like a sparrow, charge the hawk as if it were the same size, inflate herself with courage. "Just leave my daughter alone," she snapped back at him.

Labriola stepped toward her, and she felt the force of all the violence he'd known. It came at her like a wind, dry and brutal, and she lifted her hand as if against a blow.

"Don't touch me," she blurted out.

Labriola seemed to expand on a breath of hatred, grow immensely large in his fearful rage and spite. "You tell that daughter of yours she better keep her fucking mouth shut."

Celia stumbled backward as Labriola pressed forward relentlessly.

"That bitch is going to pay," Labriola screamed. "That fucking bitch that left Tony."

She turned and headed down the stairs, moving far more quickly than she'd have thought possible, her arthritic limbs now scared into obedience, lubricating her arid joints with panic's slithery oil.

"And if anybody gets between me and that worthless cunt, they're going to pay too," Labriola bellowed.

She reached the bottom of the stairs, then hurled herself down the walkway and through the gate, Labriola's voice still rushing at her like a snarling dog.

"You tell *that* to your fucking daughter."

She knew he'd stopped at the top of the stairs, but she

didn't dare look back to make sure, afraid that such a glance might inflame him further, send him flying through the clanging gate and after her again, his breath upon her back like a raging bear. And so she raced on down the street, her legs aching beneath her weight, her ankles shooting tongues of pain into her fleshy calves, until she finally stopped beside a tree, darted around it, then pressed her back against it, exhausted, panting, her mind still whirling in the aftermath of a meeting she'd thought might go well but which she would now remember only with a bitter taste, the last sweet thoughts of youth now shattered beyond repair, Labriola no more than a brutal old man, and she the fool who'd loved him all her life.

SARA

HE ARRIVED with roses wrapped in clear plastic, the stems secured with a blue rubber band.

"I got them at the corner deli," he told her. "I figured they'd brighten the place up a little."

She took them from him. "Thanks."

They walked up the stairs, and she stood silently while he fumbled for the keys, retrieved them at last, then opened the door.

"Lucille used to have a vase in the kitchen," he told her. "Top shelf."

He found the vase, filled it with water, stuffed the flowers into it, and returned to the small living room, where he stood, glancing about. "You can rearrange things any way you want," he said. Then he placed the vase on the small wooden table next to the front window. "Place could use a little light," he said as he threw open the curtains.

A bright shaft of light swept down in a gleaming slant.

"I've never seen the curtains open," he said, turning to her. "Lucille was, I don't know, she didn't like too much light. Actually, she didn't like any at all." He looked at the flowers. "Lucille didn't like flowers either."

"Why was she so unhappy?" Sara asked.

"I don't know," Abe answered. He faced the window. "Nice street. So, what do you think of the place?"

"I like it," she said.

He moved to the piano and put down the music he'd brought. "I was hoping you'd sing again." Before she could answer, he placed the music on the music stand. "I put them in the order I think they should be sung," he told her. "I mean, if it were an act."

She started to say no, to repeat once again that it was impossible, but he sat down and placed his hands on the keyboard. "Ready when you are."

"I can't," she said.

He looked at her sternly. "You have to," he said. "You have to, Samantha, or you'll"—his eyes appeared almost to melt in the intensity of what he said—"or you'll give up on everything."

Tentatively, she stepped over to the piano, looked at the music, and began, singing softly at first, her eyes meeting his briefly, then leaping away.

She finished four songs before he said "Okay, that's enough for now" and lowered the top back over the keys. "What you need is an audience," he told her. "Feedback." Before she could respond, he plunged ahead. "I don't mean a full act. Just a few songs for a few people. The late-night crowd." He smiled. "How about tonight?"

She felt her stomach draw into a knot.

"What's the matter, Samantha?"

"I can't."

"Why not?"

"I have to stay . . ."

"What?"

She shook her head.

"Hidden," Abe said. "Isn't that what you told me when I offered you a job? That you couldn't take it because you had to stay hidden?"

She nodded.

"Who are you hiding from?"

She turned away, but he took her shoulders lightly and drew her back to him. "Some guy after you? Boyfriend?"

She shook her head.

"Husband?"

"No."

She tried to turn away again, but he held her more firmly. "You in trouble with the cops, something like that?"

A short, aching laugh broke from her. "No," she said. "Not the cops."

"Who, then?"

A small wall seemed to give way inside her. "My father-in-law," she answered quietly. "He's a bad man."

"Who is he?"

She shook her head adamantly, and he knew absolutely that she would not reveal the name.

"Okay," he said, "but bad man or not, you can't hide forever. And besides, you have to make a living, right?" He didn't wait for her to answer. "So here's what you do. You come in around midnight. There'll be just a few people in the place. You'll sing a few songs. Just for the regulars. No advertising. Nothing to draw attention to you." He didn't ask her to accept or refuse the idea, but simply rose, walked to the door, then stopped and looked back at her. "It's what you want more than anything, isn't it?" he asked. "One more stab at singing . . . or maybe just . . . happiness?"

She settled her gaze upon him in a way she hoped did

not make her appear broken, did not ask for pity, but just a chance to make it work. "Yes," she said.

ABE

HAPPINESS.

Where had that word come from?

On the walk back to the bar, he realized that he'd not thought of happiness in years, that happiness was like childhood, a place he could not return to or recapture in the present. A dark wonder settled over him as he recognized that he couldn't actually remember the last time he was happy, though he suspected it had been the years during which he'd tried to make it, have his own group, cut records, tour, be *known*. He'd stopped trying for any of that years before, and the truth of why he'd stopped had tapped lightly at the door of his consciousness ever since, though he'd rarely let it in. Now he did. It was laziness, pure and simple. Even if he'd actually had talent, making a name for himself would still have required more energy than he'd ever had.

For a moment he considered his talents. They were few and modest. The greatest one, he decided, was just the talent for going on.

SARA

SHE WASN'T sure why, but suddenly all the reasons she should keep her head down only made her want to lift it more. She knew that to show up at McPherson's, even if only for a few songs before the usual crowd, was dangerous. You never knew who might wander in. Certainly Labriola himself never frequented such places. It would be far more likely for Tony to show up, probably alone, taking the off chance that she might have returned to her old life. It wasn't likely, of course, and yet it was something she had to consider.

So why had she not simply refused to do it? It would have been easy to do, and as she stood by the window, staring down at the street, she imagined having done just that. Abe would not have pressed the issue. He would have taken her refusal at face value and left the apartment with no further word.

But she'd said yes to the proposal, regardless of the risk, and she knew now that she'd done it because to have done anything else would have been to retreat even further into the netherworld she occupied now, to abandon all future hope of a happy ending to her life.

She felt the weight of the pistol in her hand, heard the chilling voice, *Kill him!* Now she knew precisely why she hadn't done it then or later. Against all odds, against the terrible urgency of the murderous voice in her head, she had glimpsed the precipice, felt her feet poised at its jagged edge, but at the decisive moment also glimpsed the hope she would forfeit if she leaped, and so had said, to her own astonishment, *Not yet*.

TONY

HE STEERED the boat out of the marina and into the choppy waters of Long Island Sound. Caruso stood a few feet away, the collar of his jacket raised against the wind despite the fact that the cabin was entirely enclosed.

"You know, I never cared for the water," Tony told him.

Caruso watched the churning waters apprehensively. "I fucking hate it, being in a fucking boat."

"Why's that?"

Caruso looked embarrassed. "I never learned to swim."

Tony revved the engine, and the boat lurched forward so abruptly that Caruso grabbed the metal railing to his left. "Jesus."

Tony turned the wheel to the right and the boat made a broad loop, bouncing roughly in the churning waters until it came to a halt and sat, weaving unsteadily in the heaving waves.

"Okay, here it is," Tony said. He shut off the engine and faced Caruso. "I know Eddie talked to you. I know because I told him to do it. So if anything happened to him, I'm to blame."

Tony could see that Caruso was trying to play it cool, but that he was nonetheless growing edgy and uncertain.

"I wanted Eddie to talk to you and find out what was going on with my father," Tony continued. "I know he's looking for Sara, and I figure he'd put you on the job."

Caruso's eyes drifted over to the roiling, foam-spattered sea. "I told you all that."

Tony guessed that Caruso was trying to calculate exactly how much he could tell him without betraying the Old Man.

"You think I'm just a gofer, right?" Caruso asked sharply.

"I know you work for my father, that's all," Tony answered.

"Everybody thinks I'm just a fucking gofer," Caruso said. "But I ain't. He gives me important things to do. Looking for your wife, he wouldn't put me on that. He'd say, 'Vinnie, find a guy to do this thing.' That's what he'd say. And that's what I'd do."

"Is that what you did?"

Caruso looked as if he'd been challenged to stand and

deliver. "Yeah, as a matter of fact. Goddamn right I found a guy."

"So it's not you that's looking for Sara?"

"No."

"Who is?"

"Like I just told you, some other guy."

"What's this other guy's name?"

"I don't know."

"Vinnie, don't fuck with me," Tony warned.

Caruso's eyes swept over to Tony, fear like small blue flames leaping inside them. "I swear I don't know," he said.

"But you told Eddie about this other guy?"

"Yeah."

"What did you tell him?"

Caruso didn't answer.

"What did you tell him, Vinnie?"

Caruso drew in a deep breath. "If your father knew that I was—"

Tony stepped over to him. "Listen to me," he said. "I know you work for my father, but this thing's between my wife and me. It's none of his business, but he made it his business anyway. Just like he has since I got married. And it wasn't any of Eddie Sullivan's business, but I pulled him into it. So the thing is, I got two people to worry about now. And the whole fucking thing is because my father stuck his nose in where it didn't belong, and I let him do that. The whole thing is my fault, Vinnie. My fucking fault. And so it's for me to straighten this thing out, you understand?"

Caruso remained silent, and so Tony drew in closer.

"He's a bad man, Vinnie," he said.

Caruso chuckled. "No, he ain't."

"My father is a very bad man," Tony repeated emphatically.

Caruso waved his hand. "He's been good to me, your father, treats me like a—" He stopped. "Treats me good is what I'm saying."

It was then Tony saw it, the weird loyalty Caruso had for the Old Man. "You don't owe him anything, Vinnie. You know why? Because he wouldn't lift a finger for you. And something else. No matter what you do, he'll never give a shit about you."

"You don't know what you're talking about, Tony," Caruso said in a voice that struck Tony as curiously child-like, a piece of wishful thinking, like a little boy clinging against all evidence to his belief in Santa Claus.

"Yeah, I do," Tony said almost gently. "I do know because he's done it before."

"Done what?"

"Gotten a guy to try to please him, do everything he could to please him," Tony answered. "And this other guy did his best too. Because he was like you, Vinnie. He just wanted to feel like the Old Man loved him."

Caruso looked at him doubtfully. "What guy you talking about?"

Tony felt relieved that he'd finally figured it out, the whole rotten scheme. "Me," he said with a small, sad smile. "That other guy was me."

DELLA

SHE COULD hardly believe the urgency in her mother's voice, the way she'd demanded that she drop everything, pack Nicky into his car seat, and come right away. You'd have thought her house was on fire.

But the house looked just the same when Della brought the car to a halt in front of it. Despite the chill, her mother was sitting on the stoop, loosely wrapped in an old wool coat, and looking uncharacteristically tense.

"What is it, Ma?" Della cried as she got out of the car.

Mrs. DaRocca stood up immediately. "Just come on in," she said harshly.

Della scurried to the other side of the car and whisked Nicky out of the car seat. By the time she'd turned back toward the house, her mother had already disappeared inside.

"I got to talk to you, Della," Mrs. DaRocca said once Della came into the house.

"Okay, so, talk," Della said. Nicky squirmed madly in her arms. "It's past his nap time."

Mrs. DaRocca waved Della into the living room. "In here."

Della followed her mother into the living room and slumped down on the old blue sofa by the window. "You okay, Ma?"

"I'm fine," Mrs. DaRocca said. "It's you I'm worried about."

"Me?"

"Because of that neighbor of yours," Mrs. DaRocca said. "The one who took off. She didn't turn up yet, did she?"

"No," Della said. "What's going on, Ma?"

Rather than answer directly, Mrs. DaRocca said, "Stay out of it, Della. 'Cause it's not safe, getting involved in it."

Della studied the worried look on her mother's face. "What happened, Ma? And don't say nothing happened, because I know something did."

Mrs. DaRocca shrugged. "I talked to him."

"Him?"

"Labriola."

"Tony?" Della shrieked. "Why?"

"Not Tony," Mrs. DaRocca said. "The father."

Della's eyes widened in astonishment. "You what?"

"I went to his house," Mrs. DaRocca continued. "I spoke to Leonardo."

"Leonardo? You call him Leonardo? What, you know him somehow?"

"A little," Mrs. DaRocca said without emphasis. "From the old days."

"What old days?"

"In school. We was in school together. Our Lady of Fatima. We was—how you call it?—chummy."

Della sat back, drained by astonishment. "Chummy? You and Leo Labriola?"

"He was a nice boy in them days," Mrs. DaRocca said. Then her face turned grave. "But not no more. Which is why I'm telling you to stay out of this thing with the neighbor."

She felt her mother's dread wash toward her like a wave of blood across the floor. "What happened, Ma? What happened when you talked to . . . Leonardo?"

"Nothing happened," Mrs. DaRocca answered. "But you get a feeling when you talk to a person, and the feeling I got was you should stay out of his business. It's got nothing to do with you, that woman."

"Except that she's my friend."

Mrs. DaRocca looked at Della with all the authority of an old-world mother. "Della, stay out of this."

Her mother's words were heavy with warning, and because of it, she knew.

"He's going to hurt her," she said. "Labriola's going to hurt Sara."

"He didn't say that," Mrs. DaRocca said quickly. "He didn't say nothing like that, Della."

"But you saw it, didn't you? You saw it in his eyes."

Mrs. DaRocca didn't answer, but the truth was in the

grim look on her face, the stiff posture. The old fear of Sicily lay upon her shoulders as thick and visible as the black scarves of women she'd seen in pictures from the island.

"Would he kill her?" she asked.

"Della, he didn't—"

"Ma, listen to me. You spoke to him face-to-face. Would he kill her?"

Her mother didn't speak, but the slow crawl of her hand to her throat provided the only answer Della needed to glimpse her best friend floating facedown in the river.

"Oh my God," she whispered.

The old woman placed her hand on Della's. "Listen to me," she said. "It ain't your business. She left her husband. That ain't your business. Even what Leo does about it, Della, even that ain't your business."

Della thought of Sara, then of Labriola. She had not been able to imagine why Sara had left Tony, nor why Labriola was so determined to find her. Now she could.

"It ain't your business," her mother repeated.

Della rose to her feet. "Yes, it is," she said.

MORTIMER

MORTIMER WAITED glumly for Caruso to arrive, his eyes surveying the Port Authority crowd, people who had normal lives, didn't have to sit in crummy little diners, and whose ordinary, everyday troubles Mortimer suddenly envied, because they seemed like such small potatoes compared to his own.

As for Caruso, he'd sounded weird on the phone, so whatever he had on his mind, whatever had made him insist on this stupid meeting, no way was it good.

Mortimer was still considering all the ways it could be bad, when Caruso swept into the seat opposite him.

"I had a talk with the husband," Caruso said quickly. "And we got a problem." His voice was tense, like his body, everything wired. "A serious problem." He reached for a napkin and twisted it violently. "Have you talked to Batman lately?"

"Yeah," Mortimer answered.

"So, what did he tell you?"

"He needs more information," Mortimer answered. Perhaps that was the key, he thought. If there were no more information, then Stark could get out of the deal, simply do what he'd already threatened and pull out of the whole lousy scheme. "If he don't get more information, then he's gonna—"

"No, not that," Caruso interrupted. "I mean, did he say anything about some guy?"

"Some guy?"

"Some guy he maybe spotted."

"What are you talking about?"

"Some guy he maybe caught following him."

Mortimer felt a keen pain in his side, the slash of a knife. "What makes you think somebody was following him?"

Caruso crushed the napkin in his fist. "Somebody *was* following him, Morty. I know that for a fact."

"How do you know that?"

"Because I set it up," Caruso answered. "Mr. Labriola wasn't satisfied when he had that meeting with you. He still wanted to know who Batman was. So I put this guy on his trail."

Mortimer stared at him, baffled. "Whose trail?"

"Batman's."

"How do you know who Batman is?"

Caruso sucked in a frantic breath. "I didn't have no

choice, Morty," he said hurriedly. "Mr. Labriola, he don't make suggestions. He gives orders, and if you don't do what he says, bad stuff can happen."

"That don't answer my question how you know who Batman is."

"Okay, all right, I know 'cause that day you met Mr. Labriola up on Columbus Circle, when you got out of the car, I tailed you down to the Village. To this bar. I figured maybe the barkeep was Batman."

"Barkeep?"

"The guy owns that fucking bar on Twelfth Street."

"Abe? He ain't got nothing to do with this."

"Okay, so now I know it was the other one."

"What other one?"

"Chelsea. White-haired guy. Silver. Hi-yo Silver, you know? Him."

"Jesus," Mortimer breathed. "Jesus Christ."

"To tell you the truth," Caruso said, "I always figured it was the white-haired guy, you know? And Mr. Labriola, he's all lathered up about this thing, and so I ask myself, how the fuck can I do my business and keep an eye on this guy, and maybe the other one too. You see what I mean, Morty? No fucking way. So that's when I decided to farm it out."

"Farm it out?"

"Subcontract it, you might say. So, the thing is, I give this guy a choice and he picked Hi-yo Silver. Which, it looks like, turns out to be Batman."

"That was stupid, Vinnie," Mortimer said.

"I know, but the thing is, what would he do to this guy, Batman? If he noticed he was being followed?"

"What makes you think he'd do anything to him?"

"Because he's missing, this guy," Caruso said.

"Missing?" Mortimer worked to get his mind around this new wrinkle. "He just vanished?"

"Yeah." Caruso leaned forward and lowered his voice slightly. "So the thing is, I figure Batman maybe did something to him?"

"Like what?"

"Like whatever it is that's caused him to come up missing. I mean, you know, like whacking him."

Mortimer snorted. "You're fucking nuts."

"I'm serious," Caruso insisted. "The guy is missing is what I'm telling you."

"So what?" Mortimer demanded. "Jesus, Vinnie, this guy comes up missing and you automatic gotta lay it on me."

"Not you."

"Same as me, Vinnie. Adds up to me."

"I'm asking, is all," Caruso said soothingly. "Just asking."

Mortimer was not soothed. "And I'm telling you that there's no reason my guy would do something to some fucking bastard that was just poking around," he said adamantly.

"You're sure about that?"

"Yeah, I'm sure."

"Okay, but could you check it out for me anyway?"

"Check it out? What are you talking about?"

"Check with Batman, make sure he ain't done nothing."

"I'm telling you, he ain't. That's what I'm telling you."

"Just the same, check it out."

"How? You think I can just ask him straight out? It ain't like that with him. If he did something to this guy, he ain't gonna tell me about it."

"But you could get a hint, right?"

"He don't give hints," Mortimer said. "If he's done something to this fucking guy, he ain't gonna tell me about it."

"Shit."

Mortimer noticed that Caruso's face fell slightly. "This missing guy, you know him?"

Caruso nodded. "From the old days. He done me a favor. I figured I was doing him one by putting him on to Batman. But it didn't turn out that way, looks like." His tone darkened. "I got a feeling, Morty. I got a feeling something bad happened to this guy. And he was a good guy, the one I put on Batman. He wouldn't hurt a fly." He released a weary sigh. "Just check it out, that's all I'm asking."

Another blade of pain sliced across Mortimer's abdomen. "Fuck," he said.

"What?"

"Nothing," Mortimer said.

"So, can you check it out for me?"

"Okay, okay," Mortimer said. He pressed his open palm against his stomach. "But this is the last favor, Vinnie. You get what I'm saying? This whole deal is getting more and more fucked up."

"I know," Caruso said. "And Labriola is getting more and more steamed."

"How do you know that?"

"He calls me, says I got to report every fucking day."

"Report what?"

"Whatever's going on. He's got a real bug up his ass about this fucking bitch."

Mortimer sucked in a labored breath and thought how fucked up things got if you didn't keep your eye on the ball every goddamn second. He'd begun with a simple plan to get a few bucks for Dottie, now a guy was missing, Old Man Labriola was fuming, and God only knew what else was going on that he didn't even fucking know about. "Things are getting out of control, Vinnie."

"Yeah."

Mortimer sat back and tried to sort out the jumble in his mind. Finally, he said, "What do you think, Vinnie, can we get out of this deal? I mean, suppose I just told Labriola it's over. Deal's off. Give back the money. All the money. Every penny."

Caruso shook his head. "That wouldn't do no good. He wants that fucking woman is what he wants. He don't give a shit about nothing else. He's all lathered up, like I said."

"What's his beef with her?" Mortimer asked. "I don't get it. It ain't like she left *him*."

Caruso shrugged. "All I know is, he's gonna find her, Morty. And there ain't nobody can stop him."

STARK

HE OPENED the door and the light swept over the crumpled parka, the dusty jeans, the wrinkled, grease-stained shirt, and up the bare naked feet that now trembled slightly against the white plastic bands that held them in place against the metal legs of the chair.

"Who sent you?" Stark asked.

No answer came, but Stark could hear the man's rhythmic breathing. He lit a cigarette and blew a column of smoke into the blackness. He'd held the man all night, simply left him tied in a chair, sitting in the darkness, in his underwear, barefoot, vulnerable.

"I need a name," Stark said.

The feet moved, but there was no other response.

"Who sent you?"

Stark waited for a reply, though he knew it would be incoherent, at most a grunt. The tape would make any more articulate response impossible.

"Are you the woman's husband?"

The man strained against the bands that held him to the chair.

"Or do you just work for him?"

The man's head trembled, and beneath the tape his lips fluttered briefly then grew still.

Stark stepped over and raked a single finger down the man's jaw. "Who do you work for?"

The man made no effort to speak but only glared silently, his jaw now set and rigid, like a fighter readying for the blow.

"Did you really think you could do it?"

The man shifted his eyes to the right and stared at the room's blank wall.

"Did you think I would lead you to a woman and then let you hurt her?"

The man drew his gaze back to Stark, staring at him intently, as if trying to see into the working of his brain. Then he closed his eyes.

EDDIE

IN THE darkness Eddie tried to imagine the man who stared at him from just beyond the closed lids of his eyes. He couldn't see him, but he knew he was there, towering over him. He could hear his steady breathing. Slowly, the man himself swam out of the darkness, vaguely translucent, an afterimage in Eddie's mind. He was tall with silver hair, and his eyes were blue, and he wore clothes that Eddie had only seen in movies and on brief trips to midtown Manhattan. He was one of *those* people, the ones who controlled things, and beside whom everyone else felt small.

And he was smart too. Eddie knew that much. He'd

turned the tables on him, accused him of following him so he'd be there when Tony's wife was found, be there because he was going to hurt Tony's wife. *I know this game.* That's what the man had said. *I fell for it once, but never again.* But none of that was true. Eddie knew that much. None of it was true because the man with the silver hair was working for Tony's father, one of his thugs, a guy he'd hired to track Sara down.

In his mind Eddie recalled Sara as she'd appeared the last time he'd seen her. She'd seemed sweet and lovely, and she'd smiled at him and said hello but he knew that even if she'd hardly noticed him or treated him badly he'd still be holding out the way he was because it really wasn't about Sara. It was about Tony, this guy who'd stood with him when his father died, and sent him a Christmas card, and sometimes took him out for a steak and fries. Tony, who'd visited him in the hospital when he got hurt on the job and seemed to know when he needed a hand. Tony had done all of that despite the fact that he was busy and his business was in trouble and he had worries of his own, and so it was clear to Eddie that you knew who your friends were not by their favors but by their sacrifice.

"Who sent you?"

He opened his eyes and the silver-haired man was peering at him, his face very still and menacing, like a snake poised to strike.

"Who sent you?"

The silver-haired man ripped the tape from his mouth with a fierce, violent jerk.

"Who sent you?" he repeated, now very sharply.

Eddie closed his eyes again and thought of Tony at his side, and it seemed to him that in the end a friend could be judged only by how much he was willing to lose. He drew a steely breath, opened his eyes, and glared defiantly at the man whose face was very near him now, and in which he saw a terrible capacity for violence. He never used bad language, but just this once it seemed okay.

"Fuck you," he said.

ABE

HE SAT down behind his desk and stared at the pile of bills, the liquor stacked high in cardboard boxes, the calendar that hung from the wall like a condemned man. Nothing would change in this room, he thought, if nothing changed in his life. Someone would simply come in one day and find him curled over the desk or sprawled on the floor. That was the curtain he saw. End of Act Three.

And so he reached for the phone and dialed Lucille's old number.

"Hello."

"Samantha, it's Abe."

"Oh, hi."

"Listen," he began, then stopped and drew in a quick, uncertain breath. "Listen, about tonight. I thought maybe you should start off with something lively."

"Okay."

"Something to get their attention, you know. And then maybe end it with a ballad. Tug the heartstrings, you know?"

"All right."

There was a pause, and he knew she was waiting for some final word. He considered his options for a moment, then charged ahead like a man out of the trenches.

"And one more thing," he said. "I was thinking maybe we could have dinner before you come to the bar. You know, talk things over. Then we could go to the bar and maybe we could sit around awhile, and then, whenever you feel like it, you get up, do the songs."

"Okay," she said.

He gave her the name of the restaurant he'd already chosen just in case and told her to meet him there at eight. When she said fine, he hung up and sat back in his chair with a modest sense of achievement, not the thrill of winning the race, but at least the knowledge that when the starting gun fired, you came out of the gate.

DELLA

IT WAS *her business*, she thought, *but what could she do about it?*

She sat at the table, Nicky now sleeping soundly, and smoked the first cigarette she'd had in three years. She'd bought the pack at the convenience store on the way back from her mother's house, asking for it guiltily, like a teenager hoping the orange-haired clerk behind the register wouldn't demand proof of age.

After that she'd driven directly home, put Nicky down for his afternoon nap, then wandered into the kitchen to light up. She knew why she was smoking. Nerves. She couldn't get the look on her mother's face out of her mind, the terrible, hopeless fear she'd seen in the old woman's eyes. And something else too, Leo Labriola, the way he'd grabbed her arm and written his number on her wrist. The remembered violence of that act, the nip of the pen in her flesh, now seemed more real than anything around her. He knew his business, Labriola, she thought, knew exactly how to terrorize people, make them cringe.

Labriola was capable of anything. That much was absolutely clear now. Whatever feeble hope that he was all bluff and hot air, a posturing old man who could rage and bluster with the best of them but in the end do nothing, all she'd used to convince herself that Sara wasn't really in danger, all of that was gone, and she was left only with the certain knowledge that the danger she was in was even deeper than she'd supposed. Not only would Labriola hurt her, he would enjoy doing so, and that enjoyment would itself blossom and expand, urging him to greater outrages against her. He wouldn't just kill her, Della decided, he would torture her. He would beat her up or burn her with cigarettes or pass a blowtorch up her arm or use a chain saw the way Colombian drug lords did to the people who crossed them. She'd read about these things in books and magazines, and she knew they were true, that some people were capable of indescribable cruelty, and that Leo Labriola was that kind of man.

She crushed the first cigarette into the saucer she'd commandeered for an ashtray, then lit another one and tried to find a way out of the situation that would somehow save everyone from harm. It was all she wanted, just that simple measure of getting everyone through this thing—Sara, her mother, Mike, Nicky, herself—everyone through this thing unharmed.

But how?

She considered the situation, trying to focus on a solution, a way out, but each time, the situation itself exploded into a thousand glittering shards. This flying apart happened, she thought, because she simply lacked the capacity to think. Bright people saw the world with a clarity that was beyond her. They could find a pattern, chart a road through the entangling forest. But she saw only what was directly before her. It had always been that way, she thought. It was as if her brain were a gigantic eye that could detect only the brightest colors, all subtlety and shading beyond her view. She was like a ship that sailed from island to island on a journey that moved from Big Thing to Big Thing. GET A BOYFRIEND. MARRY. HAVE KIDS.

The trip had gone remarkably smoothly, she realized, the sea always calm in a world without storms and where night never fell. But now everything was storm-tossed and she could feel a terrible blackness approaching. She remembered Sara talking about a play in which, at the end, the whole house was turned upside down, everything falling on top of everything else, and it seemed to Della that her own house might do the same thing; one wrong move and everything she loved would be annihilated.

Maybe the thing to do, she reasoned, was to rate love. Make a list of people you cared for. The one you loved the most was at number one. Next was number two. And if helping the third person on the list put the people at one and two in danger, then you just didn't do it. Number one for her, she decided, was Nicky. Number two was Denise. Then Mike. Her mother, grudgingly, made number four. Okay, she thought, if helping Sara endangered the others, then I won't help Sara. That was simple enough, wasn't it? Yes, she thought, momentarily pleased with the little mathematical scheme she'd worked out. Then, in the midst of that satisfaction, blurring the clarity of rated love, another calculation emerged. Herself. Where did she fit in the scheme she'd worked out? Who would she be—what would be left of her—if she turned away from a friend in danger, made no attempt to warn her, save her, but simply closed the door, turned out the light, and with that gesture switched off the power to her heart?

STARK

THE BUZZER sounded unexpectedly, and like all such surprises, it was unwelcome. He walked to the door and opened it.

"Sorry to bother you," Mortimer said. He took off his hat but didn't leave it on the rack by the door. "You busy?"

Stark closed the door, leaving the two of them in the shadowy light of the foyer. "What is it?" he asked.

"It's about my friend," Mortimer told him. "The one you're helping out."

"Did he give you more information?"

Mortimer shook his head. "The thing is, he's in a bind. Complications. He's got complications."

Stark said nothing. Instead, he worked to conceal the raging sense of betrayal he felt in the certainty that Mortimer had lied to him.

"So, that's what we need to talk about," Mortimer said.

Stark faced him squarely in the foyer's shadows. "Talk," he said.

MORTIMER

TALK.

That was all Stark said, and at that instant Mortimer thought, *He knows.*

But he was not sure what Stark knew. Only that he knew something, and that what he knew was very bad. He could see how bad it was in Stark's pale blue eyes. Because of that, Mortimer knew that his own next words were crucial, that they had to give Stark the impression that it had all been a mistake, that whatever Stark had discovered, Mortimer had also discovered it, that they'd both been fooled, not that one had attempted to fool the other.

"I'm not sure he's playing straight with me," Mortimer said. His fingers squeezed the hat. "My friend, I mean. What he tells me, I can't be sure it's on the up-and-up." He watched Stark, straining to see some sign of a reaction, but the man peered at him silently, and with what now appeared a sad contempt. "About the job, I mean," he added, trying hard not to sputter or to cringe despite the fact that he felt like a third-grade kid before a disapproving teacher. "The thing is, I ain't sure we're the only players."

"The only players?"

"I get the feeling he might have some other guy working this thing." Mortimer stopped and waited, but Stark continued to stare at him without expression. "You ain't seen no sign of that, right? Some other guy?"

"Why would you think your friend had a second man?" Stark asked.

"I don't know," Mortimer answered. "Just a feeling that—" He stopped again, staring now into Stark's stony features. "Anyway," Mortimer said quietly. "That's where I'm at in this thing."

"Which is where, exactly?"

"Where I said. I don't think I'm getting the straight story."

"So your friend is lying to you?"

"Well, maybe not exactly lying. Just not telling me everything."

"There's no difference between those two," Stark said sternly.

Mortimer saw something register darkly in Stark's face, a look he'd never seen before, that of a man who'd suddenly glimpsed another man's demise, knew the hour and the manner of his impending death. "I wish I could get you off this thing," he said.

"It's too late for that." Stark said it grimly.

Mortimer glanced down the darkened corridor that led to the right and noticed a black curtain hung across it.

"What's the matter?" Stark asked sharply.

"Nothing," Mortimer answered.

"In that case," Stark said. He opened the door and a wide swath of light passed over them, deathly pale, with swirling flecks of dust. "Unless there's something else."

Mortimer faced Stark in the mottled light. "No. Nothing." A grave premonition swam into his mind, the dreadful sense that he would never see Stark again. "Sorry for how this turned out," he said.

For an instant, he thought he saw something move across Stark's face, some glimmer of affection shaded by regret. Then it passed, and Stark stepped back into the shadowy depths of his apartment, and closed the door.

Mortimer had never been so coldly dismissed, but there was nothing to be done about it. And so he walked out of the apartment and down the stairs, where he turned right, thinking that he could use a drink, maybe a little talk with his best friend, Abe. At the corner he glanced back toward Stark's apartment, recalled the black curtain that hung over the corridor, and wondered if his first suspicion could possibly be correct.

The light changed, but Mortimer remained in place. He knew he had to focus on the situation, and so, walking now, he started first with a chronological arrangement of events, recalling how Caruso had brought up the missing wife. No. It hadn't begun there. It had begun with his owing Labriola fifteen grand, and what that meant was that everything that followed was his fault. If he hadn't bet on Lady Be Good, he'd never have gotten into this position.

But Lady Be Good had been a good bet. Several of the old stoopers at the track had told him so. So, when you looked at it, it was really their fault for giving him a bad tip. He shook his head, realizing that he'd done it again, gotten completely off the track.

And so he started again, this time carefully recalling the stages by which he'd gotten into this bind. Sure, it came back to owing Labriola fifteen grand, but that really didn't matter now. What mattered was that at the end of the process, everybody would be okay. Except the woman, of course, because what happened to her didn't really matter. Why should it, because when you got right down to it, it was all her fault anyway. If she hadn't taken a fucking hike, none of this shit would have happened.

Bullshit, he thought. He shook his head at the absurdity of his own conclusion. It wasn't the woman's fault at all. Like everything else, it was his fault, goddammit. Every fucking bit of it was his fault and nobody else's. He'd gotten into debt with a rotten old hood, then tried to pay off that debt by lying to Stark and cheating him, and now he had to fix it because Stark had gotten wind of something screwy in this thing, and God only knew what dark and bloody thing he'd done to the guy he'd caught following him.

Mortimer's mind raced through the grim possibilities—everything from kicking his ass to cutting his throat—but he couldn't determine the likelihood of Stark doing one thing over the other.

But the real question, Mortimer decided, was why Stark had done anything at all. What threat had he perceived in the guy he'd caught tailing him? He was just an ordinary guy, according to Caruso. And yet Stark had gone after him hammer and tongs.

Why?

The answer came with such force and certainty that

the word itself escaped Mortimer's mouth and hung in
the late-morning air like a strand of Marisol's coal-black
hair.

   Lockridge.

TONY

HE COULDN'T stop thinking about Sara, about the
fact that if something really had happened to Eddie, then
she was in more danger than he could possibly have imagined. Before now he'd feared that one of his father's
goons might strong-arm her. It might stop at intimidation,
or it might involve grabbing her arm and giving it a
painful squeeze. All of that would be wrong, he knew, and
none of it would ultimately work. You didn't keep a wife
that way. Well, some people did. His cousin Donny kept
Carla that way. And, of course, his father had ruled with
the same iron fist. But he did not want to be his father, or
have a wife who lived with him the way his mother had
lived with the Old Man, cringing, terrified, reduced to
shadow, a mere reflection of her dread. He wanted Sara
the way she was when he'd first met her. He wanted the
young woman who'd stood alone before an old piano and
sung her heart out. Her courage astonished him suddenly, the sheer grit she'd had to have just to do what
she'd done that night. He had taken that brave young
woman, so perfect, and chipped away at that perfection,
coaxing her to the suburbs, reducing her to baby factory—
or at least trying to—and then, when no babies came,
he'd rubbed her face in this failure, as if she were the one
who'd done everything wrong, she the one who'd ruined
his life.

   He went to his car and drove away, leaving his employ-
ees to fend for themselves. Suddenly it didn't matter if

they came in late, lay down on the job, misplaced some form, or sent a load of fish to the wrong restaurant. He'd run the business the way he'd run his marriage, under the sword of his father's instruction. *You have to show the people who work for you that you've got the muscle,* his old man had told him. *You have to show that woman who's boss.*

And so he'd done that, Tony thought. For sixteen years he'd worn the pants, laid down the law, gotten his way. And now he'd reached the end of the way he'd gotten, the barren crossroads of his life.

He drove aimlessly along Sunset Highway, all the way to Montauk Point, where he stood on the beach and watched the waves tumble one after another onto the vacant shore.

It was noon by the time he returned home. He hadn't intended to go there. There were bars and diners where he could have sat through the afternoon, the night, even the early-morning hours. And yet, here he was, staring at the empty house, the gray, cheerless windows, imagining the bedroom where she'd never sleep again. But dire as that reality was, it was not nearly so dark as what might yet happen to Sara. He knew that she'd wanted only to leave him. She'd taken not a dime of his money. She'd left the Ford Explorer in the driveway. What else could her message have been but that she wanted nothing of him and nothing of his. She had wanted only to be rid of him and had probably never guessed that anyone else might be looking for her. Certainly she would not have dreamed that the Old Man would have hired some thug and set him loose like a dog in the woods.

Something moved behind his car. He twisted to the rear and peered through the back window, where he saw Della coming toward him.

"Hi, Della," Tony said as he got out of the car.

A thin smile labored to hold its place on her lips, then expired. "I need to talk to you, Tony."

"You want to come inside?"

She shook her head.

"Okay," Tony said. "What's on your mind?"

DELLA

SHE KNEW exactly what was on her mind, but the words were a problem. How do you tell a man that his father is a crazy old bastard, completely out of control and dangerous and who, at that very moment, was scaring the living hell out of her?

"Have you heard from Sara?" Tony asked.

She'd not expected the sudden change in his voice, the way the tone went from a question to a plea. But it was the question itself that caught her off guard. She'd come to tell him that his father had confronted her, and later her mother, and that these confrontations had really frightened her and so she'd decided that he needed to know about them. That was as far as she'd intended to go. Certainly, she'd had no expectation of admitting that Sara had called her, even hinted at where she was and what she was doing. But Tony had asked her outright, and so she knew that the moment had come—the moment of truth, they called it in the movies—when you had to confront the full and awesome nature of your peril or live a coward all your life.

"Yes," she said. "Yes, I have, Tony."

His eyes caught fire, and she saw in that instant the depth of his love and the torment of its loss. "Is she okay?" he asked softly.

"Yeah," Della answered. "She's fine."

She expected a volley of questions to follow, hard and

blunt, raining down upon her like a hail of bullets. But instead, Tony shrank back against the car, folded his arms, and let his head droop forward for a moment. "Good," he said.

"I don't know where she is," Della said. "Just that she's okay."

Tony drew himself up and settled his gaze on the empty street. "That's all that matters."

She had never heard a man say a more wholly selfless thing. She'd thought he was like his father, filled with the Old Man's seething violence, but now he seemed merely broken, and in his brokenness curiously baffled, like a man who'd been badly beaten in some bar brawl and was struggling to understand how the argument began.

"You and Mike," he said. "You're happy?"

"Yeah."

"That's good." He started to speak, then stopped, and in that awkward gesture Della saw the young man Sara had first met, so vulnerable and uncertain, seeking love, infinitely kind.

"The thing is," he began, then stopped, glanced once again into the night, then back to Della. "Before you know it, things get out of hand."

"They do, Tony."

"And the years go by, you know?"

"They do, yeah."

He gazed at his shoes, kicked lightly at the cement pavement. "So, that's how it goes." He studied the deserted yard. His face grew somber. "You think she might come back, Della? On her own, I mean."

She shook her head.

"No, I don't either," Tony said. "So, what now? You got any ideas?"

"Just one thing, Tony," Della said. "You gotta be careful about your father."

"My father?"

"He's scary, you know?" The rest burst from her in a torrent. "The thing is, I told my mother about him coming over. I know that before I told you he didn't come, but he did. And, Tony, he was really scary, and so I told my mother about it and she went to see him 'cause it turns out they knew each other in high school, and so she figured she could put in a word for me."

"A word about what?" Tony asked.

"Like, leave me alone. That kind of word. Because, the thing is, he grabbed me. When he came over that time. And so my mother went over to tell him to, you know, leave me alone, but she didn't get anywhere with that because he was the same way to her. You know, like real threatening."

"He threatened your mother?"

"He scared her," Della said. "And she came back and she told me to just stay out of it because he—your father— he was . . . dangerous."

"Dangerous," Tony repeated softly.

"Yeah, Tony. So that's why she said I should stay out of it."

Tony's gaze was oddly admiring. "Why didn't you?"

"I couldn't do it," Della answered. "Because . . . if he'd hurt me, and then my mother, well, I had to think what he might do to Sara, you know?"

Tony looked like a man who'd long expected terrible news but was only now getting the full report of just how terrible it was. "Thank you," he said quietly, then reached out and touched her arm. "Thank you, Della."

TONY

HE'D BEEN waiting for almost half an hour when his father's dark blue Lincoln turned into the driveway. The

Old Man drove the car himself now, the days when he'd been chauffeured around by some gorilla long gone. Tony knew that even in the old days his father had never been very high in the criminal pecking order. He'd carried himself like a big shot, though, smoked expensive cigars and dressed in fancy double-breasted suits, and hired muscle he didn't need, usually some has-been boxer who chauffeured him from one crummy shylocking operation to the next. But now the great Leo Labriola was alone behind the wheel, a big, blustering man still, but one without backup.

"What are you doing here?" the Old Man said as he pulled himself out of the car. He was wearing flannel trousers and a floral shirt. In such attire he looked as if he should pass the autumn of his life playing pinochle in a retirement community in Florida instead of hiring some goon to track down a woman.

"What?" Labriola snapped. "What you looking at?"

"Nothing," Tony said with a shrug.

"You curious?"

"What?"

"You curious where I been?"

"No."

"With Belle," Labriola said, his eyes daring Tony to say a word about it. "She blew me."

"Jesus," Tony said disgustedly.

"You don't like it?" the Old Man barked.

Tony shrugged again. What did it matter what he liked or didn't like about his father's life? Belle Adriani had been the Old Man's mistress for as long as Tony could remember, a bleached-blond club dancer with long fire-engine-red fingernails and a perpetual pout. Labriola had picked her up when she was twenty and had kept her as his personal sex slave ever since. Once he and his mother had run into them at a local street fair. His mother put her hand on Tony's arm, led him in the opposite direction, and never uttered a word about it.

"Belle does what I tell her." The Old Man laughed. "Not like that fucking hayseed you married."

"We need to talk," Tony said.

Labriola scowled, then elbowed past Tony and headed up the cement walkway that led to the house. When he reached the front steps, he turned toward his son. "Okay, so? Talk."

"It's about Sara," Tony said.

The Old Man waved his hand. "That's being taken care of."

"How is it being taken care of?"

"I told you I'd find her."

"How are you going to do that?"

"What difference does it make how I do it as long as it gets done?"

"You know anything about Eddie?"

"You mean that mick works for you? What about him?"

"He's missing."

Labriola laughed. "So what? Jesus, some fucking mick works for you goes missing and you think I know something about it? What's the matter with you, Tony? What I got to do with this guy?"

"I need to know who's looking for Sara," Tony said.

Labriola glared at him. "You don't need to know nothing I don't want to tell you."

"Who's looking for Sara?" Tony demanded.

"What's that got to do with this fucking mick?"

Tony started to answer, then stopped. If he told the truth, Caruso's head was on the block.

"I want you to stop looking for Sara," he said instead.

Labriola squinted, as if against an unexpected flash of light. "You what? You want me to stop looking for that—"

"Don't call her names," Tony blurted out.

"What, you a tough guy all of a sudden?"

"I mean it," Tony said firmly. "Don't call her names."

"You're still pussy-whipped, Tony. She's still got you by the balls."

"Stop looking for her," Tony said.

Labriola's face had become a smirking mask. "What, you think you can find her? You couldn't find your own dick, Tony. And what if you did find her? You gonna beg her to . . ." He studied his son's face for a moment, as if trying to read the mind behind it. Then he shrugged. "Okay," he said lightly. "Okay, fine, Tony. You find her." He grinned malevolently. "Good luck," he said, then turned and trudged up the stairs, his great arms pumping massively, as if warming up for some final title fight, the great belt in contention now, the championship of the world.

FIVE

Someone to Watch Over Me

MORTIMER

HE TOOK his usual place at the dark end of the bar, and it struck him unpleasantly that he had always tended toward shadowy corners. Like a bug, he thought.

Jake stepped over and poured a drink. "You look like shit, Morty." He gave the bar a quick wipe, then slid over a bowl of beer nuts. "Like shit," he repeated like some doctor who was making sure his professional observation had not gone unnoted.

"Yeah," Mortimer said. He knocked back the round. "Where's Abe?"

"Back in his office," Jake said.

"I hear he's got a girlfriend," Mortimer said, allowing himself the small pleasure that Abe had shared this intimacy. But that was what best friends did, wasn't it, share things they didn't share with other guys? It was the only thing that gave relief, he decided, the warmth of friendship, all that trust. "He told me about her," he added as if displaying a medal he'd won for good service.

"She's probably gonna work here," Jake said absently.

"Doing what?"

"Singer, I guess."

"No shit," Mortimer said.

Jake indicated Mortimer's empty glass. "Another?"

"Why not?"

Jake poured the drink and Mortimer took a quick sip. "Is she any good, Abe's girl?" he asked.

"She ain't bad. Coming in later tonight, Abe says. Gonna do a couple numbers."

Mortimer rolled the glass between his hands and watched the amber liquid slosh back and forth. He could feel the weight of the pistol in his jacket pocket. He knew it wasn't much to offer, just a way for Abe to defend himself if some tough guy showed up and started throwing his weight around. You wave a gun in a guy's face, and he cools down right away, starts figuring the odds, decides the guy holding the piece is one serious bastard, and that the lady in question is by no means worth taking a bullet for.

And as for the piece, Mortimer thought, hell, he didn't need it anyway. He wasn't going to shoot anybody at this late date, and if somebody wanted to shoot him, so what? They'd shave off a few weeks at the most. And bad weeks at that. Hospital. Dottie fretting. Fuck it, Mortimer thought, now feeling oddly urgent about getting the gun to Abe before it was too late, doing just one good thing while he still could.

He slid off the stool. "So Abe's in back?" he said hastily.

"Yeah," Jake said dully. "Probably mooning over the broad."

Mortimer didn't like Jake's attitude, but what could you do with a guy like Jake, a dry kernel of a man, probably without a friend in the world. At least, Mortimer concluded, nobody could say that about *him*. Suddenly the pistol was like a gold watch after a long career, the physical proof that he had not lived in vain. After all, how many guys in New York City actually had an unregistered piece he could give to a friend? Not many, Mortimer told himself. You had to have lived a certain way to have an unregistered piece at your disposal. Thinking that, Mortimer abruptly decided that perhaps his life had always been headed for this moment, when he'd have a piece he could pass on, and touching it now, as he made his way toward the back of the bar, it felt like the one sweet fruit of a long, dry season.

"Hey, Abe," he said as he stepped into the office.

Abe sat behind the desk, papers spread over it.

"So, how you doing?" Mortimer asked.

"Okay," Abe said. He looked surprised to see him. "And you?"

"Good," Mortimer answered, amazed that it was the truth, that he actually felt okay despite the fact that the dark eddies of his last conversation with Stark continued to drift through his mind. But again, what was the worse Stark could do? Fire him? So what. Shoot him? Same answer. The good news about reaching the end of the line was that there just wasn't all that much anyone could do to you.

Okay, so nobody could really do anything *to* you, Mortimer concluded, but you could still do something *for* somebody. On the bounce of that notion, he stepped forward with a springiness that surprised him, took the pistol from his pocket, and placed it on the desk. "This is for you."

Abe looked at the gun as if it were a coiled rattler.

"You said you could use a gun," Mortimer reminded him. "So there it is."

Abe stared at the gun. "Morty . . . I didn't really . . ."

"My gift to you," Mortimer said. "In case that fucking guy tries to muscle in on your girl."

"Morty, I don't want a—"

"I wouldn't give it to nobody else, Abe," Mortimer said quietly.

"Yeah, but—" Suddenly Abe stopped, and Mortimer noticed a curious softening in his gaze, as if something had just come to him, a different take on things.

"Yeah, okay," Abe said quietly. "Thanks." He gingerly reached for the pistol, like a guy picking up a scorpion, and put it in the top drawer of his desk. "Thanks again," he said with a quick smile. "You're a . . . a good friend, Morty."

Mortimer smiled brightly and sat down opposite Abe's desk. "So, tell me about this woman, Abe. You didn't tell me much last time."

"She's nice," Abe said.

Mortimer waited for more, but when Abe kept the rest of it to himself, he said, "So, tell me about her."

Abe shrugged.

Mortimer smiled. Abe was playing it close to the vest, but he could see that his friend wanted to spill it all, that he just needed a little encouragement. "Jake says she's a singer."

"Yeah," Abe said, adding nothing else.

"Jake says you're going to hire her," Mortimer coaxed.

"If she'll take the job," Abe said.

"Why wouldn't she?"

"She's got a few problems," Abe answered with a slight shrug.

"Like what?"

"Left her husband," Abe said hesitantly.

"Plenty women do that," Mortimer said in a worldly tone.

"Yeah, but it wasn't a clean break."

"How so?" Mortimer asked, happy that the conversation was going so smoothly now.

"She's sort of on the run," Abe said darkly.

"So the husband's after her," Mortimer said.

"That's what you'd think, right?" Abe answered. "But not in this case."

Mortimer smiled. Now he was getting to the true heart of it, to those little intimacies friends shared. "So, who she running from?" he asked.

"Her father-in-law," Abe said. "She's pretty scared of him."

Mortimer watched Abe silently for a moment, a dark possibility suddenly sputtering to life. No way, he thought, no fucking way. Then he considered the fact that life had always managed to twist around and bite him in the ass. Take Cajun Spice, for example. What were the odds that fucking soap bar would surge ahead at the last minute, beat Lady Be Good, empty the coffers once again, leaving Dottie in the lurch?

"So, when did she show up?" he asked tentatively. "This woman."

"Couple days ago," Abe said. "She was staying at some hotel in Brooklyn, but I set her up in Lucille's old place. I figured it'd be safer for her, you know?"

Mortimer's eyes fled to the wall calendar that hung to his right. "Lucille's old place," he whispered almost to himself. "Jane Street, right? I heard her say that once. Over a Chinese laundry."

Abe nodded. "Place was paid up to the end of the month."

"Jane Street," Mortimer repeated softly.

Abe looked at him quizzically. "You okay, Morty?"

Mortimer nodded heavily, the full weight of what he'd feared now falling upon him. "This guy she's running from. The father-in-law. She say who he was?"

"No," Abe answered. "She wants to keep me out of it."

Mortimer drew in a slow breath as he figured the odds

that Abe's girl was the one Leo Labriola was looking for. "Yeah, well, maybe you should do that, Abe," he said cautiously. "I mean, it ain't your business, right?"

Abe looked surprised by the advice. "Of course it's my business."

"Yeah, but a guy like that, dangerous . . ."

Abe gave a theatrical wink. "So what if he's dangerous? Thanks to you, I got a gun, remember?"

Mortimer suddenly felt a slicing pain in his belly.

"Morty?" Abe said. "You look a little—"

"I'm fine," Mortimer said quickly. He waited for the throbbing to pass, then got to his feet.

"You sure you're okay?" Abe asked.

"Fine," he repeated as he turned toward the door. Fucked again, he thought.

SARA

SHE'D DECIDED on "Someone to Watch Over Me" as her final number, accompanying herself on Lucille's piano as she rehearsed it by fingering the melody line, then sounding the appropriate chord. She couldn't get the easy flow of Abe's accompaniment that way, but she could at least make sure her voice hit the notes. The fact that it had hit them, each and every one of them, gave her a measure of confidence that she could pull it off. After all, she didn't have to do that much, she told herself, just stand in front of a few people, pretend she was an amateur, see what happened.

She considered running through the songs again but decided not to. What if she didn't do them as well this time, maybe missed a few notes. That would bring her down, make her less confident than she was at the moment. Besides, a singer could over-rehearse. She'd learned that from the old singers she'd known the first time she'd come to New York. You could over-rehearse and lose your energy, the fresh face of your act, get every detail of the routine so thoroughly nailed down that it left no room for you to let go, soar, spontaneously take the song to some new, surprising place.

She glanced at the clock. It was three-thirty. Normally, she'd have had to start dinner now, along with finishing up whatever small chores she'd started during the day.

She recalled how she'd made work for herself in the past, creating little jobs to fill her hours. Other wives used alcohol or the occasional affair, but she'd relied on a host of small projects to keep busy. She'd wash the Explorer or clean the pool or hose down the area around it. Tony would have been willing to hire someone to do such things, or even do them himself, but she'd never brought them up. She needed such petty tasks to keep her sane. They were what she did instead of drink or meet a guy at the local motel. For the rest, she'd relied on Della, the talks they'd had as they strolled the neighborhood streets or sat in Della's kitchen, sipping coffee in the afternoon. It was the only thing she missed, a friend she could talk to.

She picked up the phone and dialed the number.

DELLA

SHE JUMPED when the phone rang, and in that instant recognized how deeply it had sunk, the sense of dread that had settled upon her since talking to Tony. If it were Sara, she decided, she would tell her everything, warn her that the Old Man was looking for her, do whatever she had to do to protect her from him.

"Hello."

"Hi, babe."

The sound of Mike's voice, so firm and familiar, filled her with joy, and she wanted only to know that he was safe and happy and would always, always, come home to her.

"Mike," she blurted out desperately, "are you okay?"

"What?"

She realized Mike had heard the frenzy in her voice.

"What's the matter, Della?"

"Nothing, sweetheart. I was just thinking about you, that's all."

"Thinking about me?"

"Wondering how you were."

He laughed. "I'm fine."

"You'd tell me, right, if anything was wrong?"

"Of course I would. Della?"

"Yes."

"Anything wrong on your end?"

"No."

"You sure?"

"Everything's perfect."

"Because you sound a little . . ."

"Mike?"

"Yeah?"

"Could we go out for pizza tonight? All of us?"

"Sure, why not?"

"Good."

"You're sure everything's okay?"

She thought of what she'd done, how she'd talked to Tony, and how she'd tell Sara everything, too, if Sara called. She'd done her duty while at the same time trying to keep Mike and her children safe. A wave of high achievement washed over her, the sense of having looked danger in the eye, maybe even stared it down.

"Everything's perfect," she said quietly. "It really is."

SARA

THE LINE was still busy. She returned the phone to its cradle, glanced toward the window, and reveled in the clear midafternoon air beyond it. She thought of going out, then the dread swept down around her, the fear he might be waiting for her out there, the Old Man or whoever he'd sent to do his work.

But it was a fear she had to put behind her, she decided, and so she lifted her head as if on the shoulder of a bold resolve and headed for the door.

Once outside, she turned right and walked to the corner, where she stopped, peered into the window of a florist shop, and thought of the roses Abe had brought to the apartment, a gesture so sweet, she thought now, that she'd felt herself crumble a little, some of the day's panic fall away.

"Nice flowers."

She jumped, then turned to face a small man in a worn suit, his features so dark and gloomy, his voice so oddly cold, she knew absolutely that he was Labriola's man.

"Nice flowers," he repeated.

She felt her body stiffen. "Yes."

"You like flowers?"

She stepped back slightly, her attention entirely focused on the man who peered back at her from beneath the broad brim of a rumpled black hat, his face strikingly melancholy.

"Yes," she told him. "Yes, I do."

A thin smile glimmered on the man's face briefly, then vanished. "Well, have a nice day," he said.

"Yes, you too," Sara answered.

The man touched the brim of his hat, then turned and headed in the opposite direction down the street, one shoulder lower than the other, as if bearing an invisible weight.

Sara stood in place until he reached the far corner, then disappeared around it. She wanted to believe that the man was only a Village oddity, a sad figure in his dark suit, but not in the least connected to her or Labriola, just a strange little man, nothing more.

Yes, she told herself, *believe that.*

She continued on down the street, trying to get the little man in the rumpled hat out of her mind, but his face kept returning to her, superimposed over other faces, Caulfield, Labriola, men she'd fled, men bent on harming her.

At the end of the block she stopped and glanced back down the street, half expecting to see the man in the rumpled hat lurching behind her, or quickly dodging behind a tree to conceal himself.

But she saw no sign of him, no indication that he'd been anything but a sad-faced man who'd commented upon the flowers in the florist's window. And yet she could not get his image out of her mind, the feeling that he had purposely approached her, as if to get a better look, then lumbered away to call whoever had hired him to find her.

She looked down the street once more, then left and right along the side streets, then up ahead. Again she saw no sign of the man who'd approached her. But again she could not rid her mind of the dark suspicion that she had been found.

CARUSO

LABRIOLA'S VOICE exploded through the phone. "Get over here!"

"You mean—"

"Right now!"

"Okay, sure, I'll—"

Click.

The phone felt like something stiff and dead in his hand.

Shit, Caruso thought, fuck.

He rushed to the car, Labriola's voice still scraping across his mind, harsh and demanding as always but with something different in it this time, a voice that seemed on fire.

The old neighborhood held its usual familiarity, mostly stubby brick buildings from before the war. He remembered playing stickball on these same streets, remembered the day his father had gone out for beer at that little deli right there, remembered watching him from that window, the one on the fourth floor, watching as he walked past the little store, checking his wallet as he turned the corner. He'd watched it for a long time after that, but his father had never come back around it again. What had he been? Four years old. And yet it was the one image that returned to him most often, his father, tall and lanky and always smiling and throwing him in the air, this man who seemed to hold eternity in his grasp, turning the corner as he thumbed the bills in his old brown wallet, head down, counting, with not so much as a quick glance back toward the little boy who watched him so adoringly from the fourth-floor window.

If the guy had just hung around, Caruso thought now, then everything might have been different. He'd have had a father and wouldn't have had to hit the streets at thirteen, become a bagboy for Mr. Labriola, collecting his winnings, making his payoffs, greasing the palms he wanted greased, making the loans he okayed, chasing deadbeats, slapping them around a little when they didn't pay—all of it done with a loyalty he couldn't bring himself to question.

He swung onto Flatbush Avenue, Labriola's voice

screaming in his ear at what seemed an even greater volume than on the phone, a voice so loud and raging that by the time Caruso brought the car to a halt behind the dark blue Lincoln, he could have sworn Labriola had actually cracked his skull and was stomping on his brain.

Labriola jerked the door open as Caruso reached the bottom of the stairs.

"Get in here," he shrieked, then turned briskly and stormed back inside.

The interior of the house swam in a murky light and had a dank smell, like brackish water. Labriola stood, naked from the waist up, at the center of the living room, his body so massive, so terribly there, everything around him seemed blurred and out of focus.

Caruso stopped at the French doors that divided the room from the adjoining corridor and stood like a dog, awaiting some command.

"What the fuck did you tell Tony?" Labriola demanded.

"Me?" Caruso asked weakly.

"Who else I'm talking to, Vinnie?"

"I didn't tell him nothing."

"You didn't tell him nothing?"

"No."

"You didn't tell him nothing, Vinnie?"

"Nothing, I swear."

"I'm gonna ask you one more time. What the fuck did you tell Tony?"

Caruso swallowed hard. "You mean about—"

"The bitch!" Labriola screamed. "You told Tony I had somebody hunting down that fucking bitch wife of his, right?"

Caruso shook his head. "No."

Labriola stared at him grimly, then abruptly turned to face the window, his hands behind his back, fingers entwined, the muscles of his arms and shoulders rippling wildly, as if small creatures were scurrying for cover beneath his skin.

After a moment he faced Caruso again, his eyes redrimmed and furious, a rage that looked drunken, and thus all the more terrifying for being sober. Then suddenly the frenzied twitching stopped, as if some invisible ointment had been applied to his flaming skin.

"Okay," he said with a dismissive shrug.

Caruso stared at Labriola without comprehension, feeling like someone who'd been hurled forward at breakneck speed, then suddenly stopped.

"I said okay," Labriola told him.

Caruso blinked rapidly. "Okay like . . . everything's okay?"

The rage flared again. "No, fuckhead," Labriola yelled. "Okay like get the fuck out of here."

Caruso glanced down and saw that Labriola's gigantic hands were balled into fists. They hung at the ends of his arms like weighted boxing gloves, illegal in the ring, the ones that hit like thunder and sent showers of blood and sweat splattering onto the mat.

"What you waiting for, Vinnie?" Labriola fumed. "You waiting maybe I should kick your fucking ass?" He stepped forward like a man out of a cloud of smoke. "What?" he screamed.

Caruso felt his stomach coil in dread, and yet he didn't move. Something had changed, and he knew it. Something in the way things had always been, the way he'd assumed they'd always be between himself and Mr. Labriola, the way the Old Man had always let him in on whatever was gnawing at him.

"I was just wondering," Caruso began hesitantly. "About Tony's wife."

Labriola took a second measured step toward him. "What was you wondering, Vinnie?" he asked sharply.

"Just about—"

Suddenly Labriola lunged forward, his body lurching across the room, huge and bearish. His great, hairy paw seized Caruso by the throat and hurled him back through the French doors and into the wall behind them.

"What's your fucking job, Vinnie?" Labriola screamed. "What's your fucking job in this thing, huh? With this bitch?"

Labriola's face was only inches away, and Caruso had to tilt his head backward to bring the Old Man's glittering eyes into focus. A wafting sourness came from Labriola's mouth, a sickening combination of beer and whiskey, which suggested that Labriola had simply slugged down whatever his hand grasped, seeking only the bleariness of alcohol.

"Well, you gonna answer me?" the Old Man demanded.

"Find her," Caruso said weakly. "I'm supposed to find her."

"What else?" Labriola stepped back, yanked Caruso forward, then hurled him back against the wall again. "What else?" he shrieked.

Caruso's mind searched frantically for an answer but came up empty. "I don't know," he whispered.

Again Labriola jerked Caruso forward and again plunged him backward against the wall. "What else, Vinnie?"

"Nothing," Caruso sputtered. "You ain't told me nothing else."

Labriola released him, stepped back, then lightly slapped his face. "That right, Vinnie?" he taunted. "Nothing else?"

Labriola's eyes looked different than Caruso had ever seen them. They gleamed hotly, red and leaping, like torches at the entrance of a dank, steamy cave.

"You ain't got to do nothing else?" Labriola asked.

It was not a question, and Caruso knew it. It was a demand for absolute commitment.

"Whatever you say," Caruso whispered.

"That's right, whatever I say," Labriola snarled. "And you know what I say, Vinnie? I say, 'Take care of it.'"

"It?" Caruso asked.

"Who you think?" Labriola asked darkly.

Caruso tried to get his bearings, arrange his thoughts. "Right," he said tentatively, buying time. "Take care of . . . it."

Labriola whirled around, marched to the small table beside the sofa, yanked open the drawer, plucked out a single bullet, and carved something onto its metal casing with a small pocketknife.

"Put out your hand," he told Caruso.

"I don't know if this is—"

"Put out your hand," Labriola commanded.

Caruso did as he was told, then felt the cold weight of a single thirty-eight cartridge drop into his open palm.

"Look at it," Labriola said.

"Mr. Labriola, I don't think I—"

"Look at it!" Labriola screamed.

Caruso glanced at the cartridge, saw that Labriola had scraped the word "cunt" on the casing. He felt his lips open in dreadful understanding, the Big Assignment now suddenly his, but not the kind he'd ever expected or wanted, a bullet in the head of some fucking deadbeat or screwup. He looked at the cartridge, the jagged letters. *Cunt.* The word screamed in his mind. *Sara Labriola.*

"You got a thirty-eight, right?" the Old Man asked.

"Yes," Caruso said in a voice that barely reached a whisper. He could feel his knees begin to buckle, and he knew he had to get control of himself, shore up the crumbling walls, put the initial shock behind him, then take the fatal step. "A thirty-eight." He closed his fingers around the shell. "Right."

"You don't put nothing in it but that one bullet," Labriola said. "You put in more than one shot, it means you ain't sure you can do it in one shot. You don't do that, Vinnie. You make sure you do it in one shot. Like a pro."

"Like a pro," Caruso repeated softly, his mind still whirling with the job he'd just been given, some part of it still not sinking in . . . that it was Sara.

"You got a problem, Vinnie?"

Caruso felt his whole body as something immovably heavy. "What?"

"You got a problem with the job?"

With enormous effort Vinnie managed to shake his head. "No," he answered quietly.

"Good, 'cause when it's done, you bring the empty casing back to me, understand?"

"Yes, sir," Caruso said softly.

"That's like her head, Vinnie. That's like you bring me back that cunt's fucking head."

"Yes, sir," Caruso repeated.

Labriola placed his hands on either side of Caruso's neck, drew his head forward, and kissed him on both sides of his face.

Caruso felt the rough dry lips and scratchy stubble, smelled the odd, revolting sweet and sourness of the Old Man's breath.

"You're like a son to me, Vinnie," Labriola whispered.

Caruso curled his fingers tightly around the cartridge, squeezing out all hope of refusal. "A son," he said.

STARK

AS HE ran the water over the towel, he thought of Marisol. Where was she now? he wondered, and the range of possible answers paraded through his mind. He saw her as mere earth, as ash, as smoke, then in wasted but recognizable remains, and finally, at the end of a long series of progressively more vivid mental photographs, he saw her waiting in some other world, dazzlingly beautiful as she lifted her arms toward him. He remembered the joyful relief that had broken over her face as he told her that it was over, that he'd confronted the man who sought her, forced him to relent, and so knew absolutely that she was safe.

But Lockridge had not relented. Instead, he had gone back to Henderson and reported everything Stark had told him, then listened to the grim instruction and steeled himself to obey it, *All right, we do it tonight.*

The towel was soaked with water, and as he walked toward the man tied to the chair, Stark heard its heavy drip splatter against the concrete floor. It was a method he'd used only once before, and it had worked quickly. Only one application and Lockridge had given him Henderson's name, then pleaded with Stark to let him live.

"Who sent you?" he asked as he stepped over to the man in the chair.

The man began to shake despite the fact that he was clearly trying to control it, a futile effort Stark could see in the white-knuckled grip of the hands to the metal arms of the chair.

"I want his name."

The man was shaking so fiercely, the metal chair rattled with his convulsions, and Stark marveled at the way the human body reacted to terror. The jerking head, the legs racked in violent spasms, the clawing fingers, all of it orchestrated by small, childlike whimpers.

He placed his hand on the naked shoulder, and the man jerked away as if a red-hot iron had been pressed against his skin.

"Are you Mortimer's friend?" Stark demanded. "Or do you just work for Mortimer's friend?"

He took the picture Mortimer had brought in the packet from his "friend" and held it before the man in the chair.

"You see this woman? Who's looking for her?"

EDDIE

WHO'S LOOKING for her?

He heard the question but had no way to answer it. Mortimer? Was that a real person or someone the silver-haired man had made up?

"Who are you working for?" the man asked.

So far the man had not actually hurt him, but he knew that he was going to because the darkness and the fear and the long hours of being strapped to a chair hadn't worked, and so the next step had to be taken.

The next step would be pain.

Suddenly he felt his body as something other than himself, the cage that held his soul. It was his body that would betray him, his body that would recoil at whatever was done to it and finally force him to say the name the voice demanded.

"Who are you working for?"

He wanted to answer, but he knew that it would do no good. It would be like answering his father when his father was drunk; it would only inflame him, egg him on to something worse than just yelling.

"Who are you working for?"

The name wailed like a siren in his mind, loud and jangling and demanding to burst from his lips.

Tony.

Just one name and it would be over. One way or the other it would be over.

Tony.

He wanted to say it. His body wanted him to say it. But what would happen then? He didn't know. Nor did he know who the silver-haired man worked for, or what, exactly, he was after. He knew only that he wouldn't tell him anything, and that by this silence he would protect Tony, and maybe Sara too.

He felt the wet towel cover his face, the silver-haired man behind him now, tightening it so that the wet drew in against his mouth and nose. He sucked at the cloth and tasted warm, salty water, sucked again, and felt the air constrict so that he could get only half a breath. He jerked his head right and left, but with each movement the cloth only tightened until half a breath became little more than a fruitless sucking at the wet, thick cloth. The pain began in his chest and seized upward like a sharp tool raked across the tender inner folds of his throat. His vocal cords throbbed and his tongue caught fire and the raw meat of his flesh hissed and boiled until his body suddenly convulsed and he felt the pulpy inside of himself like a gorge in his throat, rising like lava into the red cavern of his mouth, filled now, and spewing, but still locked inside by the suffocating cloth.

Then he felt the cloth go limp and drop from his face and the steaming vomit that filled his mouth spewed out and dripped in a warm, sticky stream down his naked chest and over his bare, trembling legs.

"Who are you working for?"

Tony's name leaped like a flame in his brain and rose

like a boil on his flesh and shook like a tattered shroud in the retching gasp of his breath, but still he did not speak.

MORTIMER

HE SAT in the diner and played it over and over again in his mind, the way she'd come down the stairs, glancing both ways, like a frightened bird. Even so, he hadn't been sure until he'd stepped right up to her, gotten a good look, compared it with the picture he'd seen, and made the positive ID.

Sara Labriola.

Abe's girl.

Abe . . . His best friend.

Mortimer shook his head. So what now? he wondered. What could he do about this broad who'd run out on her husband, which, goddammit, she shouldn't have done, because now she'd landed Abe in this same river of shit everybody else seemed in one way or another to be drowning in.

"Jesus Christ," Mortimer muttered under his breath, "of all people, Abe."

So, okay, at least one thing was clear in this fucking mess, Mortimer decided, he had to get Abe out of it. The woman was trouble, big trouble, and as long as she was around, Abe was in trouble too. But how could he get Abe away from her? Especially since, if he were any judge of such things, Abe was already ass-over-teacup in love with this broad. No way would he just walk away from her, and if Caruso or Labriola tried anything . . . He stopped, now seeing the pistol he'd given Abe in none other than Abe's hand, aimed at Labriola or Caruso or maybe the two of them, his finger pulling down on the trigger. Holy shit,

Mortimer steamed, they'd blow Abe's head off if he pulled that fucking gun on them.

Okay, Mortimer thought desperately, okay, think, for Christ's sake! Find a way out of this!

As he considered the situation, it seemed to him that Labriola was the real problem, the only guy in the whole deal that gave a good goddamn if this broad came back or didn't come back. So the thing to do was get the Old Man to let go of this thing. He had to stop looking for this woman, because if he found her and came after her, Abe would try to stop him . . . with that fucking gun!

Mortimer tried to calm the storm within his brain. Caruso, he thought, Caruso was the only way to get to Labriola. But what could he offer Caruso that might persuade him to go back to Labriola, make him call the whole thing off? The guy, he decided, the guy Stark had probably nabbed off the street and now had behind that goddamn black curtain. Caruso clearly had a thing for that guy. Not sexual. Nothing like that. Jesus Christ, no! But a thing for him like a guy can have for another guy. Like friendship, that sort of thing. The kind of thing he, Mortimer, had for Abe, a need to make things okay. So, okay, maybe he could trade the guy for the woman, get Caruso to call Labriola off the woman if he, Mortimer, agreed to get the guy Caruso was looking for away from Stark, hand him over to Caruso safe and sound. It would be tit for tat: Caruso gets his friend and Abe gets his girl. Not bad if Caruso could just convince Labriola to give up on this thing, or maybe just that the woman had simply vanished, no way to find her. Dead end, so to speak, so the Old Man should just forget about it.

Mortimer thought it through again, decided it was worth a chance, grabbed his cell phone, and dialed the number.

Caruso answered immediately.

"That guy you told me about," Mortimer said, "the one missing. Friend of yours. I think my guy may have him."

He'd expected to hear a little jerk of relief or excitement in Caruso's voice, but all that came back was a flat monotone. "What makes you think so?"

"I went over to his place . . . Batman's," Mortimer continued. "And there was this curtain pulled across the hallway. A black curtain. Thick. I think your friend may be back there somewhere."

"Go on," Caruso said, his voice still weirdly mechanical, like some human part of him had dropped away so that he was now flying on autopilot.

"Something wrong, Vinnie?" Mortimer asked.

"Get to the point, Morty," Caruso told him.

"The point is, I figure your friend is still alive," Mortimer said. " 'Cause my guy, he wants to know who sent him, you know?" Again he expected Caruso to react strongly to this, but he could sense no reaction at all. It was as if Caruso had taken some kind of pill that numbed him somehow.

"It goes back to this thing that happened years ago," Mortimer said, keeping Caruso on the hook while he looked for a way to get to his point. "Another missing woman. He found her, but somebody was following him when he found her, and the way it worked out, this woman he found, she ended up dead." He waited for a response, but none came. "So he maybe figures the same thing here. That this woman might get hurt. He'd try to stop it, Vinnie, is what I'm saying."

"He can't stop nothing if he ain't found her."

"No, but that guy he has, this friend of yours, you're worried about him, right?"

"If he got nabbed, he got nabbed. Nothing I can do about it."

Mortimer felt the door close on his first idea of getting to Caruso; then he grasped for another. "Well, if you ain't worried about that guy, there's another guy you should be worried about."

"Who?"

"You, Vinnie," Mortimer said, now desperately trying to keep one step ahead. "Because if this friend of yours breaks, he could connect you to this woman. And if she gets hurt, my guy would—"

"What happens to her is none of Batman's business," Caruso said sharply.

"He's already made it his business, Vinnie," Mortimer said emphatically. "That's what I'm trying to tell you. That woman gets hurt, there ain't nothing he wouldn't do. He ain't sane when it comes to shit like this. On account of what I told you, is what I'm telling you. He ain't . . . rational is what I mean. So, the way I figure it, we got to make sure nothing happens to that woman once I find her."

"Once you find her?" For the first time, Mortimer heard something spark in Caruso's tone.

"Yeah."

"You looking for her, Morty?"

"Huh?"

"You said once *I* find her, not Batman. You, Morty."

Mortimer swallowed hard. "Yeah, right."

"What makes you think you can find her?"

"Nothing," Mortimer said. "No reason."

Caruso's tone grew hard. "Bullshit."

"What?"

"You know where she is, don't you?"

"Vinnie . . . look . . ."

Caruso's voice grew strangely urgent. "You know where she is, Morty."

Mortimer knew he'd inadvertently dug a hole he

couldn't get out of, one that suddenly seemed deeper and darker than he'd guessed. "Maybe."

"Don't tell me maybe," Caruso barked. "You know where she is, Morty."

"I think I know," Mortimer answered softly, stalling for time. "Which means that we could be out of the woods on this thing, providing."

"Providing what?"

"Providing she don't come to no harm," Mortimer said. He waited for Caruso to react but again found only silence. "So what I figure is, I'll check her out, this woman I'm thinking about, and if it's her, then maybe we could come up with some way to make sure nothing happens to her."

"I got to see her myself," Caruso said.

"Why?" Mortimer asked.

After a pause, Caruso said, "So I can tell Labriola you done your job. That way, you keep the money. And you and me, we make sure the woman ain't hurt, so Batman's satisfied, and everybody wins, right?"

Everybody wins. Mortimer thought through the solution Caruso had just offered and concluded it might work. "Yeah, okay," he said. "I guess it's okay you see it's her."

"So, where is she?" Caruso asked.

Suddenly Mortimer felt something tighten around his brain, a leather strap going dry.

"Where is she?" Caruso repeated.

"Vinnie, you won't tell the Old Man, right?" Mortimer asked.

"No, I won't."

"Because you do, and something happens to her, my guy'll—"

"I told you I wouldn't tell Labriola," Caruso said sternly.

"You gimme your word on that?"

"My word."

"Okay," Mortimer said, then stopped, desperately trying to think the whole thing through again.

"Well?" Caruso snapped.

Mortimer started to give Caruso Lucille's address,
then stopped again and drew in a deep breath. Not there,
he thought, someplace public, so he could get a good look
at Caruso when Caruso got a good look at Sara Labriola.
"Okay, this woman that could be her, she'll be at that bar
you followed me to. McPherson's. She's supposed to do a
little act or something. Sometime tonight. I don't know
when exactly."

"Okay," Caruso said.

"I'll meet you at the bar around seven," Mortimer
said. "We can wait around till she shows up."

Caruso's response fell like a dead man's hand. "No,
you don't need to be there, Morty."

A bell went off in Mortimer's head, a warning that
whatever dead end his own fucked-up life had led him to,
there were now other people with their backs to the same
dark wall. "What's going on, Vinnie?"

"Nothing," Caruso said quickly. "If it's her, it's over."

"Providing she don't get hurt," Mortimer reminded
him.

"Right," Caruso said dryly, and on that word, hung up.

ABE

AS HE strolled the aisle at Macy's, hoping to find just the
right shirt and tie, he suddenly felt a terrible jeopardy.
Something else, too, the inevitable approach of failure,
loss, ruin. But what else could he expect, suddenly getting
a thing for some woman he didn't know, a married
woman, a woman on the run? How could he expect a

happy ending to a story that began with so many things already lined up against it? But then, he'd always chosen badly, and gotten worse, a history that had continually repeated itself, and which no doubt explained the downward pull of his mind, its assumption of unhappy ends.

For years he'd believed that his doomed take on things had begun when Mavis left him, and not just left him for anyone but for another piano player, though this time she'd chosen a guy who was *really good*.

But he was no longer sure his downward cast of mind had begun with Mavis. After all, by the time she'd skipped, he'd already figured out she wasn't much of a woman.

No, it wasn't Mavis, he decided now. It was just the way life had settled over him. The words of "But Beautiful" declared that love was a heartache either way, and it seemed to Abe that he'd come to apply that notion to every aspect of life. He was like Lucille when The Weight fell upon her, only he didn't have the excuse of bad chemistry. He had created The Weight, especially when it came to women. So much so that if the woman didn't go for it right away, he just took a hike, washed his hands of the whole thing. If she had a boyfriend . . . sayonara. Who needs the competition. If she had a few issues, good-bye, toots. Back to the bills in the back room. The slightest problem, and he headed for the hills. How many chances for happiness had he lost by giving up so quickly? he wondered. Too many, that much was sure. Too many to sing that song again. And so this time, he decided, issues or no issues, he would put up a fight.

Suddenly he thought of the gun Mortimer had given him, and the gift, along with the idea behind it, struck him as curiously admirable. Here was a guy, Mortimer, who unquestioningly assumed that if you loved someone, and someone else tried to take her from you against her

will or tried to hurt her in some way you . . . well . . . you
blew that worthless fucker's head off is what you did.
Because you had this love, and nothing was going to stop
you from defending it. Not the law, not good sense, not
even your fear of the consequences. If someone came for
the woman you loved, you did something about it. Never
mind what happened later, all the hand-wringing and
second-guessing, and maybe even regret. At that moment,
in that situation, you threw away the rules, because the
only rule was love, and the rule of love was that no one
took the one you loved from you if she didn't want to go.

But would he really do that? he wondered. If
Samantha's father-in-law showed up, backed him into a
corner, gave him no other option, would he really go that
far, reach for a gun? He didn't know, and that uncertainty
struck him as an accusation. He didn't know because he
was civilized, and because he was civilized he would calculate the odds, try to reason through the consequences,
a process that would turn him into some lousy broker,
gauging profits and losses, the opposite of a passionate
man, which was, he realized, the kind of man he most de-
spised, but also the kind of man he was, and hated being.

So that was it, he decided, that was what he wanted,
that was what would make him happy, just to know for
sure that if things really came to a head over Samantha,
he would risk it all for her.

STARK

THE MAN in the chair didn't move or speak, so different from Lockridge, who'd broken immediately. After only
one application of the towel, he'd sputtered Henderson's
name, the Paseo del Prado hotel where he was staying,
then told how Henderson had taunted Marisol as he'd

beaten her, humiliated and degraded and repeatedly stran-
gled her to unconsciousness then revived her for more,
until Henderson had finally said, "This bitch won't die"
and cut her throat.

This bitch won't die.

The last words Marisol had heard on earth.

Stark's gaze settled on the man in the chair. "Who do
you work for?" he asked.

The man remained silent, motionless.

"Who do you work for?"

The man sat rigidly in place.

"Who do you work for?"

The man's head lowered slightly, as if considering the
question, then lifted again in what Stark saw as a gesture
of defiance.

It was late in the afternoon now, and Stark knew that
the night that lay before him would be grim. The man in
the chair was weakening in every way but in his spirit. His
body was racked by hunger and exhaustion, and Stark
knew that a sense of doom was surely settling in, the certainty that he was going to die.

Death.

His own death beckoned him softly, just as it had several days before, promising an end, but also, as he began
to imagine it, a beginning, a return, as he let himself envi-
sion it, to the arms of Marisol.

He knew that every religion proclaimed the possibility
of such miraculous reunions. Perhaps, he thought, perhaps it could be true. Perhaps only a veil separated one
world from another, life's longing and inadequacy from
the ecstatic fulfillment that waited on the other side. If
it were true, Stark reasoned, then why had he gone on,
since nothing but the slender line of his tiny throbbing
pulse kept him from Marisol.

The man groaned slightly, drawing Stark back to earth. He hardened his voice and prepared to reapply the towel.

"Who do you work for?" he said.

EDDIE

TONY.

That was the name the silver-haired man wanted. But he couldn't say it. He couldn't give Tony up. Because Tony was his friend and had always been nice to him, helped him out from time to time, told him that he was going to give him a raise so he could buy a new car. Eddie concentrated on these things while the man asked him over and over to give him a name.

He moved his naked toes because they were the only parts of his body that didn't hurt, or didn't feel some aching need for relief. His stomach cried for food, and his mouth sought water, and his whole body, except for his toes, recoiled at the slightest touch or sound. He remembered once opening a clamshell on the beach and touching the tender, pulpy inside with the tip of his finger. The clam had drawn in at that slight touch, and that was how he felt now, like a clam taken out of its shell, utterly vulnerable to everything.

And yet, at the same time, something very deep seemed whole and protected and beyond anything that could be done to harm it or cause it to collapse. He knew that Father Mike would call that part his soul, but he wasn't sure that this was really what it was. Maybe it was just stubbornness or pride. No, he thought, it wasn't that. It was just that he didn't want to fly apart.

Years before, Father Mike had told him that a man was like a dandelion. Delicate. A breath of wind could tear it apart. But a man who knew himself was like that same plant, only made of steel. It still looked frail. It still looked as though it couldn't stand up to much. But it had a coating around it. The coating was invisible, but it sealed all the small fibers in a case that nothing could break. And this invisible case that surrounded you was your soul, and when it was pure, nothing could get to all the little fibers that were inside it.

"Who do you work for?"

He closed his eyes and imagined himself as a dandelion blowing in the wind, all the ones around him tearing and shredding, but himself standing firm and whole and not ever giving in.

MORTIMER

HE'D WANTED to go home after talking with Caruso, but something in their conversation continued to gnaw at him, a little sharp-toothed beast that wouldn't stop nipping at his mind. It was Caruso's tone, so oddly distant, like a man under anesthetic, some part of him gone numb. Why was that? Mortimer wondered now. What the fuck was going on? He thought of Abe, of all that could blow up in his face if Caruso showed up at the bar, tried to strong-arm the woman. He thought of the gun and raged at himself for giving it to him. What did Abe know about guns, for Christ's sake? He was just as likely to put a bullet in his foot as plug Caruso or Labriola or whoever else tried to get between him and the broad.

Fucking gun, Mortimer thought, his mind now swinging in a different direction as he labored to find a way out for Abe. He could rush to McPherson's, tell Abe to get out of town and take the woman with him. But where would they go? It didn't matter really. Labriola would find them eventually. And besides, Caruso would know who'd tipped Abe off. Even worse, this solution, which it couldn't even be called a solution but Mortimer could find no other word to use, this solution still left Stark behind that black curtain, doing God-knows-what to the poor helpless bastard Caruso had put on him.

Okay, Mortimer thought, first things first. Deal with one thing, clear that up, then go to the next one.

He decided the first thing to deal with was Abe, and what mattered with Abe was getting that gun.

He found him at the bar, all decked out in new clothes, a sure sign that he was still falling.

"You're becoming a regular, Morty," Abe said.

Mortimer nodded. "Looks like you're going out. That girl you mentioned, the singer."

"Yeah, we're having dinner before she comes here."

Mortimer smiled faintly. "That's nice," he said, "that's real nice, Abe." He cleared his throat slightly. "So, this girl, you said some guy was after her."

"That's what she's afraid of, yeah."

"But he ain't found her, right?"

"Not yet, I guess."

"And he ain't likely to, don't you think?"

"I don't know."

"What I mean is, you probably don't need that gun I give you, right?"

Abe turned to him slowly, his eyes suddenly very intent. Morty knew he'd rushed it, tipped Abe off somehow.

"What are you getting at, Morty?" Abe asked.

Mortimer shrugged. "Nothing, except I was thinking it maybe ain't such a good idea, you having that gun."

Abe's gaze intensified. "Why's that?"

"No reason in particular."

Abe drew in a slow breath. "So, what brought about this change of heart, Morty?"

"Nothing," Mortimer answered quickly.

Abe's eyes were like probing needles. "You know something, Morty?"

Mortimer tried for a dismissive chuckle. "Me? No, I don't know nothing."

The needles sank deeper. "It's what you do, though, isn't it?" Abe asked. "Find people?"

Mortimer nodded, now regretting that he'd ever told Abe anything about his work, even though the things he'd told him were mostly lies, or at best exaggerations.

"Have I got a problem, Morty?"

"Problem, no."

"How about Samantha?"

"Who?"

"The singer."

"Oh," Mortimer stammered. "No, she ain't got no problem."

"So it's like you said, probably nobody's going to show up, right?"

"Right," Mortimer said, though he could tell Abe hadn't bought it.

"So since nobody's likely to find Samantha," Abe said, "no harm in me keeping the gun. 'Cause there won't be any reason for me to use it, right?"

Mortimer said nothing, and he could tell that this only deepened the grave suspicion he saw in Abe's eyes.

"Right?" Abe asked pointedly.

Mortimer nodded heavily, giving in. Jesus Christ, he thought, what do I do now?

TONY

TIME WAS running out. He knew that much for sure. Time was running out for Sara. He saw his father's face, heard him say "Okay" in that way he'd always said it and not meant it. On that word he'd pledged not to look for Sara, but it had been a lie. He was still looking for her. He would never stop looking for her. He couldn't imagine why he'd fallen under this obsession, or why, with each passing hour, he seemed more furiously driven by it.

So time was running out for Sara.

He picked up the phone, dialed Caruso's number.

"Hello."

"Vinnie?"

"Yeah."

"Tony."

Silence.

"I got to talk to you."

"We already talked."

"No, listen. I talked to my father. Things are bad, Vinnie."

Silence.

"Things are real bad."

"It ain't my business, Tony, what goes on between you and your—"

"Yeah, it is, Vinnie. Because it concerns you."

"No, it don't. It don't have nothing to do with me."

"If he finds her, then you're in it too," Tony told him. "You know you are, Vinnie."

Caruso said nothing.

"Okay, how about this," Tony said. "You and me, we go see my father. Talk things over with him."

"What things?"

"The whole thing about him looking for Sara," Tony explained. "I'll tell him that I told her to leave. That I kicked her out. I'll tell him I don't want anything to do with her."

"He won't believe you, Tony."

"Vinnie, please. You don't know what he might do if he finds her."

Caruso said nothing.

"He's not right, you know," Tony added. "Not right in the head."

"Whether he is or not, that ain't my business."

"What is, Vinnie? What is your business in this thing?"

"What I already told you. I hired a guy, that's all."

"Vinnie, listen to me. He didn't just hire that guy to find Sara. What good would that do? He hired him to . . . do something else."

Caruso gave no response.

"It could be anything," Tony continued. "But nothing about it is good. Not for me. Or for you. But most of all, not for Sara."

"It ain't my business, Tony," Caruso repeated.

"But suppose I could stop him, that's what I'm saying," Tony told him.

"He wouldn't listen to you."

"Okay, maybe not to me, but what about you, Vinnie?"

"Me?"

"Maybe he'd listen to you," Tony said.

Caruso laughed sourly.

"I mean it, Vinnie," Tony said. "He trusts you. You know, to think things through. Give him advice."

Caruso said nothing, and in that brief silence Tony wondered if he'd actually struck a chord. "Maybe this whole thing with Sara is some kind of test," he continued. "Of you, Vinnie."

"Me?"

"To see if you can really be trusted," Tony said. "Not just to do the muscle work. But for your judgment, you know, for your . . . brains!"

"To see if I'd stop him, you mean."

"Right."

Caruso said nothing, but Tony could almost hear his mind working the problem, reaching a decision.

"So, will you help me here, Vinnie?"

"I don't know, Tony," Caruso said softly. "If he thinks I . . ."

"You don't want to see Sara hurt, do you?" Tony asked. "Or my father?" He heard Caruso release a weary sigh. "Please, Vinnie, let's try one more time to end this thing."

The silence that followed seemed to last forever.

Then, "Yeah, okay," Caruso said.

SARA

SHE SAT at the table by the window and wondered what she should do, whether she should meet Abe at the restaurant or call now, cancel everything, not just dinner, but her songs at the bar, say thank you but good-bye, and disappear from his life.

She knew that the man in the rumpled black hat had unnerved her. But she also knew that even if the man had not suddenly appeared, she would have been attacked by the very fears that paralyzed her now.

One fact loomed over all others—she was a woman on the run. In her mind she saw Labriola's face as it had swept up to her in the corridor, his voice slurred and drunken, *You giving Tony what he needs?*

She'd pushed him away, headed toward the den, but he'd grabbed her and jerked her around, *You know what I say, right?*

Again she'd pushed him away, this time harder, so that he'd stumbled backward, a curiously surprised look on his face, his eyes gleaming with a strange, mocking admiration, *You got some fight in you, Sara.*

But did she really, she wondered now, did she really have any fight left in her?

She rose, walked to the back of the room, then returned to the window and sat down again, her gaze on the street. For a moment all the mistakes she'd made fell upon her in a heavy rain of self-accusation. She'd been driven from her home by Caulfield, driven from New York by her own need to be taken care of, then driven from Long Island by the certainty that if she stayed there, she would be destroyed one way or another.

But what life had she wanted? she asked herself now. The answer was obvious and absurd. She had wanted the Big Happy Ending, the one where she wound up a Big Name Singer, but also a wife and mother, a perfect life.

She glanced about the cramped little room where that long pursuit had finally landed her. She considered how little she had, how reduced her prospects, and these bleak considerations led her to decide that she would meet Abe at the restaurant, sing a few songs at the bar, because, when you looked at the way things were, what did she have to lose?

Nothing, she thought. So if on one of the Village streets below, tonight or on some other night, the little man in the black hat came up behind her and put a bullet in her head, so be it, since no matter how you added it up, that Big Happy Ending was well beyond her now.

MORTIMER

SHIT, MORTIMER thought. He'd blown it, and he knew he'd blown it. He'd burned his cover, clued Abe in to the fact that he knew something, and worse, tipped him off in such a way that made him hang on to that fucking gun.

Okay, so, what now? Mortimer labored to put two and two together. Abe had the gun. Caruso was set to show up at the bar. Caruso might try to strong-arm the woman. If he did, Abe would try to stop him.

For a moment Mortimer saw guns blazing, glass shattering, bullets tearing into wood and upholstery ... or worse.

The only way to go at it now, he decided, was to screw the deal, and the key to that had to be Stark.

He whirled around and rushed down the street, his short, stocky legs pumping frantically, until he stopped at Stark's door, rang the buzzer, waited, heard no response, then rang a second time.

The door opened and Stark faced him squarely.

"I need to talk to you," Mortimer said.

Stark stood before him like a high stone wall.

"I know you've got a guy in there," Mortimer told him.

"What do you want, Mortimer?"

"You think I put that guy on you," Mortimer said. "But I didn't. I made a bad deal. I ain't saying I didn't do nothing bad. But I didn't put that guy on you."

"Who did?"

Mortimer knew that the moment had arrived when he could no longer lie to Stark. The deal was blown, every goddamn bit of it. "The woman you're looking for, her name is Sara Labriola. It's her father-in-law that's looking for her, a guy named Leo Labriola. Not some friend of mine, like I told you. The guy you got in there, he works for Labriola's son. He don't mean to harm the woman, which I know is what you're thinking."

A low moan broke the deathly silence. It came from down the corridor, a soft wail behind the black curtain.

"Get him out of here," Stark said. He opened the door and stepped into the apartment. "Get him out of here now. Then come back."

Mortimer did as he was told, moving quickly down the corridor, past the curtain, and into a room where he found a man bound to a chair.

"Just a second," Mortimer said as he loosened the plastic cuffs.

"Who are you?" the man asked weakly.

Mortimer gathered up the man's clothes and helped him dress. "I'm getting you out of here now," he said.

The man looked at him blearily.

"You got a car?" Mortimer asked.

"Yeah."

"I'll walk you to it."

The man shook his head. "I don't think I can—"

Mortimer placed his hand firmly on the man's back and urged him forward. "Walk, goddammit!"

They walked outside, then like a sober friend escorting a drunk one, they staggered to the parking lot where the man had left his car.

"Keys," Mortimer said.

The man sunk his hands into the pockets of his trousers and rummaged around until he found them.

"Get in," Mortimer said as he unlocked the door and yanked it open.

The man slumped down behind the wheel. "What's . . . what's—"

"Everybody's fine," Mortimer assured him.

The man looked at him doubtfully.

"Everybody's fine," Mortimer repeated. He grasped the man's shoulder with affectionate respect. "You done good," he said quietly. "I seen guys break, but you done good."

The man nodded heavily. "You're sure . . . everybody's . . ."

Mortimer nodded. "Go home," he said, then watched as the man pulled himself into the car, hit the ignition, and headed north up the avenue. At the far corner the car took a right, moving east now, toward the river. One problem down, he thought, but plenty more to go.

ABE

HE COULDN'T believe he'd actually done it, drawn Mortimer's gun from the desk and dropped it into his jacket pocket. He wasn't even sure why he'd done it, save that something in Mortimer's manner had alarmed him. Normally, he would have called the cops, but in this case, what would he have told them? *Hey, fellas, there's this woman I like and we're going out to dinner tonight, so, would you mind sending a couple of guys in flak jackets and packing Uzis over to this little bistro on Bleecker?*

The other option would have been to leave the gun in the desk, but at the fatal moment, as he'd stood thinking it all through, he'd suddenly seen Samantha, her eyes filled with terror, a guy coming toward her, and known absolutely that if he allowed her to be taken from him in such a way, two things would happen. First, he would never see her again. Second, he would never look at his own face in the mirror without disgust. It was one thing to live in fear of losing money or a friend, of losing your health or losing your youth. One way or another, you would lose all those things anyway. But while you lived, you could not fear yourself, fear that you were nothing.

He reached the restaurant and went inside. He'd picked the place carefully, a small French restaurant just off Grove Street. It had lace curtains on the windows, and the square tables were placed at sufficient distance from each other to encourage quiet talk. That was, in fact, exactly what the restaurant guide had said, that it was a place where a man and a woman could actually hear each other talk. The lighting was soft, with candles on each table that gave off such a sweet romantic glow that as he waited at the table in the back, Abe wondered if, perhaps, the room was too romantic. After a few moments of deliberation, he decided that it definitely was, but that it didn't matter because he'd already signaled his state of mind by putting on crisp new trousers, a white shirt, tie, jacket, all of which made him feel not just dressed but costumed.

And so he stood up, stripped off his jacket, and hung it loosely over the back of his chair. Then he unknotted his tie and rolled it up and stuffed it in his jacket pocket. The final touch was rolling his sleeves up to the elbow. There, he thought, what you see is what you get.

A waiter approached. He was dressed in pressed black trousers and a short white jacket. "May I get you a drink, sir?"

"No," Abe told him. "I'm waiting for someone."

She arrived a few minutes later, wearing a black cocktail dress that looked new. She'd added a string of pearls, too, and black pumps. Her hair fell in a dark wave to her shoulders. As she moved toward him, shifting among the tables, he thought that in all likelihood he would never breathe again.

"Sorry I'm late," she said as she swept up to him.

"You're not late."

She glanced about a little nervously, like a woman who hadn't been alone with a man in a long time. "It's very nice," she said as she sat down. "Is it a favorite spot?"

"I picked it from a book."

"Really? Why this place in particular?"

"The book said no bugs."

She laughed, and her laughter loosened something in him, a little knot of jumpiness and self-doubt.

He hazarded a smile. "New dress?"

She smoothed a nonexistent wrinkle with a quick sweep of her hand. "I thought it would be good for tonight."

"It looks great," Abe told her.

"The pearls are fake," Sara said.

"But the face is yours, right?"

She laughed again, and again something loosened slightly inside him.

The waiter appeared. "Cocktails?"

"What'll you have?" Abe asked.

"Vodka gimlet," she said.

"Okay, the lady'll have a vodka gimlet," Abe told the waiter. "I'll have straight rye."

They talked idly until the drinks came, and watching her, listening to her, Abe felt himself falling and falling and knew no way to break his fall.

He lifted the glass the waiter had just set down. "So, what do we drink to?" he asked.

She lifted the gimlet, and he expected her to toast the new job or New York or, worst of all, "our friendship," but she said simply, "To happy endings," and touched the rim of her glass to his.

CARUSO

LABRIOLA'S LINCOLN rested like a huge blue coffin in the driveway of the house. Sitting in his car, Caruso could see the front window, the Old Man pacing back and forth behind it, usually with a can of beer in his fist. He wore a white sleeveless T-shirt, his huge, muscular arms fully exposed. He seemed to shake the house as he moved, and Caruso could not imagine how awesome his physical presence must have been to Tony, and how different from the feeling of utter vacancy Caruso had experienced after his father left, the empty chair at the kitchen table, the car missing, along with the money his mother kept in a shoebox in the closet, everything gone with the old man around that distant corner, the whole idea of Dad.

Briefly he replayed the conversation he'd had with Tony, all that stuff about maybe the Old Man wanting to be stopped, wanting Caruso himself to stop him, the whole thing some kind of bizarre test. He'd let himself believe the whole fucking story for just long enough to say yes to Tony, agree to meet him here, have yet another talk with the Old Man. But now he doubted every word of it. Now it all sounded like bullshit. The Old Man didn't want to be stopped. The Old Man wanted ... What did he want anyway? Sara Labriola dead, that's what. But why? That was harder to figure out. What good would whacking Sara do? No good, Caruso reasoned, no good at all, to anybody. But maybe that was the point, Caruso thought, that it being good for something had nothing to do with it. The Old Man wanted it, that's all. He wanted Sara dead. He hated her fucking guts and he wanted her dead. But why? Caruso wondered again briefly, then dismissed the thought. It didn't matter why. The Old Man wanted her dead. End of story.

Caruso glanced in the rearview mirror. At any moment Tony's car would pull up behind him, the headlights momentarily illuminating the dark interior where Caruso waited, smoking nervously, now convinced that it was all a bad idea, that he should never have agreed to meet him here. For what good would it do, after all? Labriola had told him what he had to do, given him the assignment he'd waited for all his life. He could feel the heaviness of the thirty-eight, cold and stonelike in his trousers pocket.

He drew it out, threw open the cylinder, and stared at the single bullet Labriola had given him and which he'd dutifully inserted. One shot, that was all he had. He knew that this was part of the test, Labriola's way of making certain that he placed the barrel directly at the back of Sara's head before he fired. There could be no second attempt, no way to make it good if you fucked up the shot.

But what about all the things that could go wrong? Caruso asked himself. A person could suddenly shift right or left just as you pulled the trigger. A person could stumble and fall right in front of you and you'd be standing there like a complete asshole, the goddamn pistol in your hand and the person already on the ground. Standing there . . . with one lousy shot to do the job.

Tony's words sounded in his mind. *He's not right, you know. He's not right in the head.* He decided that Tony had a point. The Old Man's insistence on his having only one bullet in his piece, the way he'd carved that ugly word on its casing, all of that added up to a nuttiness that even Tony couldn't guess. Okay, Caruso thought, so, yeah, Labriola has a screw loose, but that was no reason to be nutty yourself. And whacking somebody with only one bullet in your piece is as nutty as a guy could get. Fuck it, he thought, no way. Besides, how would Labriola know if he had just the one bullet or if he brought a fucking rocket launcher, as long as the job was done. With this conclusion, he leaned over, flipped open the glove compartment, grabbed five cartridges, loaded the pistol, then tucked it into the waistband of his trousers.

Tony arrived seven minutes later. From the rearview mirror Caruso watched as he got out of his car, walked over, and tapped at the window.

Caruso rolled it down, and a thick wave of smoke billowed out and up and was instantly torn apart by a sudden gust of wind.

"Thanks again, Vinnie," Tony said.

Caruso looked at him sternly. "I'll tell you something, Tony, you better talk to him good, because, you ask me, he ain't in no mood to change his mind on this thing."

"He hasn't told you, has he?" Tony asked.

"Told me what?"

"Told you what that guy he hired is supposed to do once he finds Sara."

"No," Caruso said. The tight wad of steel nestled against his back seemed to move suddenly, shift and stir like an animal in its earthen hole. "No, he ain't told me nothing about that."

Tony appeared to believe him, though Caruso could not imagine why, since he'd lied and lied about this thing. And not just this thing either. He had lied and lied period. It was his way of life.

"So, anyway," Tony said. "Thanks."

Tony's voice was completely different than Caruso had ever heard it. He seemed sad and broken and trapped like a rat, like a guy who'd lost the most important thing he had and could find no way to get it back. It was his wife he'd lost, of course, and for a moment Caruso wondered what it must be like to be that close to someone, want them to stay with you that deeply. Then he thought of his father . . . and he knew what Tony was going through. He wanted Sara back because nothing would ever be the same if she didn't show up again. But so what, he thought, now hardening himself for the job he'd have to do if Tony didn't get the Old Man to call it off. So what? He'd wanted his father to come back the same way Tony wanted this bitch wife of his to come back. But had he? Fuck, no. Same way with this wife of Tony's. Just wanting somebody to come back didn't mean they'd do it. And you were a sap if you thought it would. Tony was a sap, Caruso decided, and Mr. Labriola was right in despising the little prick.

He felt the pistol rustle again, jerked open the door, and got out of the car.

"Let's get this shit over with," he said sharply.

They passed through the gate, mounted the stairs, and stood silently together after Tony rapped at the door.

Standing in the darkness of Labriola's porch, Caruso felt the pistol against his backbone. It seemed rough as bricks, and as the seconds passed, it grew cold and weighty, heavier than the moon and stars, a vast, motionless planet, grim and unlighted, and he yearned for the moment when the job was finished and he could toss it over the Verrazano Bridge and be done with it.

The porch light flicked on, and frozen in its harsh light, Caruso felt utterly exposed, as if he'd already been nabbed by the cops and hauled in for a lineup, eyes watching him from behind the glare, picking him out, sealing his fate. He could almost hear the whispers of the witnesses who'd seen him do it. *Yeah, that's him. I know because of that little mustache.* Caruso glanced toward the door, caught his translucent image in the glass. Before the hit, that fucking mustache had to go.

Labriola opened the door, glanced back and forth from Tony to Caruso, his eyes cold and merciless, as if he couldn't decide which of them he detested most.

"What the fuck is this?" he asked.

"I need to talk to you, Dad," Tony said.

Labriola's eyes slithered over to Caruso. "What the fuck is this, Vinnie?"

"I just come along for the ride," Caruso said. "It ain't nothing to do with me."

"I need to talk to you," Tony insisted.

"Make it fast," Labriola snorted contemptuously, then strode back into the house.

Caruso followed Tony into the living room. It was cluttered and dingy, the tables and chairs piled with pizza boxes and white containers of half-eaten Chinese food. Beer cans and liquor bottles lay scattered along the length of the sofa, along with stacks of newspapers and magazines.

"Jesus," Tony said.

"I don't have a wife to clean up for me," Labriola said sharply. "But then, you don't either, do you, Tony?" He laughed mockingly.

Tony's body stiffened. "We have to talk, Dad."

"So you already said." Labriola rubbed his hands together. "A real heart-to-heart. Father and son. I can't wait." His eyes narrowed. "Okay, let's have it."

"I want to talk to you about Sara," Tony said grimly.

Labriola waved his hand and slumped down on the sofa. "I thought we settled that."

"I know you're still looking for her," Tony said.

"You don't know shit."

"You hired a guy, and I want to know what you hired him to do."

Labriola glared at Caruso. "You tell him I hired a guy?"

Caruso shook his head.

Labriola's eyes caught fire. "Don't you fucking lie to me, Vinnie!" he screamed.

Caruso felt as if he'd been hit by a shotgun blast. "Just that I hired a guy to find her," he sputtered. "Nothing else."

Labriola shifted his gaze back to Tony. "So, a guy's looking for her. So fucking what?"

"I want you to call him off."

Labriola laughed. "Call him off your fucking self."

"Call him off, Dad."

Labriola looked at Tony sneeringly. "And if I don't?"

Caruso's eyes shot over to Tony. Now was the moment, he knew. He'd faced it before himself. Now was the moment you either touched gloves or backed out of the ring.

"And if I don't?" Labriola repeated.

Tony said nothing.

Labriola leaned forward, grabbed a can of beer from the table in front of the sofa, and took a long, slow swig. "I got an idea," he said. "Why don't we settle this thing like men?" He rose massively and lifted his fists. "Come on, you fucking pussy, fight me."

"Sit down, Dad," Tony said. But he stepped back.

Labriola shifted his weight from one foot to the other, dancing like a boxer and throwing punches in the air. "Fight me, Tony," he repeated vehemently. "Fight me, goddammit!" He stepped forward and threw a wide punch.

Tony leaped away. "I'm not going to fight you, Dad."

Labriola stopped and stared at Tony brokenly. "Then fuck you," he said with a curious sense of defeat. "Fuck everything." He stepped back and slumped down on the sofa. For a moment he seemed to retire into his own dark cavern. Then abruptly, he threw his head back and a vicious laugh broke from him, so loud and hellish, it seemed to rattle the teardrop crystals of the overhanging chandelier.

"Mr. Labriola?" Caruso asked.

Labriola's voice broke from him like a smoking belch. "You find her yet?"

"What?" Caruso asked.

"You heard me," Labriola screamed. "You find her or not?"

Caruso felt a line of sweat form on his upper lip. "Well . . . I mean . . . uh . . ."

Labriola's eyes were leaping flames. "Yes or no!" he bellowed.

"Yes," Caruso blurted.

Tony looked at Caruso, astonished. "You know where Sara is?"

Caruso glanced helplessly at the Old Man. "You want me to . . ."

Labriola laughed madly. "Vinnie found her," he cried, his gaze now on Tony. "Well, hell, let's go pay her a little visit." He snatched a wrinkled blue shirt from the floor and began to put it on. "You're gonna get your little wife back, Tony."

Tony's eyes shot over to Caruso. "Where is she?"

Caruso glanced at Labriola, found no direction there, then returned his gaze to Tony. "The city."

Labriola suddenly slapped his hands together. "The city," he shrieked. "The little woman has gone back to the city." His eyes bore into Caruso. "Where in the city, Vinnie?"

Caruso stared at Labriola and all but shivered. "The Village," he answered softly. "I got a tip she's working at some bar there."

Labriola's eyes blazed with delight. "Back in the Village, ain't that nice." He snatched a sport jacket from the sofa and plowed like a warship toward the door.

Tony didn't move.

Labriola stopped, turned to face him, and laughed tauntingly. "What's the matter, Tony? Now's your chance to get her back." His eyes shifted over to Caruso. "Ain't that right, Vinnie?"

Caruso felt the pistol stir lethally, like a creature awakening. "Right," he said.

Labriola nodded toward the door. "Okay, let's go," he said, motioning Tony forward and out the door, then holding back so that Caruso stepped up to his side, the two of them walking together toward the door just as Tony went through it and out onto the porch.

"You bring your piece?" Labriola whispered.

Caruso nodded.

Labriola draped his huge arm over Caruso's shoulder and tugged him violently to his side. "Good boy," he said.

ABE/SARA

THEY LEFT the restaurant and headed back toward the bar, the focus of their conversation now on the songs she'd prepared. He went over the lead-ins, which would be brief, and how they had to be attuned to each other, singer and accompanist, to speed up if the other one got ahead, slow down if the other one fell behind, allow as much as possible for each other's inevitable missteps, and above all, cut each other enough slack for a little improvisation.

"What time would be good for you?" he asked as they turned onto Twelfth Street.

"The sooner the better, I guess," she answered.

At the bar, Abe introduced her to Jake, Susanne, and Jorge. After that, they took a table near the back, talked briefly, then, as if on a signal, Abe glanced at the clock. "So, ready?" he asked Sara.

"I guess I have to be," she replied.

Abe walked to the piano, and standing beside it, introduced Sara as Samantha Damonte.

Then she sang, and as she sang Abe could feel it happening, how the people grew silent as they listened, grew silent and wrapped their hands around their glasses and hoped that just for a time, just for the few minutes during which her voice poured over them, the old devouring monster would leave them be.

MORTIMER

STARK SAT in the living room, stern and upright in the leather chair, his eyes on Mortimer as the two men faced each other silently.

Finally, Stark said, "What was the arrangement? The one you made with Labriola?"

"Just that you would find this woman," Mortimer said. "His daughter-in-law. She run out on his kid. He wants to talk to her." He shrugged. "He offered thirty grand." He dropped his head slightly. "I was gonna give you fifteen, keep the rest. But things got screwed up. This other guy you had. Complicated, you know? So the thing is, I figure I'll just tell Labriola that the deal's off. That you're out of it. Maybe you got sick, something like that. Dying. Anyway, you can't do the job."

Stark studied Mortimer's face a moment, then rose, walked to a small wooden cabinet, took two glasses, and poured a splash of scotch in each of them. "The whole thing reminded me of Marisol," he said as he handed one of the glasses to Mortimer.

Mortimer took a quick sip. "Yeah, I figured you thought it was maybe like that."

Stark returned to his seat, leaned back in his chair, and crossed his legs. "Is it?"

Mortimer took another sip from the glass.

"You know where she is, don't you?" Stark asked.

Mortimer looked up from the glass.

"I want to see her," Stark said sternly.

Mortimer stared at Stark silently, helpless against the fierce nature of his purpose, the odd nobility he added to every word he said.

"Where is she?" Stark asked.

Mortimer put down his glass. "She's working at a bar in the Village."

"Who else knows this?"

"The guy, the one who works for Labriola."

"How does he know?"

"I told him."

"Why?"

"To get you out of the deal," Mortimer said. "He wouldn't do it otherwise. But he won't tell Labriola where she is."

"What makes you think he won't tell Labriola?"

"He won't," Mortimer said. Suddenly he heard Caruso's voice, the tone of finality within it, the sense that something had changed. "I mean, he told me he wouldn't let Labriola . . . hurt her."

Stark's gaze would not be turned aside. "Hurt her?" He leaned forward. "Mortimer, is this woman in danger?"

Mortimer saw Sara as she made her way down the block, toward the florist shop on the corner, so utterly exposed. He knew how it would go down, that Caruso would watch her in the rearview mirror of his car, wait until she reached a predetermined distance, then fall in behind her, steadily increasing his pace, reaching for his pistol as he did so, finally pressing the barrel so close to the back of Sara's head that a wisp of her hair actually touched it.

"Mortimer, is this woman in danger?" Stark's eyes bore into him.

Mortimer shuddered with the vision of what happened after that, Sara Labriola stumbling forward, a geyser of blood shooting from the back of her skull.

"Is this woman in danger?" Stark repeated.

Mortimer could scarcely imagine how badly things had gone or how out of control they'd now become. He took a moment to retrace the steps that had gotten him to this place. A death sentence from a doctor, a need to leave Dottie a few bucks, then a ridiculous bullshit scheme to cheat Stark, all of it finally leading to the terrifying truth that Sara Labriola, his best friend's woman, was in dire peril.

"Yes," Mortimer answered softly.

Stark grabbed the telephone and thrust it toward Mortimer. "Call Labriola, or whoever this guy is who works for him," he said. "Tell him I want to have a meeting with the two of them."

"I ain't got a piece," Mortimer said weakly.

Stark looked at him darkly. "I do," he said.

CARUSO

CARUSO GLANCED back to where Labriola sat sprawled in the backseat of the car. "Batman wants to have a meeting," Caruso said, the cell phone held a couple of inches from his right ear. "Wants us to come over to his place."

Labriola laughed. "You hear that, Tony? The guy I hired to find your wife, he wants to have a meeting. Ain't that interesting?"

Tony said nothing, but merely sat, tense and agitated, like someone who'd set upon a course he now doubted.

Labriola chuckled. "What's the matter, Tony? You don't look all that sociable."

"I just want to talk to Sara," Tony answered weakly.

"Sure you do." Labriola laughed. "But first I want to see the guy I forked all that cash over to." He turned to Caruso. "Tell him okay. Tell him we're on our way."

Minutes later they were rumbling over the Brooklyn Bridge, the skyline of Manhattan a glittering wall before them.

Labriola drew in a long breath. "I hate Brooklyn," he said quietly. He leaned forward and squeezed Caruso's shoulders. "I hate Brooklyn, Vinnie."

"Yes, sir," Caruso told him.

Labriola dropped back in the seat, his gaze curiously lost and bleary. "Tremont was nice," he added.

Ten minutes later, Caruso guided the Lincoln over to the curb on West 19 Street.

Labriola rolled down the window, thrust his huge head out into the night, and glared at the building, his anger returning suddenly, burning off the oddly meditative mood that had briefly settled over him. "I ain't walking up five fucking flights to meet this asshole," he snarled.

"He lives on the first floor," Caruso told him quietly.

Tony jerked open the back door. "Come on, let's get this over with. I just want to talk to Sara."

"Talk to her," Labriola laughed, his great bulk still slouched in the backseat. "You need to fuck her is what you need."

Tony whirled around. "Why do you talk like that?" he asked fiercely. "Why do you say things like that to me?"

Labriola's eyes caught fire. "What a worthless piece of shit you are, Tony," he sneered.

Tony's face stiffened, and for a moment the two men stared silently at each other. Then Tony turned around and headed up the stairs.

Labriola watched him briefly, then turned to Caruso, grasped his shoulder and gave it a painful squeeze. "Don't fuck up."

"I won't," Caruso promised.

Labriola jerked open the door and surged out into the night, his heavy bulk lumbering up the stairs.

Caruso sucked in a troubled breath, pulled himself from behind the wheel, and headed up the stairs behind Labriola. The buzzer was already ringing by the time he joined him on the landing.

The door opened and a tall man in a dark suit appeared, his blue eyes ghostly in their icy glint.

"You Batman?" Labriola laughed.

"What?"

Caruso released a nervous little chuckle. "That's what I called you," he explained. "Mr. Labriola don't know you by no other name."

The man's eyes shifted over to Labriola. "Leo Labriola," he said.

"Yeah, that's me," Labriola said gruffly. "And this is my son, Tony. It's his wife that's missing."

The man in the dark suit nodded. "Stark," he said.

"So," Labriola said, slapping his hands together. "We gonna stand in the fucking street all night, or what?"

Stark smiled quietly. "Please come in," he said.

Caruso trailed along, following Labriola and Tony into the shadowy interior of Stark's apartment, where Mortimer stood silently in a far corner of the room.

"Would anyone like a drink?" Stark asked.

"We ain't here to socialize," Labriola said. He stepped forward, leaving a space between Caruso and Tony. "I paid you a lot of money, but you didn't find my son's wife."

"No, I didn't," Stark replied evenly. He nodded toward Mortimer. "But my assistant, Mr. Dodge, did."

"Mr. Dodge," Labriola bellowed. "You trust your . . . assistant?"

"Yes."

"You trust him like I trust Vinnie?"

"I would trust him with my life," Stark said.

Labriola laughed. "Okay, so this fucking guy . . . Mr. Dodge . . . he wouldn't short you, would he?"

Stark smiled. "I said I'd trust him with my life. Not my money."

Labriola's eyes seemed to leap with canine joy. "So you already know about this fucking guy? How he was gonna short you?"

"I know that he found the woman you're looking for,"

Stark said. "And I·know that you're going to forget that he found her."

Labriola seemed unable to process Stark's response. He glanced back and forth between Caruso and his son, then leveled his eyes on Stark. "What the fuck are you talking about?"

"I'm talking about a woman," Stark said coolly. "Her name is Sara, I believe. And she no longer exists for any of you."

Tony stepped forward slightly. "I'm not looking for her," he said. "You see her, you can tell her I'm not looking." He turned to Labriola. "Let's go, Dad."

Labriola didn't move. His eyes remained on Stark. "Who the fuck you think you're talking to, asshole?" he sneered.

Stark's voice turned steely. "Here's what's you do," he said. "You. Leave. Sara. Labriola. Alone."

Labriola squinted hard, as if trying to bring something very small into focus. Then he glanced unbelievingly at Caruso. "You hear this fucking guy?" he bellowed. "You hear how he talks to me?" He laughed, but edgily, as his gaze shot from Caruso to Tony, then back to Stark. "You a fag?"

Stark faced him silently.

"I asked you a question," Labriola said. "Are you a fag?"

Stark gave no answer.

" 'Cause you must be a fag if you think you're gonna fuck with *me*."

Stark stared at Labriola without expression.

"Or maybe you think *I'm* a fag," Labriola sneered. He stepped forward and with surprising speed yanked a thirty-eight snub-nosed pistol from his jacket pocket and aimed it at Stark. "You ready to die, fuckhead?"

Stark said nothing, but Caruso saw a dark gleam come

into his eyes, as if something important had suddenly occurred to him.

"I asked you a question," Labriola said.

Stark faced him silently.

Tony eased forward and stretched his hand toward Labriola. "Give me that, Dad," he said.

Labriola jerked the gun from his son's reach. "Shut the fuck up, Tony," he barked, his eyes still on Stark. "You look a little fucked up, Batman," he said. His eyes slid over to Caruso. "This guy look a little fucked up to you, Vinnie?"

Caruso nodded.

Labriola thrust his hand forward, snapped back the pistol's metal cock, then stepped forward and pressed it against Stark's forehead. "Check this asshole out, Vinnie."

"Stop it, Dad," Tony said.

Labriola paid no attention. "Do it, Vinnie!"

Caruso came around behind Stark and began patting him down, then suddenly stopped cold and drew a nine-millimeter automatic from beneath Stark's arm.

"Gimme it," Labriola snapped.

Caruso placed the pistol in Labriola's outstretched hand.

Labriola stepped back and smiled at Stark. "Nobody fucks with Leo Labriola."

"What now?" Stark asked coolly.

Labriola laughed. "What now?" he asked mockingly. "Now we go for a little ride."

ABE

HE WAITED until the lights went on in Samantha's apartment. Then he turned and made his way back to the bar. As he walked, he replayed the events of the last few days, how she'd shown up out of the blue, the way she made him feel. He didn't know whether anything would come of it, but who ever knew if anything would come of anything, or if what came would last, or even be all that good? But what the hell, he thought as he turned onto Twelfth Street, all life really gave you was a chance not to fuck it up.

At the bar Jake was counting the receipts and Susanne was clearing the last of the tables.

"She done good," Jake said. "The crowd really seemed to like her."

Abe nodded, then glanced over at the now-empty tables, recalling how conversations had trailed off during her first song, fallen silent for the last two. "Yeah," he said, "yeah, they did."

Jake and Susanne left a few minutes later, and Abe returned to the piano and played Samantha's closing number, remembering the way she'd sung it, how she'd made the lyrics seem like the sum total of what a person could learn.

He'd just played the final chord when he heard the door open at the front, realized that he hadn't locked it after he'd let Jake and Susanne out.

CARUSO

HE STOOD obediently behind Stark and Tony, guarding them from the back, while Mortimer and Labriola stepped inside the bar. Over their shoulders he could see the barkeep moving toward them.

"I can't serve you, Morty," the barkeep said when he reached them.

"We have to talk," Mortimer said gravely.

Before the barkeep could answer, Labriola said, "You

got a table for—what we got here?—four of us . . . plus you . . . so that means a table for five, right?"

The barkeep looked at Mortimer uncomprehendingly. "Just do it," Mortimer told him.

"Yeah, just do it," Labriola said coldly.

The barkeep didn't move. "I think you'd better go," he said.

Labriola laughed harshly. "Go? You don't even know me, and you're telling me to get out? That ain't very nice." He drew the pistol from his jacket pocket. "Like I said, fuckhead, table for five."

The barkeep didn't move, and Caruso thought it would all end at that instant, Labriola blasting the barkeep first, knocking him backward and over the nearest table, then turning to the others, dropping them where they stood, Stark and Mortimer, both of them staggering backward under a hail of bullets, geysers of blood shooting from their chests, all of it a scenario Caruso knew he was helpless to stop, the Old Man's rage now at full throttle, hurling everyone toward disaster.

Then, suddenly, Mortimer's voice broke the silence. "Abe," he said quietly, "please."

The barkeep nodded softly, then turned and headed toward the back of the bar, walking slowly, like a man to his execution.

"Okay, let's go," Caruso said. He turned around and jerked Stark and Tony forward, then walked behind them, at Labriola's side, until they reached the back of the room, where they gathered around a wooden table.

"Sit," Labriola ordered. He wiped his mouth with his fist. "And hurry up about it."

Caruso lowered himself into a chair off to the side and watched as the barkeep, Tony, Stark, and Mortimer took their seats around the table. He could feel the air heating up around him, a hundred desperate voices in his head, a babble of notions, all of them aimed at escape, until the futility of it all silenced them and he felt himself sink into that silence, cold and wordless, as if already dead.

"Got a regular powwow here, don't we, Vinnie?" Labriola asked as he plopped heavily into a chair.

Caruso nodded stiffly, his neck locked in the tension of the atmosphere, every bone aching.

Labriola placed the pistol on its side, laid his hand over it, and stared at the barkeep. "Okay, here's the deal. My son here, his wife left him, and he don't want to do nothing about it. But the way I see it, this woman fucked my son when she left him. And so she fucked me too. Only that was a mistake, 'cause I ain't like Tony." His smile was a sliver of ice. "So, can you help me out here, Mr.—"

"Morgenstern," the barkeep said.

"Yeah, right," Labriola said. "My point being, this woman, my son's wife, she should have had a little talk with her husband before she run out on him. 'Cause it ain't respectful, running off like that, without a word. Now, my son, he'd let her get away with it, because he ain't got the balls to do nothing about it."

"But you have," the barkeep said suddenly.

"You goddamn right I have," Labriola said. "Big fucking balls, asshole."

Caruso saw the barkeep's hand drift toward the end of the table and remembered those fingers at the piano keys. That was what he must be imagining at the moment, he thought, the fact that he was in danger of never doing that again, that one wrong word or movement, and those same fingers would never dance around the keys again. But so what, Caruso decided, shoring himself up for whatever lay ahead, loading the whole bunch of them into a car crusher if that's what the Old Man had in mind.

Labriola was talking again when Caruso returned his attention to him.

"Now, you know where she is, right, my son's wife?" Labriola said. "I mean, she works for you, so you know where she is." He lifted his hand like a flat stone to reveal the pistol coiled beneath it. "And I'm sure you don't mind telling me where she is, right?"

The barkeep's hands reached the curved edge of the table and stopped. "No, I don't mind," he said almost cheerily.

Caruso could hardly believe his ears. Here he was, ready to put a bullet in the fuck, and the barkeep was saving him the trouble, caving in even without the Old Man popping him one. He glanced to his right, saw Labriola grin, and grinned with him.

"Good," Labriola said.

Caruso turned back to the barkeep, who was sitting silently, staring at Labriola.

"Well?" Labriola blurted out after a moment.

"Well what?" the barkeep asked.

"I thought you was gonna tell me where she is, my son's wife," the Old Man told him.

"I am," the barkeep replied casually. Then his eyes froze. "For a price," he added.

"A price?" the Old Man barked. "You ain't getting a dime out of me."

The barkeep shrugged. "I don't want money."

"What you want, then?" Labriola asked.

The barkeep looked at Mortimer, then back toward Labriola. "One of those big balls you got," he said.

Shit, Caruso thought, seeing the slaughter once again, everybody dead, the Old Man standing in the lightly waving reeds of the Meadowlands, sipping whiskey from a bottle as Caruso hauled one body after another from the back of his blue Lincoln Town Car.

Labriola sat back slightly, lifted the gun from the table, and aimed it directly at the barkeep's head. "You're one dumb kike," he said.

Suddenly, Tony leaned forward. "Let's go, Dad," he pleaded.

"Go?" Labriola yelped.

"I don't want to talk to her, Dad."

Labriola shook his head. "What a pussy you are, Tony."

"Dad, please, you can't."

Labriola whirled around. "Can't what, Tony?" he asked icily. "What, you giving the orders now? Telling me what I can't do?" He looked at Caruso. "What do you think, Vinnie, you think maybe I should show this little fuck who's the boss?" He glanced at each man in turn, his lips curled down in a sneer. "Teach all of you who's the fucking boss." He shot his gaze over to Caruso. "Gimme your gun, Vinnie," he said. His hand shook violently, like a ragged cloth in a tearing wind. "Gimme your fucking gun!" he screamed.

Caruso drew the thirty-eight from his waistband and handed it to Labriola.

Labriola glared at the barkeep. "Let's start with you, Mr.—Morgenstern." He spun the chamber. "There's only one bullet in this fucking thing. You got the balls to pull the trigger?"

"Dad, stop it," Tony said.

Labriola spun around and cracked the pistol against the side of Tony's head. "You sound like that bitch wife of yours, Tony."

Tony lurched backward, his hands to his head, blood seeping through the closed fingers.

Labriola laughed. "Stop it! Stop it!" he repeated in a high, female plea. "That's all she ever said."

Tony drew his hands from his head and glared at Labriola. "What are you talking about?"

"Stop it! Stop it!" Labriola whined in the same mocking tone. "Like she thought she was boss." His eyes gleamed madly. "Like she didn't know my rule."

Tony stared at him darkly. "What rule?"

A leering grin formed on Labriola's lips. "You fuck my son, you fuck me," he said.

Caruso felt his lips part wordlessly, a terrible vision in his mind, the Old Man, drunk and raging, thudding down a narrow corridor toward Sara Labriola.

"What did you do to her?" Tony asked.

A swirl of notions spun through Caruso's mind, the Old Man's stark command that Tony was not to speak to Sara, the word he'd scraped on the shell casing of a thirty-eight, *Cunt*.

"What did you do to Sara?" Tony demanded. He started to rise but Labriola pressed the barrel of the thirty-eight against his forehead and drew him back down to his seat. "You're a pussy, Tony," he sneered. "I'd have done better at a nigger orphanage." He turned to face the others, the cold look in their eyes, how fully they abhorred him. For a moment he seemed to see himself as they did, a vision that appalled him, so he turned away and settled his gaze on Caruso. "Should I show 'em who's boss, Vinnie?" he asked quietly.

Caruso thought of the chambered rounds, the dark cathedral where they lay, a fully loaded gun, then of Sara Labriola on her back, helpless, the Old Man pressing down upon her, laying down his rule. *You fuck my son, you fuck me.*

"Vinnie, should I show 'em who's boss?" Labriola repeated.

Caruso felt something deep inside tear lose, something sharp and corroded, a long embedded hook. "Yeah," he whispered, "show 'em, Mr. Labriola."

Labriola placed the barrel against the side of his head. "I'll show you who's the fucking boss," he sneered.

"Stop it," Tony cried.

Caruso stared at Tony evenly. "Let him," he said coolly.

Tony seemed to study him for a moment, concentrated, intent, like a man trying to decipher a secret code.

"Let him," Caruso repeated.

Tony looked at Labriola, the pistol poised at his head, then back to Caruso, their eyes fixed in cold collusion.

"Let him," Caruso said a final time.

Labriola peered back and forth from Caruso to Tony, his face now locked in a curious suspicion. "Maybe I will and maybe I won't," he taunted.

Tony glanced at Caruso, then turned toward his father. "I didn't think you had the balls," he said mockingly.

Labriola's lips jerked downward in hideous contempt. "Just watch and see, pussy boy," he said.

The pistol trembled at Labriola's temple, but still he didn't fire, and in that interval Caruso saw the barkeep's hand drop over the side, and shook his head silently, a gesture he knew was full of warning but also of assurance, a gesture that said only, *Wait.* Then he looked at each man in turn, Stark and Mortimer, relaying the same message.

Finally he leveled his gaze squarely upon Leo Labriola. "Show 'em," he said.

A dry cackle burst from the Old Man's lips. "Fucking A," he cried.

Make Someone Happy

MORTIMER

AS HE closed in on his apartment, Mortimer felt a wholly foreign joy wash over him, and he thought it must be the feeling a magician gets when he reaches into the black hole and the rabbit's there, by God, just like it's supposed to be, and he pulls it out, and the people can't believe it, and all he hears in the vast dark room is the thrilling burst of their applause.

So much had gone wrong lately, he recalled, so much fear and dread, the deadly threat that still hung over him but which he'd come to live with, accept as part of his experience, a dark music forever playing in his mind.

But that was the point, wasn't it? he thought as he entered the elevator and glided up to where he knew he'd find Dottie snoring in front of the television, wrapped in a thick terrycloth housecoat, looking like nothing so much as a huge ball of thick pink twine, just to look the whole thing in the face, shrug it off, and go on.

STARK

CLEARLY SHE could not have been more surprised to see him.

"Hello, Kiko."

"What are you doing here?" she asked him stiffly.

"May I come in?" he asked.

She opened the door silently and he passed her and stood in the small, elegantly appointed living room.

"Did you forget something?" Kiko asked coldly. "Let me guess. Cuff links? Tie clip?"

Stark shook his head.

"So, what, then?" Kiko demanded.

He turned toward her slowly. "A guy pulled a gun on me," he said.

She couldn't suppress a brittle laugh.

"No, I mean it."

"A guy pulled a gun on you?"

"Yes."

"Okay, fine, so a guy pulled a gun on you."

"I thought he was going to do it."

"Kill you?"

Stark nodded. "I'd always thought I wouldn't care."

"But you did?"

"Yes. Because at that moment I thought about you."

She released another short laugh. "Okay, I'll spring for it. What, Stark, did you think about me?"

He started to answer, but she lifted her hand to silence him.

"No, no. Let me guess. It was my hair, right?"

He shook his head.

"Legs? Tits? Ass? You have to admit, it's a great ass."

"No one thing, Kiko."

"Okay, what? And this better be good."

The answer came to him so quickly, he knew that it was true.

"That I would miss you," he said.

Her eyes glistened. "So, you want a drink?" she asked.

CARUSO

HE OPENED the trunk of the Lincoln, and the sight of Labriola curled up inside it convinced him at last that he was actually dead.

"The boat's over there," Tony said as he stepped up beside him.

Caruso nodded. "I guess I loved the guy," he said quietly, his gaze still fixed on Labriola, the massive body now curiously small.

"He didn't deserve it," Tony said. He peered at his father a moment, then added, "You don't deserve anything you don't give back." He looked at Caruso. "Did you know?"

"Know what?"

"About what he did . . . to Sara?"

Caruso shook his head. "No, I didn't know about that, Tony."

"Good," Tony said.

They hauled the body from the trunk of the car, then across the deserted parking lot and over to Tony's boat. After that Caruso waited while Tony went into the warehouse and retrieved two cement blocks and a length of chain.

"Okay," Tony said. "Let's go."

Within minutes they were out to sea, the boat's white wake coiling behind as they made their way across the dark water.

"Sara will probably get in touch with me at some point," Tony said. "I'll go from there. If she wants a divorce, I'll give her one. If she wants to come back, I'll take her back."

Caruso nodded. "Whatever you say, Tony."

A half hour later Tony killed the engine and the boat came to a halt. "Ready?" he asked.

"Yeah."

They lifted the body and brought it over to the gunwale and eased it down again, so that Labriola looked as if he were sitting silently, head drooped forward, staring at his feet.

Caruso shrugged. "Well, we're both orphans now."

"Yeah."

They heaved the body over the side of the boat, then watched as the cement blocks dragged him down, feet-first, so that their last glimpse was of his upraised arms, fingers reaching for them.

"If he were alive, he'd really be pissed," Tony said dryly.

A burst of laughter shot from Caruso. "Sorry," he said, now trying to get control. "The way you said it . . . I didn't mean . . ." Another burst hit him. "I mean, I could just imagine it, you know, him all pissed off, 'You fucking bastard, put them fucking shells in that fucking gun. . . .' "

The same seizure of laughter now hit Tony. "Did you see his face? That look he had?"

"Oh, he was pissed all right," Caruso said, the two of them laughing together now, one burst following another in rippling waves.

"Jesus," Caruso said when the laughter finally faded.

"Yeah."

"So, what now?"

"We go home," Tony said.

And so they did, Tony guiding the boat landward

where, minutes later, they could see the twinkling lights of the distant shore.

ABE

HE GAVE a final glance back toward the bar, turned off the light, and headed out onto the street. At the corner he looked left and right, noted the streets were deserted, drew the pistol from his jacket pocket, and dropped it into the sewer beneath his feet. He wouldn't need it anymore, and what was the point of returning it to Morty?

He turned left on Sixth Avenue and headed south toward Grove Street, remembering how he'd dropped his hand into his lap, dragged his trembling fingers across his stomach and sank them into the black depths of his jacket pocket, reaching for the pistol. That was the moment when it had come clear to him that there was nothing he wouldn't do to keep Samantha safe. It was a story he would never tell, he decided. Not to Jake or any of the regulars. And especially not to—her real name surfaced in his mind for the first time and he found that he liked the sound of it, that it gave off a sense of something warm and solid—especially not to Sara.

SARA

SHE SAT by the window, her gaze on the deserted street below, and wondered how long it would go well at McPherson's, how long her voice would hold out, how long before something changed.

She shook her head at how grim her own thoughts were, how all her life she'd reached for the Big Happy Ending. But when you really thought about it, the Big

Happy Ending was beyond what anyone could actually expect, and it seemed to her that it was the very fear of not having it that held all other, lesser happiness in peril.

And so the point was to enjoy the small happy endings that came your way.

She looked at the roses Abe had brought, then reached out and touched them. The day came back to her, from first light to now.

She smiled.

Okay, so, happy ending, right?

ABOUT THE AUTHOR

THOMAS H. COOK is the author of sixteen novels, including *The Chatham School Affair*, winner of the Edgar Award for Best Novel; *Into the Web; The Interrogation; Instruments of Night; Breakheart Hill; Mortal Memory; Sacrificial Ground* and *Blood Innocents*, both Edgar Award nominees; and two early works about true crimes, *Early Graves* and *Blood Echoes*, which was also nominated for an Edgar Award. He is also the author of the novelization of the SCI FI Channel television event, *Taken*. He lives in New York City and Cape Cod, where he is at work on his next novel.

ELIZABETH GEORGE

"...reigns as queen of the mystery genre." —*Entertainment Weekly*

A GREAT DELIVERANCE ____ 27802-9 $7.99/$11.99 in Canada
Winner of the Anthony and Agatha Awards for Best First Novel

PAYMENT IN BLOOD ____ 28436-3 $7.99/$11.99

WELL-SCHOOLED IN MURDER ____ 28734-6 $7.99/$11.99

A SUITABLE VENGEANCE ____ 29560-8 $7.99/$11.99

FOR THE SAKE OF ELENA ____ 56127-8 $7.99/$11.99

MISSING JOSEPH ____ 56604-0 $7.99/$11.99

PLAYING FOR THE ASHES ____57251-2 $7.99/$11.99

IN THE PRESENCE OF THE ENEMY ____ 57608-9 $7.99/$11.99

DECEPTION ON HIS MIND ____ 57509-0 $7.99/$11.99

IN PURSUIT OF THE PROPER SINNER
____ 57510-4 $7.99/$11.99

A TRAITOR TO MEMORY ____ 58236-4 $7.99/$11.99

A PLACE OF HIDING ____ 58237-2 $7.99/$11.99

I, RICHARD ____ 38242-X $11.95/$17.95

....

Bantam Dell Publishing Group, Inc.   TOTAL AMT $_____
Attn: Customer Service   SHIPPING & HANDLING $_____
400 Hahn Road   SALES TAX (NY, TN) $_____
Westminster, MD 21157
        TOTAL ENCLOSED $_____

Name _____

Address _____

City/State/Zip _____

Daytime Phone (____) _____

EG MYS 2/05